FAITH, LOVE &
MURDER

To Sue,

I hope you enjoy reading my debut novel.

NICK CARD

Best Wishes
Nick Card

About the Author

Nick Card was born in Beckenham, Kent in 1977. Aged 10, he moved to Yorkshire and, as a teenager, developed his passion for creative writing.

In Hull, he achieved a Bachelor of Arts degree in Media Production. After graduating, Nick performed a selection of his poems in a variety of venues around the UK. He released his first book, *Loving, Laughing & Living*, in 2007 and this contained an anthology of his poetry. Nick was also the writer and director of numerous radio and stage plays. Two of his theatre productions, *A Grave Reunion* & *The Interview*, had a run at the Edinburgh Fringe Festival.

Nick currently lives on his own in the historical market town of Newbury.

**Faith, Love & Murder
by Nick Card**

© Nick Card

ISBN: 979-8863061665
Independently Published

The right of Nick Card to be identified as the author of this work has been asserted by him in accordance with the Copyright, Designs and Patents Act 1988.

All rights reserved. No part of this publication may be reproduced, stored in or introduced into a retrieval system, or transmitted, in any form, or by any means (electronic, mechanical, photocopying, recording or otherwise) without the prior written permission of the publisher. Any person who does any unauthorised act in relation to this publication may be liable to criminal prosecution and civil claims for damages.

Cover, layout and design by Viking Bay

This book is sold subject to the condition that it shall not, by way of trade or otherwise, be lent, re-sold, hired out, or otherwise circulated without the publisher's prior consent in any form of binding or cover other than that in which it is published and without a similar condition including this condition being imposed on the subsequent purchaser.

Dedicated to the memory of my late and
great friend John Hodowanyj. He had a brilliant
mind and I've expressed some of his ideas in this novel.

The Police Officers in Order of Rank

Superintendent Mark Jamieson

Chief Detective Inspector John Stafford

Detective Inspector James Mallen

Detective Constables

Fran Jacobs   Andy Taylor   Clara Sobers   Robbie Jones

THE WAKE

The house stood lonely on top of a steep hill. You could not possibly come across it by chance as it marked the end of a mile long cul-de-sac. This large rustic Victorian property was called Skyrise. Its location was in the largely unknown and very remote hamlet of Newcot in the southwest corner of Havantshire. The magnificent mansion boasted beauty and splendour. Its pleasing stone walls were complemented by ornate wooden balconies. As soon as the building became visible it just drew you in like a magnet. A great reward for the hardy souls who had ventured out to find the hidden home. It was like they had finally seen the Emerald City after following the Yellow Brick Road.

The whole surrounding area had a calming rural English feel about it. Beautiful, lush green fields with an array of magnificent oak trees encircled the property. Modern society, with all its haste and noise, had not touched it. In fact, nothing externally had changed in over a century. The only neighbour in the cul-de-sac was way down the road. This gave the house an ambience of peace, tranquillity and seclusion, so absolute privacy was guaranteed.

The birds were singing a medley of their favourite songs. Mother Nature seemed to be smiling pleasantly on this sunny afternoon. A distant mechanical noise was suddenly heard amongst the cacophony of natural sounds. It was Marianne

Furlow in her silver Volvo speeding towards Skyrise. She was playing out some easy listening music as she gently slowed her vehicle down to a stop.

Marianne then stepped confidently out of the car. She wore black sunglasses which matched her black dress. Her enormous house now shaded her from the warm sunshine. She removed her sunglasses and took a moment to take in some deep calming breaths. She knew that numerous people would soon be arriving. Marianne would have to put on her performance as the grieving widow.

Marianne had negotiated the ordeal of her husband's Catholic funeral without too many problems. There was one notable absentee, their son Kevin, who had called the previous night to say he was too ill to attend. The service featured hymns, prayers and a eulogy that was rose tinted to the point of pure fiction. Shortly after the traditional *ashes to ashes* cremation routine, she was able to excuse herself to prepare a few things for the wake.

Some family members felt someone really should have gone with her on such a sad day. However, Marianne insisted that she preferred to set these things up on her own. The truth was that she just wanted to have some time away from the buggers. This truth had to remain unsaid, of course, British politeness could not swallow such a harsh reality. Marianne could easily have hired out a function room in a town centre location. However, to some people's surprise, she chose to have the wake at her house. Marianne did this because it forced everyone to either drive or get a lift there. She reckoned that, as a result, people would not drink as much and therefore leave earlier.

Marianne opened the large double wooden garage door and her car was soon out of sight. She then hurried to the bathroom to carry out a quick facial maintenance featuring lipstick, eyeliner and mascara. Despite being in her 50s, she still had the ability to turn the heads of much younger men. She was blessed with a slim yet curvaceous figure, the envy of her lady friends. Her blonde hair had managed to ward away unwanted grey invaders. This was complemented by her striking blue eyes that had an incandescent glow. The beauty of her face was sealed by perfectly formed pearly white teeth that looked like something from a Colgate advert.

Marianne walked into her very spacious kitchen diner. This featured a ceiling full of wooden horizontal beams that were only just high enough to clear the head of a tall person. She opened her crockery cupboard and took out a lot of china plates decorated with an ornate floral design. They were all placed into a pile at the end of one of the three trestle tables that were covered with simple white tablecloths. She then opened the double doors of her American fridge that was full of sandwiches and a variety of finger food.

Marianne promptly placed all the food onto large serving platters with a matching design. She had previously planned the layout for the buffet, so it did not take long to set it all up on the trestle tables. Marianne then took out a range of alcoholic and soft drinks from the fridge. There was an even balance between the two to cater for all preferences. An appropriate number of wine glasses, all with attractive double golden lines at the rim, were taken out. These were supplemented by a selection of pint and half pint tankards together with cups and saucers. Everything was tastefully presented without being excessively lavish; enough but not too much.

The large dining room table could sit eight, or at a squeeze, ten people. As the weather was kind, another four or five could sit outside around the garden table. There was also plenty of space, both internally and externally, for guests to remain standing. Marianne had put plenty of thought into her detailed preparations. This included working out how her husband's family and friends would expect her to behave.

Two cars pulled up outside quite suddenly. Marianne steadied herself in the way an actress does when waiting in the wings of a theatre stage. She walked quickly to her front door and opened it. Marianne then saw her late husband's two brothers, Graham and Barry, as well as their sister Sue. All three were in their fifties, but with strikingly different appearances.

Sue was a slim brunette with alluring brown eyes. However, her years of rock and roll excesses showed in her somewhat tired looking face. Barry was a very trim man with steely blue eyes and was quite fresh faced for his age. He had benefitted from years of athleticism and exercise. Graham was a more stockily built man, not exactly fat but he had filled out somewhat. He appeared to have aged a little more than the others. This showed in his salt and pepper hair and in the facial lines that were clearly visible on his forehead.

A forced, falsely polite greeting was made before they promptly entered the property.

"The food is just through there…" said Marianne and she ushered the guests into the kitchen diner. Graham's wife Julie, and Barry's other half Mary, then came into the house. Neither of them was hard on the eye, but no match for the stunning widow who was hosting this wake. It was not long before they all had a drink in their hand. Graham, Barry and Sue were drinking wine. Julie and Mary were sticking to soft drinks as they were driving. Few words were spoken but negative emotions were absolutely screaming. There was little that the five of them had in common outside of their surname. However, they were all united by a hatred of

Marianne. Eventually Graham realised how to ease the tension of this uncomfortable moment.

"Well, as we're blessed with lovely weather, it might be nice to sit outside at the garden table," he said.

"Of course, but do help yourself to some food first," said Marianne.

The two couples quickly put food onto their plates and wasted no time in sitting themselves down outside. Sue, on the other hand, was much more indecisive over her sandwich selection. She then realised to her dismay that Marianne had remained in the room. Traditional manners dictated that some conversation was made. This was awkward as neither party wanted to engage with the other. After a heavily pregnant pause, Marianne finally decided to break the ice by showing off her expensive silver Cartier watch.

"What do you make of my new watch, Sue?"

"Very nice," Sue responded with a distinct absence of sincerity.

"I got this after Martin paid me last week…he's another one who makes monthly payments."

Marianne gave Sue a sinister and gloating smile. Sue knew what Marianne was referring to and it deeply angered her, but she fought hard not to show it. The two ladies then stumbled through a clumsy and vacuous verbal exchange. Eventually Marianne excused herself to use the toilet. Sue was then left alone standing next to a magnificent wooden drinks' cabinet. Marianne took this natural break as an opportunity to go online using her mobile phone. She proceeded to distract herself with some light nonsense from the internet. Marianne took as long as she felt she realistically could before it would appear rude. When she finally did return, Sue had joined the two married couples outside at the garden table. Marianne then heard a lot more cars arrive in very quick succession near her house and her heart sank.

The new arrivals were all relatives, friends or work acquaintances of her late husband Antony. Marianne had little or no contact with her own family. Unfortunately for her, none of Marianne's friends could get the time off work to attend. She viewed everybody present as a collection of old farts ranging from boring to dull. However, she was determined not to show her true feelings so was polite and gracious.

It was not long before the house was full of middle aged and elderly guests munching away and drinking. Marianne engaged in the tiniest of small talk with them. It really was tedious drivel and time crawled by at a pace that made snails look like Olympic sprinters. However, within all this irritating banality, everyone remained polite. They were kind enough to say how sorry they were to hear of Antony's tragic death. He had a fatal fall off a high cliff in the popular seaside town Southcliffe-on-Sea. Marianne then thanked the various relatives but gave polite assurance that she was coping and did not need any support.

Marianne frequently peered out into her garden to check on her late husband's sister, two brothers and their wives. She knew it had been a long time since they were all together at once. They were engaged in free-flowing conversation and she was intrigued. However, Marianne was not close enough to hear a single word. This frustrated her as she really wanted to catch at least some snatches of their dialogue. She was dying to know if they were discussing her and, if so, whether any secrets might emerge.

However, they remained at the garden table for the duration. They only returned briefly for more food, drinks or to use the toilet. Judging from their collective demeanours, Marianne was confident that no bombshells had been dropped. They had, in her view, wisely kept their private secrets (which all involved her) to themselves. After staying at the wake for about an hour and a half, Antony's two brothers and wives vacated the property together along with Sue. They were the first guests to leave the wake and pleasant goodbyes were said with enormous insincerity. There truly was a huge chasm between appearance and reality but social grace demanded this pretence.

Their cars then sped away into the mid-afternoon sunshine. Marianne breathed a sigh of relief as she would never see them again. She took a moment to reflect on those who had just departed. Marianne had decided that, after today, she would no longer engage in any sort of family event. This included any future weddings, christenings and funerals. She then composed herself for the endgame of entertaining the remaining guests for however long they chose to stay.

The afternoon dragged on slowly and Marianne grew tired of her performance as the grieving widow. She had to resist the urge to express her wish for everyone to leave immediately. She knew it would be considered bad form to tell them all to "sod off!" Slowly the guest numbers began to decrease but it was taking much longer than she had hoped. Eventually she was left with just one remaining guest, Antony's cousin Ernie. This elderly man was a retired postman and geographically the closest relative.

In this situation most people would have taken the cue to drink up and leave. However, Ernie lacked social grace and did not pick up on this cue. Instead, he stayed to give a lecture on his favourite subject, the railway lines of Britain. He had given her this lengthy monotonous essay on many occasions. The first time she heard it Marianne was bored out of her mind whereas now it was not quite so interesting.

Marianne worked very hard to maintain her totally false smile. It was as if a papier mâché grin had been glued to her face. *Surely, he must go soon*, she thought to herself, but this was not to be. Ernie was a widower with few friends so had no real reason to leave. Marianne held onto her temper with all her might for an uncomfortable stretch of time. Eventually there was a ray of hope amongst all her misery.

"I don't want to outstay my welcome," said Ernie.

It's a bit bloody late for that, thought Marianne but she was polite enough to not actually say so. Finally, Ernie finished his drink and after a brief goodbye, took off in his Skoda down the road and out of her life forever. The relief of seeing him go and knowing that it was all over bordered on ecstasy.

Marianne decided that before she could relax, she would firstly sort out all the mess left by her guests. The tedium of this domestic chore was eased by the witty lyrics of the Cole Porter songs that were playing from her hi-fi system. After successfully completing the task, she reached into the back of the drinks cabinet to pull out an extremely expensive bottle of sherry. She then took out her very finest crystal cut sherry glass that was nothing short of a work of art. Marianne, although she loved to drink, had stayed stone cold sober all afternoon. She had previously decided that even a couple of drinks might result in her saying something she would later regret. Marianne was very keen to deliver a fully polished performance.

At last, she could properly focus on what she really cared about; the enormous inheritance that she would soon receive. After some tactful persuasion from Marianne, Antony had agreed that the entire estate would go to her. Unusually, Antony had revealed this information to his family shortly before his death. Their son, Antony's brothers and sister were all horrified but there was nothing they could do. Marianne knew that she had been a 24 carat gold digger, but she did not give a damn. She just loved money and everything that money afforded her. Marianne would not miss her deceased husband one iota. Antony was just a means to a financial end as far as she was concerned.

Marianne was confident that she had both the looks and the personality to allure another wealthy man. He would then become her long-term boyfriend or maybe even her next husband. The combination of her new partner's earnings and her inheritance would facilitate an even more lavish lifestyle. She nearly always got what she wanted and was a master of manipulation. If social engineering was a subject, then she would have a PhD.

Marianne poured the sherry into the beautiful receptacle that was poised ready to receive the drink. She then got excited as she thought about her prosperous future and the extravagant lifestyle she would enjoy. Marianne slowly took her first sip from the sherry glass and savoured the moment. After a brief pause, she felt an agonising burning sensation in her throat. She then dropped her glass and grabbed her neck in total panic. Marianne did not understand what was happening, only that it was excruciatingly painful. She fell to the floor with a thump and then rolled around writhing. Absolute terror kicked in as she felt her consciousness ebb away.

And then, within a few minutes, Marianne was dead.

PART ONE
"ANYTHING GOES"

FRAN

Most local people were not aware that the Major Crimes Unit for the county of Havantshire was in Jessop's Green. It was a curious place that was largely made up of houses on mundane streets that snaked off from the main road. However, slightly incongruously, it also contained a huge lake, a retail park, a small pub and a railway station. These were all in the same area as the police headquarters. This random collection of elements seemed to be haphazardly thrown together without any village centre to give it a heart.

The workforce all had some kind of commute to work except for the young Detective Constable Fran Jacobs. She lived within walking distance of the building. Her home was on a quiet back street in a housing estate where almost everyone was a stranger to each other. It was the kind of place where a resident's death would only be realised when some bills had not been paid. Fran had the downstairs flat of a modest maisonette that was camouflaged by similar looking properties on her road.

On this fateful morning, in her bed, Fran was worrying about work. She was anxious about whether she had documented the evidence correctly for the team's previous murder case. Fran sometimes wished she had never become a detective constable. This was mostly because of the man who led the investigations, Chief Detective Inspector John

Stafford. He seemed to despise her and he came across as a man whose opinions seldom changed. She was mentally replaying her last reprimand by him over and over with certain phrases repeating themselves which heightened her anxiety. Fran's mind was now like an old-fashioned vinyl LP with the stylus stuck in a groove and unable to play on. Her entire body tightened up and her heart was beating hard. It was like a rock drummer was pounding away inside her chest.

Her eyes finally opened and she turned over in her bed to glimpse the electronic clock. It showed a time that was a minute before the alarm would make its jarring noise. To save herself from this screeching sound she turned it off and took a deep breath. Fran was not, and never had been, a morning person. She therefore had to wrestle with her lethargy to get herself moving. Fran switched on the bedside cabinet light and stared at the adjacent picture.

It was a small tastefully framed image of her mum, dad and sister all smiling radiantly against a serene Lake District backdrop. Fran would always spend a few moments gazing at this photograph when she woke up and likewise before she went to sleep. Eventually she dragged herself away from the cosy bed covers. Fran then slipped on her dressing gown and slippers before going into the kitchen.

The kitchen was square shaped with all the domestic appliances and cupboards tightly packed in. There were dull, neutral cream-coloured walls that matched the well-worn lino flooring. The dimensions of the room were so minute that when she stood in the centre, Fran could reach everything in there. Fran's kettle slowly boiled as she lined the bottom of a cup with coffee and just a splash of milk. After a tedious wait for the water to heat up, she gratefully enjoyed a much-needed caffeine injection.

Finally, Fran managed to properly open her eyes and walked into her modest little lounge. The room was rectangularly shaped with a matching light blue two-seater sofa and armchair. Her furniture was as tired as she currently felt. A TV and hi-fi were now opposite her, but they were both silent and lifeless. The adjacent bookcase contained numerous RomCom DVDs. There was also a generous helping of chick lit novels to help remove her from reality. Fran put her drink down whilst she opened the peach curtains letting in a dreary overcast light. Peering out of her window, Fran deeply wished she could see some trees or fields. In fact, she would settle for anything instead of the soulless industrial estate that dominated her view.

Fran then sat down on her armchair with her hot drink. She silently told herself that she really must avoid beginning each day with such a negative thought pattern. However, she had been telling herself this for the last year at least. Gone were the days when she had felt any kind of uplifting spiritual connection. She enjoyed her morning coffee and her evening wine, but the events in between were invariably disappointing.

Fran was not one for breakfast so instead went straight into the bathroom. This light green tiled room was not much bigger than a broom cupboard. Fran switched on the light and wished she saw a prettier face in the mirror. She was by no means ugly; her features were even with pleasing soft brown eyes. They were complemented by her neat straight brown hair. She was also slim and just a fraction under average height. Fran did not quite have the attractive girl next door look, but she would definitely still be up some suitor's street.

However, Fran was unfortunate enough to have a truly awful condition; she was English. Subsequently, as an

English woman, she was inherently self-deprecating when it came to her appearance. Any compliment she received was dismissed as a polite and well-meaning lie. After her usual morning dawdling routine, she realised time was ticking on speedily. She then quickly got washed and dressed. Fran made herself look acceptable, if not as beautiful as she would like. She then walked out the front door wearing her policewoman's uniform.

On her way out she saw her neighbour Harry coming up their shared path. He lived in the upstairs flat of the maisonette. Harry Anderson was a trim gentleman of advancing years with a good head of hair that appeared more silver than grey. Fran always wondered why, as a retired man, he always got up so early? If it were not for her job, then almost nothing would make Fran get up before 9am. The only exceptions would be delicious Belgian chocolate or a hot date with her beloved Brad Pitt. However, Harry was one of nature's early risers and always went on a morning walk. Fran admired his ability to stand up and face the new day instead of procrastinating like she did.

They had hardly spoken to each other even though they had been neighbours for a year. Fran felt bad about this but the few conversations they did have were awkward and anodyne. The problem was that she didn't know what to say or how to break the ice between them. She strongly suspected it was the same for him too which was a shame as he came across as a pleasant chap. Fran briefly sighed and then marched on for her ten-minute walk to work.

Fran arrived at her workplace which was surrounded by tall metal fence panels with barbed wire on top. A stranger to the area would be forgiven for thinking it was some sort of maximum-security prison. She walked over to the side of the building and used her badge to open the barrier gates. Within the grounds was a mini multi storey car park that could accommodate around 30 vehicles. This enabled the various Major Crimes Unit staff members to easily park.

Fran saw Chief Detective Inspector Stafford come out of his car and immediately felt anxious. Stafford was dressed in his customary dark blue suit and tie; in fact, Fran wondered if that was his only suit? Fran's superior was a small, thin and balding man who looked older than his age. Years of heavy smoking showed in his front teeth which were a colour somewhere between yellow and brown. Stafford's face appeared almost shrunk which gave him a rodent-like quality. His appearance was matched by his tendency to scurry around quickly. It was as if he was trying to reach a dingy sewer without being caught.

"Good morning sir," said Fran respectfully but this was met with a dismissive indecipherable grunt. Stafford then walked quickly past her and into the building. Fran surmised that she had better just get her head down to survive the day as best she could. She also went inside and up two flights of stairs. Fran used her badge again to swipe herself into the main office. The room was like a small factory of computers that were positioned on top of several rows of tables. A number of black computer chairs were all parked neatly alongside them.

Fran switched on her computer and logged in quickly. As the other staff members arrived, Fran reflected that she worked with a nice team for the most part. In fact, she might have even enjoyed working there if it were not for Stafford. His presence seemed to hang over her head like the Sword of Damocles. Fran was now focussed on typing up the various notes from their last case. She was determined to get this right, partly because it was evidence that could be used in Court, but also to keep Stafford off her back.

Fran was second guessing herself on certain aspects of her report, specifically the timings of a key incident. She was very reluctant to check this with Stafford as she did not want him to know she was unsure. Her anxiety grew as she debated in her mind whether she would risk making a mistake or risk his ire by asking for some help. After an uncomfortable inner dialogue, she figured that she would do the responsible thing. This was, of course, to run it by Stafford as the potential consequences of an error were very serious.

She stood up and walked over to his office, she braced herself and was about to knock on the door. However, Stafford opened it and walked quickly past her.

"Can I have your attention please," he called out to the office in his thin weaselly voice. To an outsider, this quiet command would have appeared to lack gravitas. However, the effect was like a Sergeant Major telling his troops to stand to attention. The sound of fingers typing on keyboards stopped instantly to create an eerie silence. Stafford paused for a moment to enable those who were looking the other way to turn round and face him.

"I need a team to go to Newcot immediately as I've just received a report that a woman has been murdered."

EVIDENCE

No-one in the team had heard of Newcot. Thankfully, the satnavs in their police cars guided them to their destination. Fran was assigned to drive Detective Constables Clara Sobers and Andy Taylor to the crime scene. They each took personal protective clothing with them for use at the crime scene.

Clara was dressed in a similar uniform to Fran. She was a young West Indian woman whose happy fresh face and easy smile radiated her upbeat and cheerful personality. She was originally from Antigua and was proud that her family home was on the same street where Viv Richards used to live. Unfortunately for her, none of her colleagues were cricket fans so they were not familiar with the great batsman. It had been years since she had last seen her mum and dad, which frequently played on her mind. However, she was glad to have found a friend in Fran. They shared the same fundamental beliefs which helped to bond them.

Andy had been a detective constable for 20 years. He was a noticeably tall, slim, middle-aged man with well-groomed blond hair. However, the combination of a thin body and enormous height gave him a somewhat ungainly physicality. Fran regularly helped him by driving her car to the local supermarket so that he could load up her vehicle with his shopping. Andy could drive but had a serious accident during a previous investigation. He was badly shaken by this and could not bring himself to get behind the wheel again. Andy had tried unsuccessfully to share his love of cult and classic films with Fran. Whenever he made a movie suggestion, she would always politely reply that she "might give it a go one day". However, they both knew full well that she would never do such a thing. Despite not having much in common, Andy still liked and respected both Fran and Clara.

In the police car the three of them reflected on the summary of evidence from Stafford that was given to them earlier.

"A lady dies from suspected sherry poisoning. Mmm OK, it's a nice clean murder at least. No dismembered body parts this time unlike our last case. God, that crime scene looked like Hannibal Lecter had just eaten a three-course meal!" said Andy whose London accent had faint echoes of his working-class roots.

"Hey man, Stafford only said that it *appears* to be poisoning," said Clara, who had a deep voice that echoed the lively calypso tones of the Caribbean.

"And he always says that we can't assume anything," said Fran who had quite a refined home counties voice. This was befitting of someone who had clearly been brought up very well.

"Yeah, I know, 'to assume makes an ass out of u and me,'" said Andy dismissively.

Fran checked her speedometer for a second and then a daft thought popped into her head. Thankfully, she was with the only two colleagues that she felt comfortable enough to express something silly like this.

"If I were to drive too fast, do you think one of my colleagues would arrest me for speeding?"

"Mmm intriguing, slap the car into Lewis Hamilton mode and let's find out," said Andy.

"Don't you dare," Clara countered, and her facial expression made it clear she wasn't joking.

"It's alright Clara, I wouldn't want to give Stafford the pleasure of putting points on my licence. But seriously, can you imagine arresting one of your colleagues?"

"I don't think you'll ever find out," said Andy.

Fran then turned her car to go up the mile long cul-de-sac that led to the murder victim's magnificent property. They got out and put on their personal protective clothing.

"You know, whenever I put this suit on, I'm reminded of 'Back to the Future'. You know, the bit where Doc Brown puts the cylinder of plutonium into the Delorean," said Andy.

"How did you ever become a detective constable? You're like a child, man!" Clara replied with warmth and affection.

"There is nothing more overrated than being a mature adult," Andy replied assertively. However, he then got his serious head on to focus on the investigation. Andy pulled out a wad of transparent bags from the glove compartment of the car.

As per normal police procedure for a crime scene, the house had been sealed off by blue and white tape. However, it could have been seen as unnecessary as they were in too remote a location to be disturbed. Fran saw Stafford speak to a young man just outside the house. A combination of policewoman's instincts and female intuition correctly told her that this was Kevin, the son of the victim. Her compassionate nature meant that she wanted her to go over and comfort this man in his hour of grief. She restrained herself though as she had been given a roasting by Stafford for doing something similar on a previous case. Fran had learnt that in these situations she had to leave her deeply emotional heart in the police car. Besides which, Kevin seemed to be coping surprisingly well.

Fran, Andy and Clara entered through the front door, one at a time in quick succession. They walked into the kitchen diner where Marianne's dead body laid on the floor. Her facial skin now had a tinge of cold grey; her eyes, though motionless, still radiated her sense of terror. A brief cursory glance would immediately tell you that she died several days ago. It was also obvious that she didn't die gently in her sleep. Adjacent to the body was the beautiful sherry glass with a spillage of the drink that had overflowed onto the laminate flooring. The investigation team therefore felt this was a strong indication that Marianne had been poisoned.

Andy carefully bagged the glass in such a way that it stayed upright. He made sure that the very small amount of remaining liquid stayed securely in the receptacle. He knew this would need to be tested to clarify the suspected poison. Clara then reached down carefully to do a swab of the sherry that was on the floor. Fran carefully collected the bottle of sherry and put into a suitable bag. Her instincts told her that the perpetrator probably put the poison in this rather than the glass. This would have ensured the fatal solution was not noticeable when the drink was poured.

Andy, Fran and Clara then checked all the doors and windows meticulously. It was soon realised that no break-in was involved. Indeed, the property was tidy and almost spotless bar the sherry glass that had now been removed. Marianne's mobile phone, laptop, tablet and chargers were all taken away in bags too. The three detective constables also looked through Marianne's bedroom. They were hoping for something like a diary or anything that might provide a window into her mind.

The painstaking investigation continued all day. Andy, Clara and Fran could feel their frustration rising. It was a tedious and uncomfortable task, bearing in mind their restrictive clothing. They had become like soulless robots sifting through all the evidence with mechanical efficiency. Finally, after his team had checked every room in the property in minute detail, Stafford instructed everyone to return to Head Office.

Fran was relieved to be released from what had felt like a prison cell. She was now free to travel back on the road with Andy and Clara.

"God, he's such a bloody perfectionist," said Andy, who was making the most of the privacy that the police car afforded him. There was a pause of mutual silent agreement before Andy continued.

"Stafford is the chief detective inspector equivalent of Stanley Kubrick. It's like we do 100 takes of every crime scene!"

"Yeah, but Andy, you know the tiniest insignificant detail can sometimes make all the difference. Look, I know it's a…" Fran abruptly stopped as she struggled to think of the right adjective.

"Ball ache!" Andy crudely interjected. After a brief pause, he became conscious of the women who were with him.

"Or the female equivalent," he then quickly added.

"OK yeah, it's tedious, but we are talking about a serious crime and we've got to get it right," Fran continued.

Andy turned to briefly stare through the car window at the pleasing early evening sunshine. Sunrays kissed the top of a large hill that they were passing. He then remembered his plans for tonight.

"I hope we get to finish soon," said Andy, whose hope was not matched by his expectation.

"Why, have you got something on?" enquired Clara.

"Yeah, I've got a date," said Andy.

"A date!" said Clara.

This was the most interesting thing that Fran and Clara had heard all day. Fran was surprised as Andy had not long split up from his girlfriend. Having whetted their appetites for some ripe and juicy gossip, Andy held them in suspense briefly before continuing.

"I've got a date with Chelsea."

"And who's 'Chelsea'?" said Fran with a mischievous 'wink, wink' undertone.

"Well ladies, 'Chelsea'…is the world's most glorious football club and tonight we're playing a key match against Liverpool!"

A groan was then heard in the car. It was the only suitable response to Andy's lead balloon punchline.

As she was about to arrive at the police car park, Fran noticed her neighbour Harry walking home carrying a shopping bag. She wanted to wave but she had to concentrate to make a turning correctly. Shortly after arriving, Stafford summoned them to a briefing in the main meeting room. There were no computers, but several rows of chairs lined up to face the presentation area. The square space had a good balance, large enough to fit plenty of people in but not so big that microphones were required. It was not impressive or aesthetically pleasing but functional and fit for its purpose.

Stafford was somewhat reminiscent of a schoolteacher as he stood next to the white board marking out a timeline for the events of the murder. Fran then noticed him squirting a bit of freshener spray into his mouth. She had seen him do this on numerous occasions; he seemed very self-conscious about the smell of his breath. Stafford then scribbled some headers that were only just legible.

```
21/09/23 Evening _ _ _ _  22/09/23 Afternoon_ _ _ _  27/09/23 Morning
Sherry Aperitif          Antony's Wake              Marianne found dead
```

Finally, he turned to face the team who had now all assembled for his debriefing.

"OK listen up everybody. Kevin, the son of the deceased Marianne Furlow, claims that she had been living alone after her husband Antony had died. For the record he only died a few weeks ago in an accident. She had his wake at her house last Friday, hence all the scraps of sandwiches and finger food we found in the bin. Kevin said that due to illness he missed his father's funeral and wake. In fact, he was unable to go to Marianne's house until today. However, he did say that he called his mum's mobile on three consecutive days before going to her house today. I've checked Marianne's mobile phone records and there are indeed three voice mail messages left by him.

Kevin said that Marianne liked an aperitif of sherry every evening around 6pm. Assuming this is true, it's most probable that she drank the poisoned sherry and died around that time last Friday. Kevin said he is the only person to have spare keys to the property and our investigation showed no signs of forced entry. Now, if no-one else has a key then there is only one logical conclusion…"

There was no need for Stafford to spell it out to the team. Everyone immediately reached the same conclusion; somebody at the wake must be the murderer. Everyone except for Fran, who was having other ideas.

RUMINATIONS

The Major Crime Unit team was dismissed shortly after Stafford's briefing. Andy rushed off to catch his train as he wanted to avoid being late for his football 'date'. Clara also hurried away as she wanted to be able to have a late dinner with her children before they went to bed. As always, Fran walked home alone and was formulating thoughts in her mind. She was quite oblivious to everything and everyone around her. This did not matter as night-time in Jessop's Green made a cemetery look like a disco.

Fran walked up the drive to her maisonette and noticed Harry's bedroom light was on. She saw him smile down at her from his window as he cradled a glass of brandy. Fran returned his smile before entering her property and taking off her uniform. She ran a bath and dropped in a lavender scented bath bomb. It fizzed up the water like a glass of vintage champagne. She wanted to create a pleasant ambience to help her relax. Fran therefore opted for a soft candlelight instead of the much harsher ceiling light.

Whilst luxuriating in the warm water and bubbles, Fran was thinking intensely. She was very focussed on the case and an hour passed by without her even noticing. Eventually, Fran got out but was a little taken aback when she realised the time. Despite possessing excellent cooking skills, she figured it was a bit late to get out her pots and pans. She needed an alternative which prompted her to scroll through some fast-food options on her mobile phone. Fran eventually settled for a Chinese take away and an order was duly made.

After changing into her pyjamas, dressing gown and slippers, Fran decided it was now her favourite time – 'wine o'clock'. As she sipped at her glass of Chardonnay, her mobile phone showed an image that made her smile. Her chosen fast-food establishment was clearly having a quiet night. The map on her screen was now showing the delivery driver on their way. She was very hungry and so followed the driver's route with keen interest until it concluded with a knock on her door.

Fran was always self-conscious about her appearance. However, she decided it would be a bit much to get dressed and 'dolled up' just to answer the door. After all, it was not likely that the food would be delivered by Brad Pitt. She therefore gave the delivery man the rare pleasure of seeing her without any make up on. Fran happily accepted the brown paper bag that contained the oriental nosh.

The chicken was a touch cold, but she was still very grateful for the convenience of this meal after such a long and exhausting day. Fran brought the candlelight, that she absentmindedly had left burning away, from the bathroom into the lounge. She then got onto her iPod and selected Ed Sheeran's *Divide* album. Fran listened to the melodic tracks whilst she played through the events of the day in her mind.

She understood why Stafford had deduced that the murderer was one of the attendees of the wake. If Marianne really had died of poison at around 6pm on the Friday, then his conclusion made sense. However, what wrangled with her was that the perpetrator must have taken an enormous chance. Somehow, they got the poison into the sherry glass or bottle (Fran was convinced it was the latter) without being seen. There were numerous guests present so how could they be sure someone would not walk in at the wrong moment?

This risk would be eliminated if the murderer was alone in the house or if Marianne was asleep in bed. However, Kevin said he had the only spare set of keys and he was in his sick bed at the time. If this was the case, then how the hell did the murderer enter the property? Assuming Marianne did not give them access then it appeared impossible as there was no sign of any break-in.

It was also reported that Marianne drank a daily sherry aperitif before her main meal. This would mean her tipple was poisoned somewhere between Thursday evening and Friday evening. Fran then considered the possibility of the sherry being poisoned in the early hours of Friday morning whilst Marianne was asleep. However, this still left the question of how did the murderer get inside the house?

Fran's mind was now like a Rubik's cube being twisted around. To her frustration she could not get the lines to sync up and solve the puzzle. She was really hooked on this case because it was unlike anything she had come across before. Fran knew that it was actually Stafford's responsibility to work everything out, not her. However, she simply couldn't stop herself, curiosity had murdered the pussycat. Fran sometimes fantasised about being a chief detective inspector herself. However, the realities of the intense pressure, long hours and tedious paperwork was a grim prospect. No, she would much rather be a sort of modern *Miss Marple* character. Fran would, of course, be much younger and not have the old-fashioned collection of tweed jackets.

After Ed Sheeran had sufficiently entertained her ears, Fran went to bed. However, her mind was still racing away like a horse in the Grand National. She eventually had to calm herself down with a cup of Horlicks. She reasoned that every one of her many thoughts about the case tonight had just been idle speculation. To really progress properly, they needed the toxicology, pathologist's, and coroner's reports. Fran knew that all of these would be available soon and was confident that the evidence would be illuminating.

The following morning, Fran needed two cups of coffee to get herself moving. Once again, her overactive mind had deprived her of the sleep that her body craved. She also forced herself to have a brief shower to help awaken her. Fran then drew upon her depleted energy reserves to leave her home. She was, at least slightly, uplifted by seeing her friendly neighbour Harry on the way there. Fran noted that for some reason she seemed to be seeing him more frequently of late.

Whilst enroute, she remembered that she still had to talk to her dreaded superior about that report from the previous case. However, this would have to wait as the focus was now on this new and mysterious murder. When she arrived in the office, she was immediately relieved by the absence of Stafford. As a senior investigation officer, he was now working alongside the pathologist, coroner and the forensic team. They were all examining the physical evidence such as Marianne's dead body and the remains of the sherry.

The entire workforce arrived shortly afterwards and the mood of the room was noticeably more relaxed. There was much more banter and humour than normal. It was as if a memo had been sent to the office giving everyone permission to smile. This bonhomie did not detract from their work as the team focussed on the chief objective of the day. They had to figure out who else attended the wake on that fateful Friday. Kevin could only think of a handful of names and had no telephone numbers for any of them. It was obvious that he was quite removed from Antony's broader family, friends and acquaintances.

Stafford returned to the office around lunchtime and did not look happy. Whilst he never looked truly happy, he was now even more miserable than normal. Fran was intrigued as to what had caused his gloomy mood, but the fear of instant decapitation prevented her from asking. A couple of hours after arriving the chief detective inspector summoned everyone back into the meeting room. An impressive looking PowerPoint presentation had been set up. Stafford proceeded to reveal the names of every single person who attended the wake. He also explained what their relationship was to both Marianne and Antony. This information had now been acquired and cross referenced accordingly. Fran noticed that Marianne did not have any friends present and she was curious. However, she quickly refocussed back on the CDI who was now concluding his briefing.

"The toxicology report has confirmed that Marianne was poisoned by a crudely made Strychnine poison. I would say anyone with a Chemistry degree could have created this potion. The report also showed it was mixed into the contents of the sherry bottle."

Ah, so it was in the sherry bottle, Fran silently thought and was pleased that she had made the correct deduction.

"However, the bad news is that there is not a single shred of incriminating physical evidence anywhere. Whoever committed the crime knew what they were doing. I think it's safe to conclude that it was pre-meditated rather than spontaneous. We have already gathered that it must be someone at the wake, the question is, which one of them is our murderer?"

Fran then weighed up in her mind whether she dared to share an idea from the ruminations she had last night. She knew she had to say this quickly or Stafford would move on and the moment would be lost.

"Sir," said Fran, who projected her voice sufficiently to bridge the 20 foot gap between them.

"Yes, what is it, Fran?"

"I know that all the evidence appears to suggest that someone at the wake must have poisoned the sherry. But it must have been risky to do this when there were so many people present? It would have been much easier to do this without all the guests there. Especially if they wanted to ensure no incriminating evidence was left. Can we be sure it really was someone at the wake? Could it possibly have been done another time?"

"Don't be stupid Fran. We've established her habit of daily aperitifs. This means there's a 24 hour window for this crime to have been committed. The house is in a very remote location and her son was not present. Now, as there was no break-in and he was the only one with the keys, then it's *got* to be someone at the wake."

"Sir, we only have Kevin's word that he never went there."

"No, we've collected lots of statements, including some guests at the wake, who have confirmed it. Marianne was called by Kevin the night before to say he was ill and couldn't make it. There's also a phone record that proved he called. Now please, I haven't got time for baseless and bloody stupid ideas."

Stafford then glared at Fran harshly and his facial expression hurt her much more than his actual words. It was as if two daggers had been thrown out of his eyes and stabbed her in the heart. She just had to look away as she could not bear Stafford's intimidating face. Fran wished she could reel the words she had just spoken back into her mouth.

Stafford eventually ended the meeting and the shift ended. Fran then went outside and breathed in the cool air with Andy and Clara. They both picked up that she had been upset by Stafford's sharp reprimand. He was still in the office and was working late as he always did. This meant the three of them were at liberty to speak freely.

"Don't take it to heart Fran, Stafford is a git with the diplomacy skills of a Dalek. If it wasn't for his great track record, he probably would have been sacked years ago."

"Thanks Andy."

Andy gave her a friendly hug, like a brother comforting a beloved sister.

"Now get yourself a bottle of wine and a takeaway."

"I had both of those last night."

"But you can do it again."

Andy smiled warmly before looking at his watch and grimacing.

"Blimey, I'd better go or I'll miss my train. This is where I really wish I could drive again, goodnight."

And with that Andy swiftly disappeared into the night. Fran then faced her other friend and colleague.

"Now look girl, it's not just you. He got all stroppy with me when I tried to get some time off to go to Antigua. I don't want you beating yourself up, just chill and forget all about it," said Clara and Fran smiled.

"Promise me…" Clara continued.

"Alright, I promise I won't beat myself up," said Fran assertively. Shortly afterwards Fran went home and beat herself up very badly.

A TEST OF FAITH

It was just as well Fran had booked the next day off work as she had hardly slept at all. As this was on top of her previous couple of sleepless nights, she was now feeling exhausted. Fran was for the most part a house-proud young woman. On a day off she would normally do some spring cleaning or, as it was now late September, autumn cleaning. However, today she took more of a bachelor approach and decided it really was not worth the effort. Besides, years of good housekeeping ensured she could slack off a bit without too disastrous a consequence.

It was late morning before Fran was able to separate herself from the warmth and comfort of her bed. She felt low and she really wanted the companionship of a friend. However, experience had taught her that any rendezvous had to come with at least a week's notice. Most of her friends either had a family or were somehow permanently busy. This is where she missed her teenage years when she could meet up with others almost spontaneously. She longed for the good old days when her social circle had the precious commodity that is time. Fran sent a few texts to some friends but received curt replies. It was obvious that they did not want any kind of conversation.

She switched on the TV but the daytime 'chewing gum for the eyes' programmes were not to her taste. Fran then had some flashbacks to Stafford from the previous night. She wished she could get him out of her head so she could enjoy her days off. Unfortunately, she had the self-destructive habit of clinging onto negative things. Fran then saw Harry come up their shared path and wanted to finally strike up a decent conversation with the man. However, once again, her shyness and self-doubt got the better of her, so instead she remained inside alone.

During the evening, Fran spent some time on the internet via her mobile phone. She went on Facebook and read all the relevant updates. This included what the girl who she sat next to her 17 years ago in her Geography class ate for breakfast this morning. After this mind-numbing social media exercise, she then moved onto dating websites. Fran swiped left and right on the profiles of various potential suitors. She did not hold out much hope for finding love online as it seemed hopeless. Despite this, Fran still kept the door open just in case she received a Tinder surprise.

The next day Fran got back into her usual clean and tidy mode. The domestic chores were all done to a very high standard. In fact, it would have earned her a rave review if the property had been let out through Airbnb. Finally, she felt in a slightly better mood than the day before although she was still quizzing herself over the case. Late in the afternoon she received a text from Clara.

> Saturday, 30 Sep · 17.17
>
> Hi Fran, Sorry about this but please could you give me a lift tomorrow. Our car is in the garage and won't be ready until Tuesday?" xx

Fran had no problems with this and confirmed straightaway. She felt she should be looking forward to their regular Sunday fixture, but her feelings were quite mixed.

Fran got up just after 9 o'clock on Sunday morning and took a bit of time to get ready. She applied a touch more mascara and lipstick then normal. Fran hoped it would help bring out her best features. She then put on some light blue jeans together with a tasteful cream jumper. Fran set off in her brown Ford Fiesta just after 10am. A few minutes later she saw her friend waiting outside on the street. Clara was dressed in a pair of casual but still quite smart looking navy blue trousers with a flowery top.

"Is it just you then, Clara?"

"Yes, I'm afraid so, the kids are sick."

"Oh, sorry to hear that, I hope that…"

Fran paused abruptly and had to make a minor but somewhat embarrassing admission.

"Clara, I'm having brain fog, what are you children's names again?"

"Well, you know I'm a big cricket fan so that's why I called my twins Brian and Lara."

"Oh right," Fran replied politely even though she failed to make the connection.

"Curtly is staying home to look after them so it's just me and you."

Fran was sorry to hear this as she genuinely liked the whole family. However, it did mean that she was now at liberty to discuss the confidential matters of the case.

"You know, out of curiosity I googled that brand of sherry," said Fran.

"Oh, is there something special about it?"

"Yes, it's extremely expensive, Amonti Sherry goes for hundreds of pounds a bottle."

"This girl liked the finer things of life."

"Yes, but I'm pretty sure a bottle like that would be kept well out of the way. She wouldn't want to share that with the other guests."

"Yeah, definitely Fran."

"So, whoever poisoned it must have known where the bottle was kept. They must have also known about Marianne's habit of having a sherry aperitif before her evening meal."

"Have you mentioned this to Stafford?"

"No, and to be honest after last Thursday night's debacle, I'm very reluctant to suggest anything to him."

"Oh, it shouldn't be like this, you are an intelligent woman who has good ideas."

"Thanks, but I…oh he really gets to me."

Clara wanted to offer some reassurance to her friend. However, she knew that Fran's insecurity was buried deep into her soul. Despite the best of intentions, kind words would not change a damn thing. There was a slightly awkward pause as both women wondered how to continue the conversation. The situation with Stafford scratched uncomfortably at Fran's heart, so to give some relief Fran then changed the subject.

"How's your family in Antigua?"

"They're good, we Skype every week and it's lovely but…" Clara's sentence trailed off abruptly.

"But what?"

"But it's never the same, the computer screen is never the same as seeing them in person."

Fran wondered what to say and was now in the same position that Clara was in only moments earlier. She wanted to offer reassurance but knew it was impossible.

Fran drove up to their destination, Midbury United Reformed Church which was located in northwest Havantshire. This House of God was now in view and they had arrived in good time for the Sunday service. Fran parked adjacent to the building that appeared more functional than holy. Her Ford Fiesta was outshone by the more impressive cars that were parked alongside hers. However, she reasoned that if Jesus rode into Jerusalem on a humble donkey, then she should make do with her modest vehicle. The double doors of the church entrance were fully opened and the two young women walked swiftly inside.

There were no ornate stained-glass windows in the church. It seemed a tad minimalist although there was a large wooden cross on the far wall of the hall. Underneath this ancient symbol of Christianity was a plush blue carpet. This carpet covered the three steps that spanned the width of the stage just behind it. In the left-hand corner was a rather tired looking pulpit. The wooden lectern was angled down to hold the Bible and the sermon papers.

A lot of chairs were set out, each one had a hymn book placed on top. The hall was about a third full, with clusters of worshippers scattered sporadically around. On the wall behind the chairs were three enormous arch shaped windows. These ensured that there was plenty of light in the room. Traditional organ music was being softly played to give a heavenly ambience. The congregation quietly waited for the Reverend Matthew Atkinson to appear. At 10.30am sharp, he duly marched in wearing his conventional black and white clergyman cassocks. He was a chubby bespectacled man and his salt and pepper hair gave a strong hint as to his advancing years.

The service followed the usual structure of a 'hymn sandwich'. The main meat of this sandwich was Matthew's sermon which concerned the power of prayer. After about five minutes Fran was indeed praying, she was praying that he would just shut up. Fran got his message very quickly so was annoyed that he continued for another 20 minutes. Matthew's words eventually became nothing more than a distant white noise to her. Fran had been taught that the path to righteousness was steep and stony. She wondered whether that was the point of her vicar's intolerable ramblings - to test her faith.

Finally, a divine peace was felt by all those present when Matthew stopped speaking. The congregation then proceeded to give a somewhat half-hearted rendition of the hymn O *Jesus I have promised*. Hymns are a well-established church tradition, but Fran could not stand her own voice. She therefore felt uncomfortable and very self-conscious when singing. This was despite her voice being masked by the collective harmony from the rest of the congregation.

Matthew gave a concluding final prayer which was mercifully short and then the service ended. Once again, this holy hour in church was something that Fran had endured rather than enjoyed. She definitely did not get the spiritual connection that her soul yearned for so deeply. Fran smiled politely to some acquaintances she had known for years, but her face was not showing her true feelings.

A couple of old ladies then went into the adjacent kitchen through a side door. Five minutes later they reappeared with a three-tiered trolley. The bottom two tiers contained a plethora of cheap but functional blue cups. The top tier had two pots of boiling water with tea bags, a jar of coffee, some milk and sugar. Everything was now ready for hot refreshments to be served. Fran had a cup of tea and put a few coins into a small dish. This proved to be a nice little earner for the church aside from the main collection in the service.

Fran then surveyed the room like a hawk hunting its prey. She was looking for Matthew as she wanted to discuss a matter that was very pressing to her. Eventually she found the clergyman who had been her vicar for the last three years. Matthew was cheerfully chatting away to the treasurer who was also his closest friend. Fran had her patience tested as she waited for their conversation to end. Eventually the two men broke free from each other and so she swooped in eagerly.

"Ah Fran, always lovely to see you," Matthew said warmly.

"Matthew, have you got time for a chat?"

"Of course."

"It's just that something has been troubling me for a while."

"Oh…what's the matter?"

"OK, well you know that in my profession I see all sorts of horrible things."

"I can imagine."

"And you also know that what happened when I was a teenager…"

Fran's sentence trailed off as she recalled a deeply traumatic experience.

"It's OK, I know what you are referring to and that was tragic," said Matthew sympathetically.

"Alright, let me tell you what I'm struggling with. We are taught to believe in a God of infinite love. But if God's love is infinite then why do all these terrible things happen?"

"It's a natural question to ask Fran, but you must remember we all have free will."

"Yes, but some people are born with pain, what about them?"

Matthew paused for what felt like an age to reflect. Fran wondered if he was ever going to answer her question, but eventually he did.

"Fran, us mere mortals are not able to understand the intricate workings of divinity. We must trust that God has a higher plan for everyone even if we cannot make rational sense of it ourselves."

Fran knew that he would say something like this, but felt Matthew's response did not really explain anything. She quickly but politely ended the conversation and walked away. It was obvious that she was not going to get an answer that would satisfy her. Fran then found Clara, who had been busy chatting with the organist. Clara picked up on the social cue and promptly left with Fran.

Fran drove away in her car and felt relieved to be leaving the church behind. To take her mind away from the frustration she had over Matthew, she focussed back on the murder case.

"You know there's one other thing that's been bugging me about this case Clara. When I saw Kevin outside, he seemed remarkably calm. It was very surprising as he had just discovered his mother's murdered body."

"Hey, you don't think he did it, do you? He's got the perfect alibi, he wasn't there."

"No, I don't think he did it, it's just, I don't know, it's just his reaction…"

"Different people express feelings in different ways. I mean Curtly always seems so chilled, but I know inside he's really emotional."

Shortly afterwards Fran dropped Clara off home. She then returned to her humble maisonette where she relaxed for the rest of the day. Fran understood Clara's point, but she still felt there was something not right about Kevin.

KEVIN

Monday morning arrived like an uninvited guest who had come to spoil the party. Fran reluctantly pulled herself out of her sleepy slumber. Once again, she stared at the picture of her family for a moment's reflection before getting ready. On the way into work, she tried to figure out what her feelings were telling her about Kevin. However, it was all too vague and nebulous to articulate with any clarity. Fran arrived at the Major Crimes Unit, walked swiftly into the office to find Andy sat down alone. He was holding a glass of water and looking unusually glum and serious.

"Hi Andy…what's wrong?" asked Fran.

"I think we're going to have our work cut out with this case."

"What makes you say that?"

"OK, all the initial interviews we've had so far show that no-one has any idea who committed the murder. You may remember Stafford saying there was no incriminating evidence found. So how the hell are we going to get a warrant to carry out an arrest? We've got nothing to go on."

"Come on, it's early days."

"Yeah, but I would have thought this case would have been relatively straightforward. Bearing in mind that it happened at a wake in a private house."

Deep down Fran had a feeling that something was being overlooked. However, she did not have the confidence to speak up, even to Andy, whom she viewed as a friend. She was feeling very insecure but then something happened that immediately perked her up.

Detective Inspector James Mallen strode into the room confidently. He looked very dapper in his smart black tailored suit, crisp white shirt and impressive gold tie. Fran could not help but to turn her head whenever he walked in as she found him irresistibly attractive. James was a fine figure of a man with an impressively toned body. He had neat jet-black hair, warm chocolate brown eyes and a smile that had a magnetic quality. However, what Fran found particularly appealing was that his good looks were complemented by a refreshing modesty. Fran was disappointed to learn that James was married. However, she still enjoyed a bit of window shopping albeit discreetly.

"Hello Fran, what's occurring?" said James. His soft lilting Welsh accent had the singsong quality that quickly changed from a lower to a higher tone. Fran could not help but to love having the attention of such a handsome man.

"Not much really but I'm good," said Fran. She knew this was a lie, but she really did not want to go into her theological issues. She also did not want to express her doubts over her abilities as a detective constable. There was a brief pause before Fran got over her shyness enough to ask the obvious question in response.

"How about you?"

"Oh lovely, I had a nice bike ride down to the valleys."

Fran deduced that James regularly exercised and this would explain his impressive physique. All she wanted to do was just gaze at him like a teenage girl with a crush. She had to control herself though as this was inappropriate on several levels. Besides which, as she had to remind herself, he was a married man.

Stafford suddenly summoned the whole of the Major Crimes Unit in for a briefing. It did not last very long and effectively amounted to him giving out orders as to who would do what. Fran had been assigned to interview Kevin; this was exactly what she wanted. However, Stafford then said he would accompany her; this was exactly what she didn't want. It reminded her of when she was at school and about to have a lesson with the awful Mr Wozniak. The only difference was that she could no longer go to her nan's for sweeties afterwards. Fran had to steel herself to stay professional and focussed. She needed to steer clear of those negative self-destructive doubts that frequently plagued her mind.

Despite her doubts she did at least have some confidence about carrying out the interview as this was her main strength. Even Stafford acknowledged that she was good at prising out information from her interviewees. Fran knew which buttons to push and how gently or firmly to press them. This was undoubtedly the reason why he had picked her for a more in-depth interview with Kevin.

However, Fran had one more obstacle to overcome first, the journey there. It was a lengthy trip to Kevin's house which could be made even longer by heavy traffic. This meant being in very close proximity to the man she loathed for what would feel like ages. Fran drove the police car and just as she left the barrier gates, she noticed Harry walking down the road. She wanted to wave to him, but she was worried Stafford would view this as unprofessional.

Stafford was swigging on his water bottle and munching on his Polo Mints. Fran was curious as to why he always did that whenever he travelled in a car. She eventually concluded it was just one of his quirks. Stafford then became busy on his mobile phone and Fran was grateful for this. As her superior was occupied, she could just focus on driving and leave him to it. However, her reprieve was short-lived as after about 10 minutes he put his phone down. Fran then had to work out what to say to this unpleasant man. It would be uncomfortable to have such a long journey with no conversation at all. She was eager to avoid saying anything that would give him ammunition for one of his cutting putdowns. Eventually Fran found a safe but relevant question to ask.

"Just to bring me up to speed, sir, what information has come from the other interviews?"

Fran had already ascertained this information from Andy. However, Stafford did not know about this conversation and it was something to break the ice.

"Nothing that is going to help us catch our killer, I'm afraid. Everyone seems to be baffled. I must admit I've been puzzling over this one myself. I mean the murderer must have known that Marianne liked a sherry aperitif every night before her meal. They must also have known where the sherry bottle is kept so they could easily drop in the poison."

Fran was proud that she had been thinking along the same lines as her superior. She kept this private glory to herself but it lifted her spirits. Fran was then able to engage in further discussion about the case more confidently. It was hardly revelatory, but it did help to pass the time. This was the object of the exercise as far as she was concerned. Eventually they arrived at Kevin's small terraced house in the quiet village of Alderham. This was located on the east side of the county of Havantshire.

Stafford got out of the car first and Fran swiftly followed him. They walked up to the two steep steps in front of an old brown wooden door. Stafford gave a succession of knocks that had a rhythmical quality. He then took out his ID badge from his jacket pocket and held it in his hand. There was a tantalising silence, long enough for them to wonder if Kevin was at home, but finally the door was opened. Kevin was a young man and the sole occupant of the property. He was dressed in old blue jeans and a scraggy dark blue jumper. Kevin appeared somewhat laid-back, not at all alarmed by the police presence. There was an apathy in his manner as well as the vacant expression in his blue eyes. This was enhanced by his distinct absence of a hairstyle and his scruffy clothes. It was as if this interview was of no real consequence – Fran made a mental note.

"Kevin Furlow?"

"Yes"

Stafford swiftly brought up his ID badge so that Kevin could easily see it.

"I'm Chief Detective Inspector John Stafford and this is Detective Constable Fran Jacobs."

"Oh yeah…well, come in," Kevin said almost nonchalantly. Kevin spoke in a voice that could only be described as nondescript. There was no trace of an accent and it was devoid of any defining characteristic. It was unnervingly cold like an android's mouthpiece was doing the talking. He opened his front door fully and gestured to Fran and Stafford to enter. They duly did so and passed through a hallway. It looked rather tacky with bare floorboards and specks of white paint dotted around. The acutely narrow dimensions meant they had to walk in single file. It was only a few steps before Kevin turned left and opened the door that was the entrance to a very small square lounge.

The room had a well-worn beige carpet with an aging cream two-seater sofa. This settee contained wine and coffee stains that clearly showed where the drinker had been clumsy. On the other side of the room was a television, a DVD player and a small selection of popcorn films piled up next to it. The sunlight shone through two grubby grey framed windows with visibly broken handles. Pressed against the wall furthest away from the windows was a small square table that could only accommodate one diner. This was covered by a white tablecloth with little spots of pasta sauce ingrained into the material.

There was only just enough space for one person to squeeze through the gap between the furniture. Having three people in the lounge made it feel terribly claustrophobic. Kevin took a chair that was placed under the table and turned it to face the sofa. He then swiftly sat down which cued the two police officers to both take a seat on the settee. A drink was offered but politely declined as both Fran and Stafford wanted to proceed with the interview. Fran knew the drill; she would ask the questions whilst Stafford would scribble down the relevant points on his notepad. The chief detective inspector was assertively poised to write, she could tell he did not want to wait much longer.

After a few moments of deliberation Fran decided that she should begin gently and compassionately.

"Firstly, we are terribly sorry for your loss," she said but this was met with a dismissive gesture from Kevin.

"Look I know you feel obliged to say this stuff but it's alright, let's just get on with it," said Kevin. Fran immediately realised that Kevin did not want sympathy or empathy. Usually under these circumstances support from a Family

Liaison Officer would at least be offered. However, it was clear that Kevin did not require this.

"OK then, were you aware of anyone who had some kind of vendetta against Marianne?"

"Vendetta…mmm…actually, I know a lot of people who detested the very sight of her. But I can't think of anyone of who would have a clear-cut motive for murder if that's what you are driving at."

"Why was she so hated?"

"Because she used people, everyone was a pawn in her game. She was so incredibly selfish. She had this overriding philosophy of 'anything goes'. This basically meant she would just do whatever she wanted and not give a damn."

Kevin had adopted a very matter-of-fact tone. Fran was a little unnerved by his candour. However, from the point of view of evidence it was good that he was so direct. Her training kicked in so she would remain completely neutral. She knew that she couldn't show any emotional reaction to his answers. Fran just focussed on extracting the information that the investigation required.

"Tell me about her marriage with your father."

"It wasn't a marriage; they just shared the same surname."

"What do you mean 'it wasn't a marriage?'"

"She fleeced him for all of his wealth and then slept with whoever she wanted."

"And did your dad ever consider divorcing her after all this adultery?"

"You would think so, wouldn't you? But she had this way, it's hard to explain exactly. She just made him feel that he couldn't live without her, that he would never find anyone else. Also, now don't get me wrong, I didn't fancy my mother or anything, but she was regarded as an astonishingly beautiful woman. From a purely physical point of view, it's very unlikely that dad would find anyone to match her. She ruthlessly exploited this too."

"How would you describe your relationship with your mother?"

This was the first time that Kevin had a delay in his response. It was also the first time that he looked uncomfortable and the mood in the room changed. Kevin looked down at the carpet for a few moments with the palm of his hand pressed against his forehead. Fran could tell this was going to be a considered answer.

"OK, well I obviously didn't like her. In the same way that she wasn't really dad's wife, she wasn't really my mother. I learnt as a young boy that she didn't want me."

"How did you realise that?"

"Due to her continued absence. She hired in endless amounts of au pairs and got family or friends to look after me. Meanwhile she would go out until all hours living it up. And when she couldn't get away, she would just plonk me in front of the TV. We never talked, not properly, not as a mother should talk to her son."

"And this made you grow up resentful?"

"Damn right it did! I know she never wanted children. It was only because of Gran and Grandad being staunch Catholics that she didn't have an abortion."

"Just to clarify, when you say 'Gran and Grandad', is that your mother's or father's parents?"

"Dad's, actually being forced to give birth was one of the very few occasions where she didn't get her own way."

"So, she would normally get what she wanted."

"Yes, she could manipulate and lie very convincingly. She was also a great one for image. We had lots of fake smiling photos in beautiful golden frames. She would always put on a good show whenever there was a family occasion. Mum could really turn on the charm like it was on tap ready to be dispensed. But it was just a front, she never had one iota of sincerity, she was a selfish bitch!"

After such a strong statement Fran was expecting Kevin to finally show emotion but he remained stony faced. *Surely this must be painful for him* she thought to herself. What Kevin had just said could be viewed as a motive for murder, but he had a cast iron alibi. Fran reckoned this gave him the liberty to speak freely without the fear of any consequences.

"The fact I left at 16 and never returned tells all you need to know. I tried to make home visits when she was out so I could just see Dad who I had a much better relationship with."

"So, you got on with your dad but hated your mum. Did you ever speak to your dad about his marriage?

"Many times, but he could not resist her. She was like a deeply delicious poison."

Fran decided this was the moment to change the subject to ask something more directly about the case.

"I see…speaking of poison, for your information it has been confirmed that your mother's sherry had been poisoned. Someone must have known where the bottle was, and that she liked a daily aperitif before her evening meal? Now, who would know that do you think?"

Kevin paused and for the first time showed a little trace of anxiety.

"OK….I must stress that I am not accusing anyone. However, Dad's sister, his two brothers and their wives would have all known this as they've had meals in that house. And yes, on a previous visit they may have seen where she kept the sherry bottle too."

It was now clear who were the main suspects for the murder.

BLOWING A GASKET

The interview ended shortly after Kevin had given this important piece of information. Fran and Stafford thanked him for his time and swiftly left. As Stafford closed the front door he paused and stared for a few moments at the lock.

"He's obviously made that a lot more secure."

"Sir?", Fran enquired as she was a bit puzzled by her superior's remark.

"You see Fran, I came here with James to interview Kevin a few weeks ago regarding his father's death. At the time, we were assisting the local police force with their investigation following Antony's fatal fall off a cliff. We noticed that his front door lock was very insecure. I heard from a mate in the Alderham force that on the night before the wake someone broke into his house. He's clearly had a locksmith round to sort it."

"I see…so Kevin was burgled then."

"Well no, that's the weird thing, there was a break-in but nothing was stolen."

They then returned to their car and Fran drove them away. Although they seldom saw eye to eye there was now something that they could both definitely agree on.

"Thank God we're out of that house, it was like being trapped in a lift," said Stafford.

"Yes, I found it hard too, sir, but we've got some useful information."

"Yes, well done for that."

Wait a minute, was that a compliment? Fran thought to herself in disbelief. It was indeed praise so she concluded that God must be smiling down on her today. Once again Stafford swigged away on his water bottle and had some more Polo Mints. After a few minutes Fran felt confident enough to share her thoughts about Kevin.

"Sir, may I just say that there is something not right about Kevin. I know he's got a cast iron alibi, but I find it hard to believe that someone could be so cold about the loss of their mother."

"Some people hate their parents; I must admit I did."

Fran was quite surprised by this statement. It was not because Stafford hated his parents, she could easily imagine that. However, this was the very first time he had shared anything about his private life. Despite her fears, today had actually gone very well. Stafford had not humiliated her and the interview gave some good insight. She noticed a lot of traffic had appeared in the last few miles. Thankfully, there was no rush to get back for any office meetings.

Fran was feeling as good as she had felt in a long time. She saw a sign that said Jessop's Green was just three miles away. At this point they were only 10 minutes' drive from their Head Office building. Stafford was in a good mood, almost uncharacteristically. Fran decided this was probably the best time to broach the subject of the report from the last case. She was looking at this from the perspective of damage limitation. Fran took a deep breath and was about to admit everything when the car started to judder violently.

"What the hell are you doing Fran?" said Stafford aggressively.

"I don't know what's happening, sir," said Fran who was now panicking.

"Oh, for God's sake, pull over."

"I can't, there's no layby."

They were still on the dual carriageway but there was no hard shoulder for a couple of hundred metres.

"Fran the car's going to bloody fall apart," said Stafford who was also panicking.

Fran looked up and could now see a hard shoulder appearing on the horizon. It would be much safer to pull over there. However, the car was now juddering to such an extent that it might not physically make it. There was no time for any kind of analysis, Fran was forced to trust her gut instinct.

"Hang on sir, there's a layby coming up. I'll pull in there."

"Oh, for Christ's sake, Fran, we'll never make it."

"We will, hang on."

Fran gripped the wheel tightly as Stafford closed his eyes. The car now had a motion that was akin to a kangaroo hopping along. Fran braced herself as the vehicle slowly crept towards the hard shoulder. At the earliest possible moment, she turned the wheel to do a sharp turn. The vehicle just got over the thick white dividing line before grinding to an immediate halt.

There were a few moments of stunned silence before Stafford opened his car door to step outside. Fran remained still and motionless, the enormous stress of this incident had frozen her solid to the spot. She gave it a minute to allow her shooting heartbeat to calm down. Eventually the realisation that they were now safe was enough for her to function on some level at least. Fran then went out to join Stafford, she saw him lift up the bonnet that now had smoke rising up from it. She did not know what to say but Stafford soon worked out what had happened.

"The gasket has blown; somebody really should have picked up on this." He then sighed in frustration before going back into the car to radio headquarters.

"Hello Control, Control this is CDI Stafford, do you read me?"

"Yes, read you loud and clear," said a slightly mechanical voice through a small speaker that was on the dashboard.

"Our car has broken down; I repeat our car has broken down. Get our coordinates and send someone down here immediately to pick me up."

"Sorry sir, I don't think anyone is free right this moment."

"Well, they can bloody well make themselves free. I'm a *chief detective inspector* and I can't just stand here on this layby for hours on end. Look, I don't care who it is, but just make sure someone gets their arse over here on the double."

It was patently clear that Stafford was not open to any kind of negotiation. An arrangement was therefore made and a police car was duly despatched.

"Sir, may I ask what you want me to do now?" Fran asked rather meekly.

"Isn't it bloody obvious Fran?" Stafford replied in a sharp tone that conveyed his annoyance. Fran immediately regretted asking it and felt her body tighten up.

"You will have to wait here for someone to tow away the car, then get someone to pick you up. As soon as you get back into the office, I want you to do a full report on this incident," Stafford continued.

She tried hard not to show it but Fran felt a sense of dread. Fran knew this report would be long and tedious. She also wondered what ramifications there might be. Police cars are supposed to be checked regularly to ensure they are always in good working order. Somebody somewhere would be held responsible for this incident and reprimanded accordingly. Stafford once again pulled out his water bottle, had a few swigs and munched a few more Polo Mints. It was not long before a police car pulled up to collect him. Fran was then left marooned on the hard shoulder with the broken-down vehicle.

An arrangement had been made with the vehicle recovery service and Fran was given an ETA of an hour. She was grateful for the delay as it gave her some downtime. Fran had to tolerate the constant sound of cars zooming past. However, this was a small price to pay to be away from her angry superior.

She then remembered that she was about to broach the subject of the report from the previous murder case. Fran immediately realised that after today's debacle it was not a good a time to tell Stafford. She was working out when to make her confession when it suddenly occurred to her that there was an alternative. Fran could talk to James about it as he was a suitable higher-ranking officer. This was a very attractive option in more ways than one.

Eventually the recovery services arrived and Fran explained to the best of her ability what had happened. The car was towed away to be repaired and Fran radioed into Control again. She patiently watched the world go by before another police car finally came to collect her.

On returning to her office, Fran duly began to fill in the report on today's vehicle incident. It was not as tedious as she feared, it was much worse. A lot of the questions seemed pointless and she felt like giving up on several occasions.

However, Fran forced herself to keep going until it was finished. Andy then arrived in the office and sat down next to her.

"Hi Fran, well Stafford's got the hump. I understand you've had some fun and games."

"You could say that, once again I'm in his bad books for asking the wrong question. Anyway, how are you?"

"Frustrated."

"Why, what's up?"

"On Marianne's computer we found a file for her computer journal, but its password protected. Stafford's convinced it will contain something revelatory. He got the IT team to try and hack into it but no joy. And this is on top of that awful event that happened on Wednesday evening."

"Oh, what happened?"

"Oh, didn't I tell you, Chelsea lost against Liverpool!"

"My condolences, Andy"

"Thank you. It's OK, I'm sure Occupational Health will provide the appropriate counselling."

Fran smiled warmly. She welcomed a bit of light banter after the stress of the car incident and the tedium of the subsequent form.

"I tell you what, why don't we both make up for our troubles by having a meal at Jac & Mac's tonight?" said Andy.

"Sure, that would be lovely."

Fran was pleasantly surprised by this offer. She had been friends with Andy for a long time but had only ever seen him socially as part of a group event. This meal out would therefore be a step forward for their friendship. Andy then proceeded to say something that intrigued her.

"I've got some gossip about Stafford."

CHEWING THINGS OVER

After work, Fran and Andy left the office together. The uplifting glow of pleasant evening sunshine greeted them outside. They wandered over to the retail park that was literally a minute or two from their workplace. Their chosen restaurant was on a long row of stores that were adjacent to a spacious car park and it had a distinctive sign.

Jac and Mac's
DINER & SMOKEHOUSE

Andy was the traditional English gentleman and opened the door to allow Fran to walk in first. He then subtly ducked his head whilst entering as his height proved to be hazardous.

A smiling and smartly dressed waiter with a bronze suntan greeted them warmly. Jac & Mac's was a stylish establishment with a retro American chic. This was enhanced by the vintage black and white pop culture photographs that were dotted around the walls. Fran and Andy were led to a booth that had bright red sofas either side of the table. The restaurant was obviously having a quiet night as there were only a few other diners present.

"You know this place reminds me of that scene in 'Pulp Fiction'. You know the one where Vincent and Mia go out for a meal and she has a 'five-dollar shake'," said Andy.

There was an awkward pause, but Andy eventually realised why Fran did not respond.

"You've not seen 'Pulp Fiction', have you?"

"No sorry, is it a RomCom?"

"Err, not exactly," said Andy who was conscious of his gross understatement. He then decided to try and tailor the conversation to Fran's film taste.

"I take it you like watching Hugh Grant be a lovable English twit for a couple of hours?"

Fran was silent but her smile answered the question.

"OK, you know that bit in 'Love Actually' where he shimmies across the door archway?"

Fran smiled again to acknowledge that she knew the scene.

"Well, I tried that move at my last birthday party – it's not as easy as it looks," said Andy.

"Oh, I wish I could have seen that," said Fran who was quite amused.

The waiter then came over and they ordered drinks before scanning the menu. The options mostly consisted of life-shortening junk food. Fran and Andy did not take long in choosing something suitably unhealthy. Pleasant conversation continued as their burger and fries arrived on wooden chopping boards. Neither party was physically attracted to the other, but this made everything much easier. It meant there was no pressure to impress so they could just relax and enjoy themselves. After a few more laughs and a second drink, Fran felt it was now time to move on from small talk to something with more substance.

"How are you going now after…?" Fran stopped abruptly as she was not sure how to ask the question.

"Splitting up with Suzie?" said Andy, who had immediately realised what she was alluding to. He took a moment to collect his thoughts before replying.

"No, I am doing better. I'm only thinking about her 20 hours a day instead of 24 so that's an improvement," Andy continued.

He took a sip of his lager and Fran could clearly see the pain in his eyes.

"Actually, I'm looking to find something to distract me from all that and I am in a bit of a quandary."

"About what, Andy?"

"Driving. Obviously, it makes my job awkward having to always get lifts everywhere. If I can just find the confidence to drive again or at least take some lessons."

"Hey, whenever you're ready, Andy."

"Thanks, but if I do, I will then have another dilemma. I'd have to work out whether it's worth the expense of buying and maintaining my own car. You see, it's not just work where I am severely limited as a non-driver. Some places are a bugger to get to by public transport especially in the evening."

"Yeah, but my car costs me thousands every year."

"Exactly and this is my dilemma, is the freedom worth the money? Answers on a postcard please."

Fran smiled and took a sip of her wine. The evening was going splendidly but there was still an unasked, and therefore unanswered, question in Fran's mind. She reckoned Andy would have to go soon to catch his train so figured she had better ask now.

"Alright then Andy, what do you know about Stafford?"

Andy took a sip from his lager before he looked his friend and colleague in the eyes to answer.

"OK, I was in my local pub the other night when I met someone who knows Stafford. Well Fran, it appears our chief detective inspector is harbouring a couple of secrets."

Andy had an innate sense of theatre, so he paused to leave Fran in suspense. She impatiently waited for his revelation; he sensed the moment for the big reveal.

"Stafford is a very heavy drinker, bordering on alcoholic."

"Really, I can't say I've noticed."

"No, this guy said that Stafford hides it very well."

"Yeah, he must do…wait a minute. Whenever I take him anywhere, he's always eating Polo Mints. And he's constantly squirting freshener into his mouth. Of course, he does this to…"

"…hide the smell of the alcohol."

"And I wonder if that black water bottle really contains water?"

"Yes, it could well be something stronger. However, to be fair, he still functions and gets results."

"Yeah, however much I don't like him, I can't deny he's good at his job."

"But that's not his only vice, Fran."

"Really?"

"Oh yes, he's also a compulsive gambler and it apparently ruined his marriage. Even though he's on a massive wage as a CDI, he actually lives in some crappy little flat."

Fran was quite taken aback by tonight's revelations. Andy gave her a moment to absorb all this information before continuing.

"You might want to keep all this in mind the next time he has a go at you. They do say 'hurt people hurt people'."

Fran knew exactly what he meant as she had seen this in action before. It gave her relief to know that Stafford was a flawed person. This would make it easier for her to detach herself from his harsh criticism. Easier, but still far from easy, as she had a personality that tended to take everything to heart. Fran then had a quick look around and in a corner of the restaurant, she noticed Harry was settling a bill. He swiftly left before she had a chance to say hello.

Fran and Andy focussed their attention back to the remaining fries that had been moistened by tomato ketchup. And then, with over 1000 calories now sitting in their stomachs, Andy told Fran some more news.

"Marianne never wrote a will. This means that Kevin, as her only son, defaults to next of kin, so he will receive the whole estate."

"You see that gives Kevin a strong motive for murder."

"Yes, but it doesn't complete the traditional murder holy trinity; there's no means or opportunity."

"Yeah, I know, he's the only one who really gains from her death, yet everything suggests he could not possibly have committed the crime."

"True, but we haven't interviewed everyone else at the wake yet. By the way, I overheard Stafford talking to James earlier. I think you will be interviewing Graham Furlow and his wife Julie tomorrow evening with him."

"Oh great, another trip out with Stafford," Fran said sarcastically.

"No, not with Stafford, with James."

Fran smiled gleefully; this was the perfect end to her day.

GRAHAM & JULIE

The following day Fran had a lay in as she was on the late shift. When she finally did get up, she had a shower and washed her hair using her most expensive shampoo. Fran took plenty of time in applying her make up as she wanted to look her best. After lunch, she walked to work with slightly more bounce than normal. Fran entered the office with a beaming smile on her face. She sat down and logged into her computer to look at her emails. Clara then came in and Fran immediately turned to her friend.

"Hi Clara, how are Brian and Lara doing now?" Fran made sure she got their names right this time.

"Yeah, they're feeling much better now, thank the Lord. After school, they're going to play cricket with their friends."

"Aw…that's good to hear."

"So, do you know what Stafford has got lined up for you today?"

Fran was then in a quandary as to whether to tell the truth or to play a little dumb. After a moment's hesitation, Fran decided she could trust Clara so, to avoid being overheard, she whispered in her ear.

"Well, I've not been told by Stafford, but Andy reckons I'll be interviewing Graham and Julie this evening with James."

"Ah, so that's why you're looking so nice today!" Clara then gave a hearty Caribbean chuckle.

"Clara!" Fran said in a kind of mock outrage. Clara knew how attractive Fran found James. It was mischievous fun, but not intended to be anything more than a joke. The tall imposing figure of Andy then entered the room. He smiled warmly at Fran with a discrete wink in his eye. Fran had never told him of her feelings for James. However, Andy guessed from her reaction in the restaurant the previous night that she fancies the Welsh detective inspector. James then strode in wearing another immaculately tailored suit that accentuated his impressive physique.

It was not long before Stafford confirmed that Fran would indeed interview Graham and Julie Furlow with James. On hearing the news, Fran focussed hard to remain pokerfaced. She did not want Stafford to know that she was already aware of this. Fran was also desperate not to give any clue as to her feelings for James. However, despite her best efforts, she still had a slight grin and a twinkle in her eye.

Later that evening, Fran got into a police car and drove away with James. Their destination was a quaint old-fashioned town called Rivermead located in northeast Havantshire. Fran knew where she was going as she sometimes visited the place on her days off. It was renowned for its charming antique shops. This would be a fairly long journey but bearing in mind her company, Fran wished they could travel all day. She wanted to enjoy a private conversation with the handsome detective inspector. However, Fran had an inherent shyness, but fortunately her Welsh superior initiated the dialogue.

"Fran, have you heard about Robbie?"

"No, what's happened?"

"He's handed in his notice and he's going to retire."

Fran was more intrigued than sad to hear the news. Robbie was, by far, the longest serving detective constable in the unit, but he was also a very quiet man. She had known Robbie for years and yet she didn't know him at all. No-one *knew* Robbie, he was just a body in a uniform that carried out the duties that his position required. Any attempt to try and engage with him on a personal level was met with an uncomfortable silence.

"Sorry to hear that," said Fran, although she was not sure if she really meant it.

"I don't suppose he'll want a party to say farewell."

"No, he'll just slip away quietly into the night."

"I always found the man a bit of a mystery if I'm honest. He's polite enough I suppose but…oh I don't know, when someone is so shy all the time you can't help but to wonder why?"

James then became conscious of the approaching interview. He felt he should instruct his junior detective constable.

"Now Fran, I want you to focus on trying to find a motive from either Graham or Julie."

"They're likely to know where Marianne stored the sherry."

"We've got no concrete evidence yet, so we've got to keep all our options open at this stage."

A few minutes later they arrived at the house that was in a distinctly affluent area. The residents of Kingsley Avenue were undeniably posh. They would spend their evenings glugging away at their fifty-pound bottles of vintage wine.

Graham and Julie were equally well-heeled and refined. They never had the family they wanted but reaped the financial rewards of remaining childless. This, coupled with their joint salaries, meant they could afford a beautiful, detached house.

It was a conventional two-storey home encircled by attractive brick and stone hybrid walls. Their front garden was of a generous size containing a veritable Chelsea Flower Show. Fran and James walked down the concrete path which split the lawn evenly in two. When they reached the porch, Julie opened the door before either James or Fran had a chance to knock on it.

"Oh hello," said James who was somewhat caught on the hop. It was like the question had been answered before it had been asked.

"Hello," said Julie in a polite but slightly matter of fact tone. She was dressed conservatively in cream trousers and a light green jumper. Julie had a pleasant enough face with glimmering blue eyes and full red lips. However, her neatly trimmed blonde hair was tinged with numerous grey streaks. This revealed that the vibrant summer days of her youth had been replaced by a more mature autumn season.

James showed his ID badge before introducing himself and Fran, and then Julie led them inside. There was a noticeably wide hallway that had laminate flooring. They went past an almost regal looking red carpeted stairway and into the lounge. This room had a very impressive cream patterned carpet. A crystal chandelier hung down from the ceiling exactly in the centre of this square space. Serene oil paintings were equally spaced out around the magnolia walls. There was also a magnificent red Chesterfield sofa suite featuring two armchairs. Everything just oozed an ambience of splendour.

Graham Furlow was sitting in one of the armchairs. He was wearing casual elasticated grey trousers and a thin red V-neck jumper. There was a touch of anxiety in his face, which he tried to disguise with a somewhat insincere smile. Fran attempted to silently reassure him with both gesture and facial expression. Refreshments were offered and gratefully accepted.

Subconsciously Fran and James were taking everything a bit slower. This was so they could spend some more time in these pleasant surroundings. Hot drinks were served in two white Royal Doulton china cups along with a couple of Bourbon biscuits. Fran had to remind herself that she was not here for some relaxing coffee morning, but for a very serious interview. James took out his pen and pad ready to make notes. Fran took the cue to begin, addressing both Graham and Julie.

"How well did you know Marianne?"

The married couple looked at each other before Julie answered this question.

"Reasonably well, I guess."

"How did you feel about her?"

There was another pause before Julie eventually spoke once more.

"OK, well I'm conscious that I am required to be honest with you. This means I will have to admit that we *detested* the woman."

Graham nodded assertively but then looked away momentarily before facing Fran once more.

"Why did you detest her?"

"She was just so selfish," Julie answered.

"Can you give me some examples?"

"Well, the obvious one being all those affairs she had without the slightest hint of remorse. But it wasn't just that, she was also incredibly materialistic. Don't get me wrong, I appreciate we have some nice things in here, but she took it to a whole different level. Marianne would buy half of Harrods on one of her shopping trips. She was also a terrible mother and took no interest in raising Kevin at all. Little wonder he grew up so angry and confused," Julie continued.

Fran wanted to steer the interview towards how the deceased affected them personally. She hoped this would reveal a possible murder motive. Fran considered subtlety but decided that a more direct approach was required.

"Did Marianne ever do anything particularly bad to you personally?"

Graham looked especially uncomfortable at this question. Julie also looked a touch hesitant but eventually she replied.

"I suppose nothing major...but she could be very disrespectful."

"How do you mean disrespectful?"

"Well like when she came round here for Graham's 50th birthday party. She got obscenely drunk and accidentally knocked our university certificates off the wall and the frames got smashed. She never apologised for that at all, and it really upset me. I'm actually very proud of my Chemistry degree."

"I see. Can you think of any...sorry, did you say you've got a Chemistry degree?"

"Yes, we both have, you see I met Graham at university."

"Oh...that's interesting...and did you go on to some Chemistry based work?"

"Errm, well I went onto become a pharmaceutical consultant whereas Graham did something else...I'm sorry but what's this got to do with anything?"

"Sorry, I was just curious, we'll move on."

Fran knew she could not express the idea that was forming in her mind as it was unsubstantiated. After taking a sip of her refreshing Earl Grey tea, Fran took a moment to reflect on her next question. She then decided she would try and bring Graham into the conversation, as she did not want Julie to rule the roost.

"Graham, what were your memories of Marianne?" Fran asked.

Graham clearly did not like that question and Fran guessed this would be the case.

"Well…what can I say, she was the wife of my brother…I can't say I know that much about her. Except that…as Julie said, she was obviously selfish. She had this attitude of 'anything goes' and just did whatever she pleased regardless of the consequences."

"Please understand, we are trying to build a picture of Marianne. Now, can you think of any notable shared experiences that you had with her?"

Graham subtly avoided eye contact with Fran, Julie seemed a bit unnerved too.

"No…not really," Graham eventually replied.

The interview then continued in a similar vein to the previous one with Kevin. Julie soon took over from Graham to answer all the subsequent questions. Fran tried to include Graham in the interview at certain points, but it did not achieve much. Even when she was able to get him to talk, he never said anything illuminating. Neither of them had any idea as to who killed Marianne or why she was murdered.

However, Fran was more intrigued by their demeanour rather than by anything that was actually said. She could tell they were both uncomfortable, although Julie was disguising it a little better than Graham. Fran wondered whether they might be hiding something. A little secret like being a murderer perhaps? It became clear the interview was not leading anywhere, so Fran brought it to a close. After briefly thanking the interviewees, she promptly left the property with James.

On the way back to their office in the police car, Fran decided to share her thoughts.

"I think we need to do some digging to see if we can unearth any secrets from those two." Fran was mindful that this suggestion would have to go past Stafford for approval.

"I agree, there definitely was guilt in their eyes. But Fran, why did you quiz Julie about their Chemistry degrees?"

"Well, Stafford said the poison was a crude concoction and that anyone with a Chemistry degree could have mixed it together."

"What, do you think one of them created the poison?"

"It's a possibility James, the poison had to come from somewhere. I mean, it's not like you go and buy a bottle of the stuff from Boots!"

"True."

Fran and James then enjoyed a comfortable silence. They crossed a bridge with an expansive river view before James continued.

"Oh, by the way, just to warn you, Stafford is in a bad mood again. The IT team still haven't cracked the password to break into the computer file for Marianne's journal. The man's going tup over it."

"Tup?"

"Sorry Fran, Welsh word. I mean it's driving him crackers."

"OK, I'll bear that in mind."

She then braced herself to broach, what was for her, a tricky subject.

"James, on my report for our last case, I'm a little unsure of the timing of when that black BMW was last seen. I'm really not sure what to put there."

"Aw Fran, I'll check that out for you, leave it with me."

"Thanks."

Fran then felt a lot more relaxed. She also felt she was making some connection with James. The detective inspector was about to take this a step further.

"Fran, can I share something personal with you?"

"Of course."

"Alright, between you, me and this car, things have not been great at home lately."

"Oh, I'm sorry to hear that," Fran swiftly replied.

She felt compelled to say this, but deep down she could not help to be pleased as it might just give her an opportunity.

THE LAKESIDE DEBATE

When Fran returned to the office, she reported back to Stafford. A further investigation was subsequently done on Graham and Julie Furlow. To everyone's frustration, the Major Crimes Team found no skeletons in their closets. Fran then expressed her idea about how one of them could have used their chemistry knowledge to a fatal effect. Stafford accepted this in theory but said there was no evidence to move forward with this line of enquiry. The atmosphere in the office grew increasingly tense. Fran could envisage intelligent detective procedures being replaced by desperate guesswork if no progress was made soon.

Eventually, Fran reached her Saturday night parole as she had been given Sunday off. It was only a brief reprieve from the prison that was her workplace. Nonetheless Fran still appreciated some time off for good behaviour. When she got home, Fran watched the sweet RomCom 'Notting Hill' accompanied by a bottle of wine. Normally this would be the perfect mood boost for her, but tonight it failed to release Fran from her growing sense of despair.

Sunday morning arrived with beaming sun rays lighting up the sabbath. However, Fran's disposition was far from sunny, something was terribly wrong. The simple act of getting washed and dressed felt like an epic marathon. She knew she was not coming down with the flu or physically sick in any way. However, emotionally speaking, Fran was under the sort of weather that Noah had to deal with when he was in his ark. She could not understand why she was feeling so bad. Fran tried to brush it off and was confident that once she reached her church, she would be revitalised.

She then drove off in her car but after a few hundred metres she changed her mind and stopped. It was no good, she just could not drive any further. Luckily, she had parked in an area that had free street parking, so she stepped out for some air. Fran needed something to calm her and the most calming thing she could think of was the nearby lake. She walked swiftly towards it and passed some strangers walking their dogs.

Fran knew that the only way to properly view the lake was from one of the seats adjacent to a café. Thankfully it was open on a Sunday, so she walked in and ordered a coffee. She sat down at an outside table that was right next to the enormous expanse of water. Fran watched some serene white swans give a sort of swimming ballet performance. It was literally the 'Swan Lake' and it helped to ease her troubled mind. The waiter brought her the hot drink and she gratefully sipped its warmth.

She had been brought up as a Christian and until now had never missed a church service unless she was ill or working. Fran took a few deep breaths as she tried to understand why she suddenly felt so averse to worshipping in the House of God. Eventually she realised that she had grown tired of the church's conventions, ceremonies and rituals. Ultimately, she only went there because she felt it was her duty as a Christian to join in with this shared religious experience. However, Fran was now fed up with unanswered questions, especially the one about pain and suffering. She was also at odds with all the sanctimonious prayers and sermons where the vicar expressed high moral ideals. For Fran, these were completely divorced from what people actually did in, what might be described as, the *real world*. Fran felt as though she had lost her map and compass. Anxiety rose within her as she wondered how she could move forward with her life? She also wondered if there was anyone who could show her the way?

"Hello Fran," said a man who was standing right behind her. She did not see who had been speaking so she turned round sharply and instantly recognised him.

"Oh, hello Harry," Fran replied nervously in surprise at seeing her neighbour.

"Is it OK if I sit next to you?"

"Yeah, sure."

Harry sat down and looked Fran straight in the eyes.

"Are you OK?"

"Yeah, I'm fine."

"You don't look it."

Fran was a little taken aback by this direct statement. She would always say she was 'fine' even when she wanted to slit her wrists. Up until now, no-one had ever challenged this polite lie that she was so accustomed to telling. However, after taking a moment, she suddenly felt she was able to tell the truth and it was liberating.

"Actually I feel bloody awful. I'm sorry, I'm so used to pretending that I'm alright, it's what I instinctively do."

"You don't have to pretend, Fran. So, what's wrong?"

This was so unlike their previous inconsequential conversations. Harry was asking real meaningful questions with a disarming sincerity.

"Oh, believe me, you don't want to know."

"What makes you think that?"

Fran took a moment before she decided that, for once, she would let go of her reserved British nature and just talk about the damned thing.

"Alright, if you *really* want to know…theological issues."

"Theological issues eh. OK, what's the problem there then?"

"Well, I've actually skipped church this morning because I'm so wound up about this. Pain and suffering; God is supposed to have infinite love yet there is so much agony in the world - why?"

"It's a fair question."

"But no-one can answer it."

"Actually, I do have an answer."

At which point the waiter arrived with Harry's cup of tea and this was placed on the table. After blowing on the top to cool it, Harry took a sip. He then briefly ran his fingers through his silver hair. Fran stared at him in eager anticipation, she was very intrigued but also a little afraid.

"You see, the whole dilemma over God and the pain and suffering in this world is predicated on a traditional religious notion. The idea that this deity, usually perceived as male, is in control of everything or at least has an overwhelming influence. OK brace yourself, here comes the bit that might prick your Christian sensibilities; God controls absolutely nothing."

Harry had the sensitivity to realise that Fran needed a moment to absorb this idea and so he paused before continuing.

"All of us have free will and Mother Nature has free reign. The trouble is when people hear the word 'God', they very often conjure up this image of a man in the sky. A man who moves us all around like pawns on a chess board. I really feel that we need to open the doors of perception to reach a new theological understanding. God is not the universal master; God is the universal soul. The essence of all life, not the controller. God doesn't float around on a cloud; God is in our hearts."

Harry drank a bit more of his tea before continuing.

"Once, or should I say *if*, you can accept that God does not actually control life, then pain and suffering is inevitable. Mother Nature and human nature make it unavoidable I'm afraid. We must let go of the idea that God will stop horrible things from happening, there's too much evidence to the contrary. You only have to watch an episode of the news to see that. No, there's no masterplan, life just happens and sometimes in a really cruel way. However, despite this, we can still find and even *create* beauty out of all the ugliness."

Harry smiled gently at Fran before continuing.

"If you can connect with the divine essence, it'll lift you to your higher self. You can then shine a light into the darkness – that's the whole point of spirituality."

Harry paused again before concluding with a simple statement.

"In my humble opinion."

Fran was not sure what to make of Harry's theology. It certainly was not something a vicar would say. However, she appreciated that Harry did not sidestep challenging issues as, in her experience, clergymen always did. The two neighbours took a moment to watch the lengthy sun rays glisten beautifully across the large oval shaped lake. They enjoyed the peace before the conversation continued.

"Don't get me wrong Fran, I would not expect you to give up your Christian conception of God just like that. In fact, you may not ever agree with me and to be fair a lot of people would struggle with what I've just said. It's too faithful for the secular but too alternative for the religious. I'm just this strange armchair theologian with some leftfield ideas."

"At least you answered my question."

"Oh, I do believe in facing up to these things."

Harry took another sip of his drink before facing Fran once more.

"May I ask, is there a reason why you are chewing over all of this?"

Fran knew damned well there was a reason. However, as this was their first conversation of real depth, she wondered if it was premature for her to actually share it. Normally, the outer layers of a person are slowly removed like an onion being peeled until you finally reach their vulnerable heart. But there was something about Harry that made her feel that she could just shortcut this process and bare her soul completely.

"Yes, there is Harry, it's something that goes back a long time. It happened on Christmas eve in 2006, the date is forever imprinted on my mind. My older sister was returning from working abroad for a few months. I wasn't feeling well so Mum and Dad left me alone in the house while they went to pick her up. A few hours later I got a call to say they had all been killed in a car crash."

"Oh God, I'm so sorry."

"It happened only a few hundred metres from here close to that blind corner near the railway station. They never found out why Mum had driven straight into a tree. But I just know someone else must have caused her to swerve into it."

Inevitably, recalling this painful event made Fran feel very emotional, so she gulped the remainder of her coffee before concluding.

"And ever since then I've been looking for…I don't know, some kind of answer."

"I see."

"Some of my Christian friends have told me that God picks his favourite flowers from the garden first."

Harry rolled his eyes and shook his head before replying.

"God is not Alan Titchmarsh!"

Fran laughed and smiled warmly at Harry.

"You know it's nice that we are finally talking, I mean properly talking, sorry it's such a heavy subject."

"Oh, that's OK with me, I like a good theological debate, always have done. This is where I differ from Joe public. They're much more concerned about other issues like whether pineapple belongs on a pizza. It's nice to have someone I can talk to about this."

Harry then frowned and Fran sensed he was having melancholic thoughts.

"In fact, it's nice to have someone to talk to at all," Harry continued.

Fran placed her arm affectionately on Harry's shoulder and he smiled in response.

"You see, when I divorced Carrie, I not only divorced my wife, but I effectively divorced my social circle. Nearly all my friends were made through her and inevitably they all sided with her when we split up. She kept the house and this was the only area where I could afford a half decent place. It was just somewhere I could escape to and get away from it all."

"Do you not have any family, Harry?"

"My relatives are either dead or don't want to know me. I don't have any friends at all."

"You do now, Harry."

Fran then smiled warmly at her new friend.

SUE

Just before she went to bed, Fran looked at the photograph of her deceased family. She remembered how difficult it was for her to move to the town where their fatal accident took place. It took a long time before her head was able to overcome her heart to accept the practical benefits. These were the relatively cheap property prices and being within walking distance of work.

Overnight she contemplated Harry's alternative theology. It was wonderful to make a new friend but that did not stop his ideas being challenging to her. The notion that God is not the omnipresent master was particularly hard for her to swallow. Fran remembered a line from the hymn *O Jesus, I have promised* that she sung when she was last in church. "O give me grace to follow, my Master and my friend." Fran had grown up with the notion that nothing happens in the Kingdom of Heaven by accident. She was repeatedly told that He has a plan for everyone. Fran knew a lot of Christians who took inspiration from these beliefs. They drew comfort and strength from believing that they are acting in accordance with the divine masterplan. This, in their eyes, meant they were fulfilling their religious duty and doing 'God's will'.

However, Fran was also conscious that her beliefs were not typical of someone of her age in British society. Most of her friends were secular and she could understand, if not actually agree with, their atheist arguments. As they saw it, events like the holocaust and the two world wars meant there cannot be any divine plan. No masterplan was tantamount, in their view, to the non-existence of God. Alternatively, they reckoned that if there really is an omnipresent master, then bearing in mind all the pain and suffering in the world, he can't be very nice.

Harry's theology was a kind of middle road between the traditional Christian and secular viewpoints. He rejected the idea of a masterplan but still believed in an underlying essence flowing through all of life. Fran had to admit that in some ways Harry's idea appealed to her as it seemed more progressive. However, changing her religious beliefs was quite a scary prospect as her faith had always been her bedrock. This divine dilemma was eventually interrupted by the grating sound of her alarm clock. Fran quickly realised the need to refocus and promptly got ready to go to work.

When she arrived in the office, Clara asked Fran an awkward question.

"Hi, how come you weren't at church yesterday?"

Fran was not prepared for this as she had been too busy chewing over the true nature of divinity. She needed to say something immediately and had desperately searched the vaults of her mind for an answer. Fran decided that there were occasions when one just had to break the commandment "Thou shall not bear false witness". Yes, she would lie, but it would be a good, pristine white falsehood.

"I ate something that disagreed with me on Saturday night, so I had to rest up yesterday morning but I'm fine now."

"Oh, sorry to hear that, but glad you're feeling better, girl."

Fran felt bad about lying to her friend, but she knew the truth would result in a heated discussion. She was keen to avoid this theological argument so she could be completely on the ball for the investigation. Stafford then marched out of his office in his customary surly manner and approached the two detective constables.

"Right, I've arranged for you two to go and visit Sue Furlow, the sister-in-law of Marianne. I want you to probe her for anything that might give us a motive for the murder because we've got sod all so far," said Stafford rather brusquely.

Fran and Clara got into a police car with plenty of time to drive to Brock Heath, in southeast corner of Havantshire, where Sue lived. Fran was driving and within a few minutes into their journey, Clara brought up a personal matter that she wanted to discuss.

"I was Skyping with my family last night; they really want to visit them. The trouble is I get terrible jet lag from long plane flights. So, to make the journey worth it, I will need two weeks' annual leave," said Clara.

"Why don't you just ask for a couple of weeks off work then?" suggested Fran.

"Oh, come on, girl, you know what Stafford's like?"

"Surely no-one can deny you seeing your family?"

"Ah, it's like he thinks we don't have lives outside of work."

"Look, what have you got to lose, Clara, just ask."

Clara smiled but clearly was still not convinced. However, Fran sensed that she had to let this go, at least for now, as they would soon arrive at their destination.

Sue Furlow's home was just outside the town centre. The block of flats was in between a supermarket and the local Job Centre. This five-storey building was surrounded by other similar properties. They were not exactly skyscrapers, but the birds would still have a decent view from the roof. The car park operated on a first come, first served basis. Thankfully, most of the residents of the block had gone to work so Fran was able to find a free space easily. There was a small panel of buttons on the side wall. Fran pressed the appropriate one for Sue and a tinny, slightly distorted voice was then heard.

"Hello," said Sue.

"Good morning, this is Detective Constable Fran Jacobs and I'm here with Detective Constable Clara Sobers, may we come in please?" Fran projected her voice in hope that Sue would hear her clearly. A sharp buzzing sound was then heard. Fran pulled at the communal door and was relieved when it opened. The two ladies then entered and went up the staircase that had a badly stained black and brown carpet. There was something undeniably rough about this place. Fran could imagine the residents' playing darts with their knives.

Sue's flat was on the first floor and she had her own private porchway. She was holding her front door open, Sue was dressed in black leggings and a scraggy looking red jumper. Her hair was unkempt, and she appeared a tad bleary eyed. Fran guessed that Sue was recovering from a crazy night on the tiles. Fran showed her ID badge, but Sue was not interested as she just wanted them to come inside so she could close the door.

Sue's flat had a narrow hallway that led to a white slightly chipped door on the right-hand side. They then entered a compact rectangular lounge diner. A small wooden drop-down leaf table was adjacent to the far end window that had a flaking frame. There was also a brown two-seater sofa that was made of faux leather and covered in rip marks. The room was enclosed by four pale-yellow walls that were covered with stains and holes. This was cheap accommodation rented out by a cash-in-hand landlord who obviously wanted to remain a stranger to the taxman.

Fran and Clara sat down on the sofa and Sue took out a chair from under her table. She did not offer them refreshments but that was perfectly fine as all three of them wanted to just get started. Fran made a judgement call that no small talk was required. Clara clearly reached the same conclusion as she was poised with her pen and pad ready to make notes.

"OK then…" said Fran but she was abruptly interrupted by Sue.

"You're not gonna arrest me, are ya?"

Fran was thrown off her stride a little and took a moment to compose herself. This clearly was not going to be a straightforward process.

"We're not going to arrest you, Sue. It's just that you were present at the wake and you obviously knew Marianne. Consequently, we do need to ask you some questions. We are just gathering evidence for our investigation, that's all. Please relax, you've got nothing to worry about."

Assuming you're not the murderer Fran silently thought to herself.

"Alright, it's just that you're coppers, you have to suspect everyone, don't ya?"

Fran had to play this carefully as Sue actually was one of their main suspects. However, she did not want her to realise their suspicion as Sue might then become guarded and omit useful information. Fran had already lied once today, but circumstances were going to force her to tell another fib.

"Sue, we really don't suspect you of anything, we just need some information," said Fran feeling her body tense up as she lied.

"Alright, what do you need to know?"

"OK, well one of the main things we are trying to do is to build up a picture of Marianne and her life. What are your memories of her?"

Sue did not engage with this question either verbally or with facial expression. She was acting as though she had not heard Fran. However, it was a case of Sue deliberately ignoring Fran rather than some kind of hearing issue. Fran decided to try asking a similar question instead, but this time on a more emotional level."

"How did you feel about her?"

"I hated her," Sue replied sharply.

"Why did you hate her?"

"Because she was a selfish bitch."

"I see," Fran said calmly. She noted how 'selfish' was the recurring complaint about Marianne. There was a brief pause before Fran decided to probe a little deeper.

"Can you give me some examples. Did she ever do anything against you personally?"

Sue grimaced and briefly looked away before answering.

"Err…well, nothing really bad I s'pose but well…she was really rude."

"Can you give me an example?"

"OK, at the wake I tried to be nice and talk to her but she…I don't know, she was just dismissive. She said that she had to go to the toilet, but I knew that was a lie. She then just buggered off for ages and left me alone in her kitchen."

"I see…but can you think of a time when something more…"

Fran then stopped abruptly and hesitated. She felt she should move on to the next point, but something was intriguing her. Eventually she decided that she would have to clarify what Sue had just said, as it could be important.

"Sorry Sue, but did you just say Marianne left you alone in her kitchen?"

Sue failed to see the relevance of the question so hesitated but eventually she answered.

"Well yeah, just typical of her rudeness."

Fran was tempted to ask Sue what exactly happened while she was on her own in the kitchen. However, Fran was worried that Sue might then realise that she was under suspicion. Fran decided that it was not worth the risk and did not pursue this any further. Instead, she made a mental note to go with the handwritten one that Clara had just made.

It then became difficult for Fran to fully concentrate as she started to imagine what Sue actually did in the kitchen. She remembered that the drinks cabinet was in this room. Sue would therefore have been close to the sherry bottle that was poisoned. Eventually Fran decided that she would bring the interview back to something Sue had said earlier on.

"Sue, just to reiterate, you said you hated Marianne. Now 'hate' is a strong word, are you sure Marianne never did anything to you personally apart from simply being rude?"

"No, no, she was just a horrible woman, that's all. Marianne just had this attitude of 'anything goes', which was just her lame excuse to dump on everyone."

As with the previous interviewees, Sue said she had no idea who had committed the murder. Fran then decided not to bother with many more questions as she felt that she had extracted the most important points. She briefly thanked Sue for her time before swiftly leaving with Clara.

Fran shared her thoughts with Clara in the police car on their way back to the office.

"OK, from the evidence that we've got, Sue is the only guest who spent some time in Marianne's kitchen alone. This means she had the best opportunity to poison the sherry."

"That's not proof, Fran."

"No, but I think we have to say she is now the most likely person."

"Mmm, but what about motive?"

"OK, we've still got some work to do there."

Fran went quiet as Clara, who this time was driving, concentrated on the road as she had a tricky right turn. Once Clara had safely negotiated that manoeuvre, Fran continued.

"Also, I'm sure Sue was lying when I asked her if Marianne had done something to her personally."

"But why couldn't Sue tell us about it?"

"Maybe it's something she doesn't want us to know about."

"Something illegal?"

"Possibly or it might just be something embarrassing. I don't know, but she's hiding something, I know she is."

"Could it relate to the murder?"

Fran considered the possibility in her mind for a few moments.

"It's impossible to say. Oh, that's the problem with this damn case. It's like a dot-to-dot picture with too many missing dots."

At this point, Fran's mobile phone made a 'ping' sound. She then glanced at it and saw she had received a text from Harry.

> Monday, 02 Oct · 11.47
>
> **Hi Fran, how are you? x**

It was a simple message, but Fran was most uplifted. She was seldom contacted by anyone unless they were responding to one of her texts. The fact that Harry had initiated this pleased her enormously. Fran promptly replied before she returned to her thoughts about the case.

When she got back to the office, Fran explained to Stafford that she suspected Sue was hiding something, but he was clearly unimpressed.

"Oh, for God's sake Fran, there is nothing concrete about this at all. It's just your gut feeling, that's not evidence. I told you that we need to find a motive, but you've given me bugger all. Now stop wasting my time with your flights of fancy and do some proper detective work."

Once again Fran felt humiliated by Stafford and immediately left his office. Andy, who had been checking his emails, then came over to reassure her as he could tell she was upset.

He then explained that he had been assigned to interview Barry and Mary Furlow with her tomorrow. Later that night, Fran decided the best way to bounce back from Stafford's harsh reprimand was to pull out all the stops for the next interview. It was clearly going to be difficult to uncover a motive for this murder. However, Fran was determined to somehow find a way.

BARRY & MARY

The following morning Fran arrived at work to find Andy was already there. Andy had one request before they set off and looked a little embarrassed when asking.

"Can I pop into Gregory's for a cheeky bacon sarnie before we go? It's just I overslept a bit and didn't have time for breakfast."

Fran considered this for a second and decided that they could just about get away with it.

"Go on then, Andy. Actually, I think I'll join you."

Fran could not remember the last time she had eaten breakfast, but reckoned it would be good to have some sustenance inside her. Gregory's' was just around the corner in the retail park. Fran parked the vehicle just a few metres away and they both walked into the small shop. The hot food had to be ordered at the counter and the middle-aged lady serving looked nervous at the sight of their uniform. She had the irrational fear that she would suddenly be arrested.

Andy ordered a bacon roll whilst Fran went for a sausage sandwich, both were garnished with a dollop of tomato ketchup. After a moment's hesitation, Fran then decided she would also have a coffee. She was a little bemused by Andy pulling out a can of his favourite fizzy drink, Dr Pepper, from one of the shop fridges. After they had both paid, Fran was compelled to quiz him over his choice of beverage. Andy took a moment before offering a robust defence.

"Well Fran, as a detective constable, you will know that there's no legal requirement regarding the time of consumption of Dr Pepper."

"OK, I won't press charges, but seriously all that fizz so early in the morning."

"Yes, but unlike the majority of the country, I don't drink tea or coffee. So, when I've had a bad night's sleep, I need the 'good doctor' to give me a sugar rush."

A few minutes later the sandwiches and Fran's coffee arrived. There were two elevated stools with cheap plastic seats adjacent to the window. Andy and Fran put their drinks on top of a convenient wooden ledge whilst they munched their breakfast. The view of the empty car park was a galaxy away from inspiring. However, Fran was much more concerned about the welfare of the man sat next to her.

"How come you didn't sleep then?" said Fran.

"It's my own fault, Fran. I really must stop having these wild all-night parties with the supermodels, or at least not on a school night."

Fran knew that this obviously fictional response was Andy's way of disguising the real truth. She therefore probed a little deeper with a more direct question.

"Are you still beating yourself up over Suzie?"

"Ooh maybe just a little…actually maybe a hell of a lot!"

"Oh Andy, you're going to have to let her go."

"Yes, I know but I've always been spectacularly crap at moving on. It's just the whole 'we've been together for 15 years so how could it end like this?' malarkey that I'm chewing over. But it's OK, when I get home, I'll watch a film to take my mind off it, something light and fluffy like 'Schindler's List!'"

* * *

Fran and Andy finished their breakfast and then set off in their police car with Fran behind the wheel. Their destination was a small historical market town called Walmsbury located in the northeast corner of Havantshire. It boasted attractive public gardens and a pleasant riverside walk. On the way there the two detectives worked out a game plan for the forthcoming interview.

"Alright, so we'll start with Chinese water torture and if that doesn't work, we'll stretch them out on a medieval rack," suggested Andy.

"Or alternatively I could ask questions and you can take notes."

"You always go for the boring conventional approach, don't you Fran?"

Fran smiled but she knew that she actually had been boring and conventional for most of her life, so could do with a bit more excitement. After briefly reflecting on this, she focussed her attention back onto the murder case.

"It seems pretty clear that Marianne was a much-despised woman so you can see why she met her grisly fate," said Fran.

"Yeah, but Stafford is getting stressed by the lack of a definite motive, we need something concrete. I mean if people just murdered everyone they didn't like, then…blimey, all the chavs would have been bumped off by now, surely? No, there's got to be something that the murderer would gain from Marianne's death or potentially lose from her staying alive."

"Mmm, unless it's something along the lines of insane jealousy or some other deeply negative emotion."

"I guess, but it would have to be something really hardcore," Andy countered.

"Agreed, I'm going to have to try and push Barry and Mary hard for some kind of motive."

Fran worked out some questions in her mind as she drove the last few miles. Barry and Mary lived in a semi-detached house that was just outside the town centre. The driveway had a steep incline and it led up to the integral garage that had a dark green door. The main property was neither attractive nor repulsive and blended in with other similar looking homes on the street. The only distinguishing feature was a collection of flowers and small rose bushes. These were dotted along a rectangular patch of earth just in front of the building.

Andy led Fran to the front door that was also dark green. He knocked on it firmly and Mary answered quite quickly. She was a middle-aged woman dressed in cream chinos and a thin blue jumper. Her clothes were on the cusp between smart and casual. She wore just a touch of makeup that made only a subtle impact on her face. Mary was just a fraction fatter than slim and a fraction shorter than tall. Her green eyes had a warm inviting glow and were by far her most pleasing physical feature.

After they had identified themselves, Fran and Andy were shown inside. They traipsed through a narrow grey carpeted hallway and into a square lounge area. There was a beige sofa suite that was comfortable without being lavish. The room only had a few square feet of open floor space. It was not exactly cramped but it certainly did not lend itself to having many guests. Opposite the sofa was a tall wall unit that housed a collection of spirit, wine, port and sherry bottles on top.

Barry Furlow was sat on one of the sofa seats. His slim figure was covered by a sporty tracksuit, the open jacket revealing a green T-shirt. Barry was due to go to the athletics club, where he worked, after this interview so he was dressed for the job. Refreshments were served before Mary joined Barry on the sofa. The two detective constables sat down on the armchairs. Andy was armed with a pen and pad to make notes. After some pleasantries and small talk, Fran began questioning both interviewees.

"How well did you know Marianne?"

"Unfortunately, we knew her pretty well," said Mary.

"'*Unfortunately*,' so you didn't like her then?"

"No, we both detested the woman," Mary said quite sharply.

"Why did you detest her?"

"She was so selfish."

As soon as Mary had said the word 'selfish', Fran knew where this was going. However, as with Graham and Julie, it was the wife of the married couple that did most of the talking. Fran then turned to Barry as she wanted to focus on him. She wondered if he could give a clue to help them find the holy grail of this case, the motive…

"Can you think of any reason why someone would kill Marianne?"

"Well, she was a horrible person."

"OK, do you remember any specific examples of the bad things she did? For example, was Marianne involved in any kind of financial irregularities like blackmail?"

Barry visibly flinched and Mary also looked uptight before eventually answering.

"Look if we had any idea as to specifically why she was murdered, believe me we would tell you". Mary spoke with such a conviction that it made it very difficult for Fran to pursue this any further. After she had taken a sip from her tea, Mary gave a concluding statement.

"All we know is that Marianne ruined many people's lives. She would always say 'anything goes' and then do whatever she damned well pleased."

Fran felt frustrated as the interview was not going anywhere useful. Mary was repeating, almost word for word, the complaints that the previous interviewees had made about Marianne. Fran was almost ready to give up when she noticed a sherry bottle on the top row of the wall unit. This bottle was right in the middle and there was something familiar about it.

"I'm sorry but what are you looking at?" questioned Mary.

She was clearly put out that Fran had suddenly stopped asking questions to stare at their alcohol selection. Fran read the sherry bottle label carefully, she was a little startled but focussed hard to remain calm.

"Amonti Sherry," Fran finally said.

"What about it?" asked Barry who was clearly nonplussed.

"Marianne used to drink this sherry; in fact, this was the last drink she ever had as it was poisoned."

"That's just a coincidence," Mary said firmly.

"OK, but why you would have the same bottle of what I know is a very expensive sherry?"

"Well…it was the only influence we got from Marianne, her taste for expensive sherry. Don't get me wrong, we only have it on special occasions. We drink it instead of champagne," Mary explained.

Fran was not sure if Mary had been totally truthful with this explanation. However, she had no way to disprove it, so she visually feigned her acceptance of Mary's answer.

Shortly afterwards, Fran and Andy thanked the interviewees and promptly left to drive back to their office.

"Mmm, I can't help thinking about the sherry bottle," Fran said wistfully whilst she drove the car.

"OK, it's a strange coincidence, but it doesn't prove anything."

"No, it doesn't, but it's just…"

Fran then slowed down the car dramatically and pulled into a layby to stop completely.

"Fran, what the hell are you doing?" Andy asked and was clearly unnerved.

Fran stepped outside to stare at two distant green hills and the pleasant valley running between them. Andy then got out and walked around the vehicle to be next to his friend and colleague.

"Fran, have you gone loopy or something, what's going on?"

"Sorry Andy but I can't concentrate on the road, I've just had an idea."

Fran looked heavenwards for inspiration as she tried to formulate her thoughts clearly enough to be able to express them.

"We've been trying to work out how the murderer got the poison into the bottle without being noticed or leaving any evidence. Well…what if they smuggled in a bottle of the same sherry but with the poison already inside it."

"Sorry Fran, I'm not with you."

"OK, let's assume that Stafford is right, and the murder really did happen at the wake. You see, it would be a faff to take the bottle out, drop in the poison and put the bottle back in exactly the same place. You would have to do this very quickly to ensure no-one saw you but careful enough not to leave any incriminating evidence. Now that would be a hard trick to pull off, it's far easier to just swap the bottles over."

"Yeah, of course, that could be done in seconds. Assuming you have the right sherry bottle."

"And Barry and Mary obviously knew how to get one."

The detective constables considered the possibility as a gentle wind briefly brushed against their bodies. Fran and Andy then got back into the car and they quickly sped away.

"There was one other thing I noticed but I know it won't wash with Stafford," said Fran.

"What makes you say that?" Andy enquired.

"Because he wants solid evidence and this is just my gut feeling. However, I've got a hunch that something has happened between Marianne and Barry. I also think something's happened between Marianne and Mary too."

"What do you mean 'something has happened'?"

"I don't know, it was just the way they flinched when I mentioned 'financial irregularities or blackmail.'"

Fran then remembered the objective for this interview.

"Stafford's not going to be happy about this. I know he was expecting me to get a possible motive out of them."

"Look Fran, if they don't know, then they don't know; that's not your fault. Besides, you've got a more plausible means of murder, that must count for something."

However, it counted for very little as far as Stafford was concerned. When she returned to Head Office, he made this patently clear. The CDI dismissed her swapping bottles idea as unsubstantiated nonsense. Fran's confidence was pretty much bulldozered, so later in the afternoon she sent a text. She really needed a swift exchange of text messages. Fran knew there was only one person who would give her an immediate response.

> Tuesday, 03 Oct 14:37
>
> Hi Harry, I can't go into details as it's confidential but Stafford is really on my back, I don't know what to do. x

> Tuesday, 03 Oct 14:38
>
> Sorry to read that Fran and don't worry I understand it's confidential. Just stay calm, stay balanced and try to keep it all in perspective. I'm sure you can find a way through this. x

Fran duly thanked him for the message but still could not decide what to do. She was about to log off from her computer when suddenly James walked up to her.

"Hey Fran, what's occurring?"

"Oh…just a bad day."

"Bad day, tell you what, why don't you tell me all about it over a meal at Jac & Mac's tonight?"

This was a most welcome surprise and Fran did not hesitate in replying.

"Yeah, that would be lovely."

Shortly afterwards they walked over to the restaurant and were greeted by the same well-tanned waiter from her last meal there. James and Fran soon settled down with their drinks and a food menu. Fran decided that this time she would go for a healthier option. She scanned the limited salad section for something that did not have a plethora calorie count. James on the other hand went for burger and fries. He clearly was in the mood for something caked in grease. They had a pleasant enough conversation and shared a few jokes. However, all the way through this there was one question that Fran was aching to have answered. After James had a pint of lager, he brought up the subject without her having to ask.

"I must admit Fran, one of the reasons I'm here with you now is because I don't want to go home."

"Oh, are things really that bad?"

"Yes, it's just horrible being in that house."

This statement was what Fran was secretly praying to hear although she could not admit it to anyone. After eating their meal, James gave her a big hug goodbye. Fran knew that he was just a man who was in a bad way and needed a bit of comfort. Nevertheless, their physical embrace was the most pleasant feeling she had experienced all year. At that moment she wished gravity was no longer a force so they could just float up to the heavens in each other's arms. However, the euphoria was short-lived as James quickly broke free and duly walked way. As she watched him disappear into the night, Fran was in no doubt about her desire. Her emotional and carnal cravings did not exactly square with her morals, but he was irresistible; she just wanted the man.

STUART

Whilst she walked into work, Fran reflected on the previous evening with James. She concluded that if his marriage really does end, it would still be useless as he is out of her league. Instead, she had better focus on the murder case or, more specifically, keeping out of Stafford's bad books. He had been particularly vicious to her as of late and she was puzzled as to why. She eventually concluded that he is under pressure and just taking it out on her.

Shortly after Fran's arrival, Stafford got the whole team together for a meeting. There was no visual display set up as he just wanted to give a debrief.

"We have now interviewed every single person who attended the wake as well as all the relevant family, friends and acquaintances. I'm afraid we still have no clear-cut motive, only that Marianne was a deeply despised woman. We also have no physical evidence that is of any use either. Our IT team have been unsuccessful in trying to hack into Marianne's computer journal. The file is extremely well protected and trying to extract the password is proving to be a nightmare. We're going to have dig a bit deeper to find something, really anything, to move forward with this case."

Stafford then proceeded to give out tasks for everyone bar Fran. She thought for a moment he had overlooked her but eventually her turn came.

"Fran, I want you to come with me to interview Stuart Larkin, the nearest neighbour to Marianne. In fact, he's now the only person to live on that road."

Fran nodded in acknowledgment but said she needed to nip to the loo. This was a lie as she did not need the toilet at all, but she was desperate to just have some time on her own. The prospect of spending a few hours with Stafford crippled her with dread. Fran locked herself into one of the cubicles and sat on the seat. She felt her entire body tighten up as negative thoughts traumatised her mind and took deep breaths.

Fran wondered if any of the female police officers might come in to genuinely use the toilet. To keep up the pretence, Fran flushed it and waited for a few seconds before leaving the cubicle. When she came out, she realised that there was in fact no-one there. Fran then allowed herself a little more time to finally compose herself. Eventually she joined Stafford in a police car and was ready to drive away.

Whilst driving, Fran noticed Stafford swigging from his water bottle and munching on a few Polo Mints. She wondered whether his water bottle contained something alcoholic. If so, then Stafford really must be desperate to start drinking so early in the morning.

"OK Fran, let's hope you don't blow a gasket this time."

This remark really stung her for it was obvious that the previous debacle was just a mechanical fault. The insinuation that this was somehow of her doing was grossly unfair. Fran was so enraged that she felt like stopping the car and abandoning Stafford in a strange town. She even fantasised about smashing the vehicle into the nearest lamp post out of protest. Fran hid all these dark thoughts behind a fake pokerfaced expression, *just get through this* she silently told herself.

"Alright, now the man we are seeing today has Asperger's Syndrome, there will be a support worker present. You're going to have to use some tact, do you think you can do that for me?" said Stafford. His question had a condescending tone that grated on Fran.

"Of course, sir," she replied rather meekly.

"Unfortunately, the man who supported Stuart on the day of the wake has since left the care team. He did not leave any kind of forwarding address, he's just somewhere in Scotland apparently. The mobile number they gave me for him is out of service. He doesn't do social media, so we're going to have a hard time tracking him down."

"I see."

"I admit it's a long shot, but I feel it's worth talking to Stuart. As he was Marianne's only neighbour, he might know something revealing about her. Alternatively, he may have seen something that happened on the day of the wake."

"But he wasn't there sir."

"No, but he might have seen the guests that were driving up the road. Like I said Fran, it is a long shot, but I want to cover all bases."

"Very well sir," said Fran. She concluded from this remark that Stafford was now getting desperate.

Fran then focussed on the journey to Newcot and on arrival drove up the extremely long cul-de-sac to Stuart's home. She then parked in a suitable place next to a disused barn opposite. Stuart lived in a small, detached bungalow with a gravel driveway. There was a wooden trellis on the front wall with an array of colourful plants growing up it. In many ways it had all the hallmarks of a classic English country village home, only in a very remote location.

Fran and Stafford scrunched over the pebbles that led to a white front door and the CDI knocked firmly on it. A young casually dressed Indian lady opened it. Identity badges were then shown before Fran and her superior entered the bungalow. They walked straight into the lounge as there was no hallway to negotiate first. The white ceiling had three rustic wooden beams that spanned its width. There was a brown carpet and a green two-seater sofa suite.

Stuart Larkin was a small, tubby middle-aged man with unkempt brown hair. This was matched by his scruffy beard that lacked an even shape. He wore brown trousers with an old grey jumper and was sitting in his armchair. Stuart seemed content enough reading his book on owls. He was blissfully unaware of the police presence that was now in the room.

"Stuart, the police have come to see you," his support worker advised him.

He did not respond at first, but eventually closed his book. He then turned to face Fran and Stafford. They were sitting on the sofa and the CDI was ready to make notes on his pad.

"Hello Stuart," said Fran.

Stuart did not reply verbally but gave a slight nod in acknowledgment.

"First of all, do you know why we are here today?" asked Fran.

"We have told him about it," said the support worker, who was sitting down on the other available armchair.

"Did you know your neighbour Marianne at all?" Fran continued.

Stuart looked blank and gestured with his hands to signify he was not sure.

"Marianne, the lady who used to live up the road," said the support worker.

"Oh…her…yeah…I err…" Stuart ended his sentence abruptly.

"Did you get to know Marianne at all?" Fran repeated.

Stuart's face then had the expression of immense concentration. He looked like he was trying to work out some complex scientific formula. Eventually, after further serious thought, he finally answered.

"Not really."

"OK, now Marianne, your neighbour, was killed on Friday September 22nd, so not last Friday, the Friday before. Can you remember seeing anything unusual on that day?"

Stuart was clearly nonplussed by this, so his support worker assisted him.

"Stuart, that was the day when all those cars came up the road, remember?"

"Oh…err…yeah," said Stuart.

Fran focussed back on him and looked deeply into his eyes to try to engage him.

"Now, did you notice anything odd or unusual on that Friday?"

"What…what…ermm odd? How…how do you mean?"

"Just something you wouldn't normally see."

"Err no, cars just went…" Stuart's sentence trailed off, but he signalled left and right with his hands. Fran understood that he meant the cars just drove up and then back down again later. The interview had only just started but it already seemed hopeless.

Fran continued to try and gently extract some relevant information out of Stuart, but it was clear he had nothing useful to share. She frantically tried to work out what other questions she could ask. Fran was conscious that this was their last roll of the dice as far as interviewees were concerned. A random question then popped into her head and she decided that there was nothing to lose so she may as well try.

"How about the night before, you didn't…"

"That's not relevant Fran!" Stafford firmly interrupted with a slightly raised voice. There was an uncomfortable silence before Stafford continued.

"Well, I think that's all we need from you today, Stuart, thanks for your time," Stafford then concluded.

This rather abrupt ending unsettled Fran. As they had gathered hardly any relevant information, the trip didn't seem to have been worthwhile. Fran now genuinely needed the toilet and not just as an excuse to be alone. She did not normally ask for this when she interviewed someone and felt a bit embarrassed. However, she could not ignore, what was now quite a loud call of nature.

"I'm sorry, could I please just use your toilet before I go?"

The support worker gave a matter-of-fact nod to confirm.

"I'll wait for you in the car," said Stafford in a manner that made it clear that Fran was in trouble.

Fran was shown to the bathroom by Stuart's support worker and she was not in there any longer than necessary. She then walked up to the front door and, just as Fran was leaving, she heard Stuart's support worker speak to him.

"Yes Stuart, it's OK, we can still set up the camera to film the owls overnight, don't worry."

Fran then left the bungalow and walked slowly towards to the police car. She forced herself to open the door and as

Fran sat down it felt like she had just nosedived into the jaws of hell.

"Fran, I have told you before, we are focussing *purely* on the day of the wake. I don't care about the night before; now pull your bloody socks up!"

It was not so much his words but the intense aggression behind them that upset Fran so deeply. She did not respond, not even to say sorry, she was too frightened to speak at all. The journey back was made in a very unpleasant silence.

After returning to the office, Fran focussed on her admin tasks. She only just about held it together for the rest of the shift. Fran could not bring herself to talk about it to James, Andy or Clara. There seemed no point as she felt there was nothing that they could really do to help. She was also too within herself to express her feelings adequately. Immediately after work, Fran went to Jac & Mac's on her own. This time she did not go there for a meal but for a large glass of wine. The drink disappeared very quickly and she soon needed several tissues to dry her tears.

A DAY OFF

Overnight, Fran got stuck in an uncomfortable limbo where she was neither asleep nor awake. She was several miles past the end of her tether and overwhelming depression engulfed her whole being. The bedside electronic clock counted the minutes agonizingly slowly towards the new day. Eventually Fran released herself from her mental trauma via a cup of Horlicks. She drank this in almost complete darkness and found a tranquil peace in the stillness of the night. Fran was grateful to just drift along with the gentle motion of the early hours.

She was now beginning to think a little more rationally. Fran knew that, because of the stress caused by Stafford, she simply could not face going to work the next day. However, this was her job, this is what she had to do and where she had to go. There seemed no alternative, but she eventually realised that there was in fact one way out of it, she could ring in sick.

This was not something that she could do easily. Fran had never avoided work under false pretences before. She knew that she was not actually sick, apart from being truly sick of Stafford. Fran made herself a second cup of Horlicks. She then rationalised that there would genuinely be no point in her going into the office today. Fran reasoned that she would not be able to focus. Subsequently she could easily make serious errors like missing vital information on her reports. These sorts of mistakes could have a very detrimental effect on the investigation. However, it still took a while for her to console her conscience sufficiently to accept that she would take this course of action.

Having made that decision, she then considered what she was going to say when she phoned the absence line. Perhaps she could claim she was stressed, actually that was not a lie as she was indeed extremely stressed. However, if she said that then she would have to give more details as to why, a prospect that filled her with dread. Stafford would no doubt deny everything as he is far too proud to admit any wrongdoing. She would then be forced to fight her corner, but she really did not have the strength for such a battle. The stress of explaining her stress would be too stressful.

Fran eventually convinced herself that she needed to invent a different reason to be off sick. She then ran through a list of common illnesses in her mind. It had to be something that could flare up very quickly as everyone saw she was fine when she left work yesterday. She only wanted one day off to rest and regroup, so she also needed an ailment that could pass quickly. After some deliberation, she settled on a severe migraine as it is quite plausible that this could come and go within 24 hours.

Her shift was due to start at 8am and it was good practice to give at least an hour's notice. It may be that no-one would answer and she would have to leave a voicemail message. Fran scripted out a little speech in her mind in preparation for this. It was now just a case of waiting for the right time, but that was still several hours away. Fran got increasingly frustrated as she really wanted to just get it over and done with. As she could not sleep, she put on a soppy RomCom from her DVD collection. This featured Hugh Grant using a whole load of expletives but still coming over as awfully nice. Watching several weddings (with a funeral thrown in for good measure) did indeed help to pass the time.

At 6am, Fran started to get into the zone to do something that was never her forte – to lie. Fran had frequently lied about her feelings for reasons of politeness or diplomacy. However, this was much more official and therefore deeply uncomfortable for her. She then remembered one of her friends telling her the trick is to convince yourself that you are, in fact, telling the truth. This way it would not feel wrong and you could maintain an apparent sincerity.

Fran also remembered a Peter Kay skit about putting on a 'sick voice' to make it sound like you're ill. It was important for her to come across as being in some discomfort. However, as she had hardly slept all night, Fran felt her natural tiredness should help to create the right effect.

At 6.15am, Fran decided that it was probably now close enough to her shift start time to make the call. She had to steady herself as, despite all her rationalizing, this would still be very difficult for her. Fran took a deep breath and speed dialled the absence line. The familiar ringtone tantalisingly repeated itself several times before cutting to an answerphone message. She was relieved by this as it would be much easier for her than an actual conversation.

Fran then mustered up her best 'sick voice'. She apologised and said she had a migraine but would try and come in tomorrow. After making the necessary false statement, she ended the call. The deed was done and no-one would ever know. Of course, she would have to lie a little more when she next saw her colleagues. A few more 'porkies' would then have to be told to her superior for the 'return to work' meeting. However, she could think about that later, so Fran went back to bed and dozed several hours away.

Eventually she dragged herself out of her bed to have a refreshing shower. It was a deeply cleansing experience as if her sins had just been washed away. Fran then had an early lunch consisting of a jacket potato with tuna mayo and salad. It was a simple pleasure, but this meal never failed to please her tastebuds. She then switched on Classic FM and the warm sounds of Mozart danced gently around her living room. Fran poured herself a glass of water (a mild health kick to balance out all the coffee) and drank this whilst considering her situation.

Today is a reprieve not a resolution she silently told herself as Bach joined the classical music party. Tomorrow she would be back in the ring and Stafford could well have her on the ropes again. She really needed to talk to someone, but most of her friends would either be working or busy with parental duties. The only person she could realistically speak to, here and now, would be her recently befriended neighbour Harry. She did not want to just knock on his door and impose herself, so she sent a text that briefly explained the situation. Harry kindly offered to pop down and, true to his word, he appeared a few minutes later.

Fran let her neighbour into her home for the very first time. He took a few moments to acclimatise himself with these new surroundings.

"It's a nice place you've got here, Fran."

"Thanks, I guess I could have done worse."

Fran gave Harry a cup of tea whilst she had a coffee (the mild health kick was very short-lived). Harry sensed that the moment had arrived for them to discuss her issues.

"OK Fran, so you're struggling with work…"

"Yes…believe me I would never normally throw a sickie; it's just all got on top of me."

"I see, so what's going on then?"

"Stafford is just…"

Fran could not find the words, so she just took a gulp of her coffee.

"I take it he's not very nice then?" Harry enquired.

"No, he's just horrible and I don't think I can face working with him any longer."

"Can you apply for some kind of transfer?"

"I suppose I could but I…err…oh I don't think I'm cut out for working in the police."

"What makes you say that?"

Fran considered this question and then opened a drawer in the very centre of her heart to retrieve the honest answer.

"Doubt, Harry, *doubt*. I can't trust my own judgements and in this line of work that's too much of a stumbling block."

"I see. It does seem a shame though."

"I know but I really am struggling."

"Mmm…well, there are times in life where you do have to walk away. It's what you do when you know you can't change or accept something."

"'God, grant me the serenity to accept the things that I cannot change, the courage to change the things I can…"

"'…and the wisdom to know the difference,'" Harry finished off Fran's sentence to show that he was familiar with the *Serenity Prayer*. Fran smiled warmly at him for a moment before Harry continued.

"And with this one, you can't accept your situation so you need to change what's unacceptable. But Fran, if you leave your job, what will you do for work?"

"Well, luckily, I do have a lot of savings as I inherited quite a bit from my family. I can dip into that, get some temp admin work and then eventually find something permanent. It will probably pay less than my current wage but I'm sure I'll survive. I may just have to lay off the champagne and caviar."

Fran smiled and paused before giving her concluding sentence.

"I value my mental health much more than money."

"Absolutely, and it will help you to get through this period knowing that it is temporary, not permanent. However Fran, this is a major change, are you sure you're ready to completely give up your career and not look at any alternatives in the police?"

Fran grimaced, it had taken years to secure a position in the police and now she was on the verge of throwing it all away. In one single fleeting moment she allowed her mind to go past the point of no return and make a definite decision based on self-preservation.

"Yes…yes, these doubts have been building up for a while. It's not for me, Harry, I just can't do it. I will see this murder case through but then I'll break free."

Fran had not needed advice but more of a sounding board and Harry fulfilled this function very well. She now had a game plan and knew how she would move forward.

THE FUNERAL SERVICE

On her way into work, Fran rehearsed in her mind the lies she would tell regarding her fictional migraine. She dreaded carrying off this pretence and anxiety clawed mercilessly at her soul. Fran was relieved when the 'return to work' meeting was done quickly. It had been a long time since she had been off sick so there was no suspicion. Stafford wanted to just get it all over with so he could focus back on the murder case. Clara, Fran, and James all asked if Fran was OK, but she managed to bluff her way through successfully. However, she was a little surprised to be approached by another colleague asking about her wellbeing.

The ever-mysterious Robbie walked up to her. His balding head now only had a sprinkling of thin white hair. He was far from tall, but his slight stoop made him appear even shorter. Robbie's face was well-weathered and you could tell at a glance that he was almost of a retirement age. However, his blue eyes still shone brightly like a ray of light beaming from the lighthouse across the dark night sea.

"Sorry you've not been well, Fran," Robbie said in his gentle southern accent.

"Oh, thanks Robbie, but I am better now."

"I don't know if you've heard but I'm leaving in a couple of weeks."

Fran did her best to act surprised even though she already knew this.

"Oh, sorry to hear that Robbie, but I'm sure you're looking forward to retirement."

"Very much so, I'm going to move to Southcliffe-on-Sea."

Fran noted that Robbie was now making this public. She did not blame him for wanting to spend his remaining years at the seaside. Fran could easily imagine him with a Golden Labrador going for 'walkies' along the beach. As was always the case with Robbie, the conversation quickly ended and he sat down at his computer to check his emails. Fran wished she could properly talk to the man but realised that, for whatever reason, he was and would remain elusive.

Having negotiated the pretence of recovering from illness, Fran could now focus on her working day. She reminded herself that her detective constable position would soon come to an end. Stafford came out of his office and approached her. Such was her relationship with him that she automatically assumed she was in some kind of trouble.

"Fran, I want you to go to Kintley Crematorium for Marianne's funeral service this morning and report back."

This was a relatively straightforward task and one that Fran relished. She could do this alone which was most appealing after her emotional rollercoaster ride. Fran drove for about half an hour and enjoyed cruising down the rural road to Kintley in southwest Havantshire. The crematorium was a large single storey building that was set back a little way from the main high street. There was a well-maintained grass area at the front. Next to the lawn was a colourful array of bushes and flowers. These encircled the property to give it a serene ambience.

Fran parked in the adjacent car park 10 minutes before the service was due to commence. She looked around and wondered if she had got the wrong address as no-one else was arriving and there was very few cars there. After some hesitation, Fran decided to go inside just to check if anyone was there. The double doors opened onto a large laminate floored hall with six rows of freestanding chairs.

Fran was relieved to see Kevin Furlow. He was dressed in black trousers and jacket with a conservative pale blue shirt. There was only a small smattering of attendees who were dotted around the room. They were all lady friends of Marianne and dressed much more brightly than Kevin. No-one from Antony's family was present and Fran made a note of this on her pad. For her report, Fran counted everyone there and the number came to nine. This included the pleasant looking celebrant who would lead the service. Fran was seated on the back row so that she could observe unobtrusively from a distance.

The hall had all the peace of a church but without the religious symbols. Indeed, today's service would be a secular humanist affair. Marianne's life would be remembered but God would be absent from the proceedings. Although Antony's family had strong Catholic roots, Marianne's belief system had been somewhere between atheism and agnosticism. This style of remembrance was therefore befitting to the deceased. Fran was the only person of faith in the room.

A selection of poems was read out by the celebrant. There were also a couple of songs played out rather than sung as would be the case with religious services. Half of the congregation (if it could be called that) were busy tapping away on their mobile phones. They appeared to be more interested in how many 'likes' their last Facebook post got. Kevin gave a eulogy that Fran listened to intently as she hoped it would give an insight into the life of Marianne. His ill feeling towards his mother was clear by the inhumanly dry delivery of his speech. Nothing bad was actually said but his lack of emotional connection was striking.

From the eulogy, Fran noted that Marianne had once been a secretary to Antony. This eventually led to them getting married. Kevin also spoke about Marianne's love of the finer things of life. Fran had already realised that from Marianne's very expensive taste in sherry. There were no major revelations, Kevin ended his short monologue and duly sat back down. Marianne's body was to be cremated and the coffin slid away behind the curtain to the incinerator. This final act was accompanied by Cole Porter's *Anything Goes*. Fran found it almost distasteful but then she remembered this was the overriding philosophy of the deceased.

Fran noted how all of Marianne's lady friends left shortly afterwards and no-one spoke to Kevin. It was clear that there was no love lost between them. Fran noted that there did not appear to be any kind of wake arranged. The service had been perfunctory, it was done because it had to be done. Few people wanted to celebrate Marianne's life; most would rather forget her. The celebrant smiled warmly before leaving through the double doors. This left Fran and Kevin as the only two people remaining in the hall. Fran felt compelled to say something and so resorted to traditional British politeness.

"It was a lovely service."

"You don't have to lie, Fran."

As with their previous interview, she was taken aback by Kevin's blunt manner. It then placed her into an uncomfortable situation as she did not know how to respond. Kevin was right, of course, the service had been as cold as arctic snow. Fran scraped the bottom of her diplomacy barrel to find something non-offensive to say.

"Well…it's over now, I'm sure you can take some comfort from that."

"Yes, I am glad to get it done, now I can get on with my life. So, how's the murder investigation going?"

The question was asked with a distant curiosity rather than any kind of eagerness for the murderer to be caught.

"Well, I'm not at liberty to say too much but we are doing all we can with it."

"I see, well, good luck. Right, if you'll excuse me, I really want to be anywhere other than here."

And with that Kevin nonchalantly left the building. Fran just could not believe how a human life could be dismissed like this. She remembered how hard she had cried at all her family members' funerals, so this apathy was really disturbing to her. After a brief reflection, Fran walked swiftly to her police car and drove back to Head Office. On her return she duly reported back to Stafford. He was neither pleased nor annoyed but just took on board the limited information she could gather from the service. They both agreed that the most intriguing aspect was how few people wanted to pay their respects. However, this still did not give a motive for her murder. It was clear to both Fran and Stafford that there was now only one place left where they were likely to find it.

THE PASSWORD

The next day Fran came into the office and it was if the air had been polluted by the collective frustration of the team.

"It's hopeless, Fran. All our evidence is as about as helpful as a comb to a bald man," said Andy.

"But we still haven't looked at Marianne's computer journal."

"Yeah, but no-one can access the bloody thing. Stafford has had all his IT guys trying to hack into it but it's just impenetrable. She obviously didn't want anyone to ever read this file."

"Which makes you wonder what's in there?"

"Exactly, but damn it, it's no good unless someone, somehow can guess the password."

Shortly afterwards, Stafford and James approached Fran. The CDI assigned her and his detective inspector to the task of cracking this password. Stafford explained that this was a last resort and that he would never normally ask them to do something like this. However, he was now forced to make an exception. It was clear that they had to access the computer journal to discover the elusive motive for the murder.

Fran was torn, on one level she was delighted to be working with James for the day. However, this task seemed to be a tall order, a very tall order, an order so tall it would dwarf Mount Everest. James brought over Marianne's laptop and placed it on Fran's desk. He plugged it into a nearby socket and loaded up the file that contained Marianne's private journal. A message appeared on the screen.

> **Please enter the password**
> *****************

"OK, I think a challenge like this requires a good strong coffee," said James.

A few minutes later two good strong coffees were placed on Fran's desk.

"How the hell are we going to do this?" asked Fran.

James took a moment to consider it and then decided on the course of action.

"Let's face it, we'll be bloody lucky to guess it blindly. Let's ring everyone who knew her to see if they've got any clue as to what the password might be."

Fran was immediately fearful of what Stafford would make of this. It would reflect badly on the team and ipso facto on him and his beloved reputation. However, James intuitively knew why Fran was anxious and sought to reassure her.

"Don't worry, this is *my* decision. I will explain it to Stafford and will take full responsibility. You are only obeying my order."

James and Fran proceeded to make numerous embarrassing calls to all the relevant people that had known Marianne. It made them both feel very amateur but there was a need for pragmatism. The initial responses were all negative. Fran and James also had to leave a few voicemail messages. Over the next three hours, they had heard from everyone who they had contacted but there was still no joy. James then turned to Fran and shook his head despairingly.

"Oh, sod this, let's get some lunch," he said and Fran needed no persuading.

James and Fran popped into Gregory's sandwich shop. They both ordered a ham salad baguette and then sat down to munch their lunch. It had been a frustrating morning and both parties needed some distraction. Initially they had engaged in some light conversation including that favourite British obsession, the weather. However, it was not long before Fran asked the question that was now in the forefront of her mind.

"Are things any better at home?"

James audibly sighed and looked out of the window for a second before turning to face Fran.

"It's over, we live in the same house but we're not husband and wife. We never kiss or cwtch."

"Cwtch?"

"Sorry Fran, another Welsh word. You would say 'cuddle'."

"I see. Oh James, I…"

Fran's sentence trailed off as she really did not know what to say.

"It's alright, I'm not the first person to have a failed marriage and I won't be the last."

"Are you going to be alright?"

"Yes, I'll cope, luckily we have a TV in the lounge and the bedroom so we can live in separate rooms."

"Yeah, but what about…"

Fran's sentence again trailed off as she was worried that she was about to ask an inappropriate question.

"Overnight? It's OK, the spare room has a camp bed, so I'm sleeping there. We can almost not see each other at all and believe me, it's much better that way."

The conversation was sombre and sobering. Fran's soft brown eyes looked deeply into his as she tried to visually reassure him. However, they both knew that this was not the time to try and expunge heartaches, so James took command once more.

"We'd better get back before Stafford sends out a search party."

And with that they swiftly walked back to the office.

"OK, so Marianne has taken her secret password to the grave," said James.

Fran decided to not point out that Marianne had in fact been cremated as it would spoil James's flow.

"This, of course, means that we have no alternative but to try and blindly guess it. Now, what kind of things do people use as their password?" James continued.

"I think I read somewhere that the most popular password is the word 'password' itself."

"Oh, she would really be a numpty to use that."

"Shall we just make sure?"

James typed it in on the keyboard, but it was immediately realised that Marianne had not been a 'numpty'.

"How about her name? Maybe with her age or year of birth?" said Fran but these suggestions were not right either.

"Names of loved ones, maybe," said Fran more in hope than expectation.

"Mmm, well we can try but it would appear that Marianne's only true love was money," said James.

However, to cover all the bases they typed in the names of all the significant people in Marianne's life. They also tried them alongside their ages and years of birth but to no avail. James was now writing down all the failed attempts in his notebook.

"Did Marianne have any pets?" asked Fran.

"Nope."

"How about hobbies?"

"Spending was her main hobby."

"Maybe she had some kind of prized possession?"

James paused for a moment, but his expression was as blank as unused printing paper.

"Her house had a name…what was it?"

"'Skyrise', good thinking Fran, let's try that."

James typed with hope, but the outcome was disappointing.

"How about her car?"

"You mean the Volvo, well perhaps, it's a lovely looking car."

The guess of 'Volvo' was rejected too.

"OK, let's get all our research on Marianne and see if there's anything else that leaps out."

Fran and James spent several painstaking hours researching everything they had on Marianne. Passwords were then typed in and a plethora of failed attempts were written down. James was not sure which would run out first, the ink in his pen or the page space in his book. Regular coffee intervals were essential to preserve their sanity. As time crept slowly into the evening the process had spiralled from painstaking to downright torturous. Eventually James realised that they needed some unhealthy finger food and pizza was the perfect solution. He then placed the order that made sure the delivery man literally got on his bike.

When their takeaway arrived, James popped outside to collect if from the barrier gates. There was no way that the delivery driver could enter the building grounds as this area was securely sealed off. Fran and James ate a bit quicker than normal as cramming the food into their mouths gave relief from their intense frustration. The pizza break was intended as a mere pit stop before battling on with more random guesses at the password. However, they both looked at each other in despair, there was now nothing left to give.

"Let's call it a night, sorry this has been such a wasted day."

"It's not your fault James. Oh, no-one is ever going to guess this damn password!"

"No, it's futile. I mean there's no set format for these things. It could be words, figures, letters, you know, anything goes."

"What did you just say?" Fran asked sharply and appeared almost startled.

"I said there is no set format…"

"No, after that," Fran interrupted.

"Oh…err it could be words, figures…"

"No, the last bit," Fran interrupted again.

"Errm…anything goes."

Fran clicked her fingers as a 'Eureka' moment had just struck her. She then launched herself into singing the Cole Porter song.

"'In olden days a glimpse of stocking was looked on as something shocking, now heaven knows, anything goes!'"

Fran was so enraptured that she overlooked her embarrassment of singing that had always plagued her in church. James stared at her as if she had just flipped her lid into the loony bin.

"Are you alright?" asked James.

"Anything goes!" Fran exclaimed.

James was very confused, so Fran decided she had better explain.

"They played that song at her funeral and everyone I interviewed said that this was Marianne's life philosophy, 'anything goes'."

"OK?" said James hesitantly as he was struggling to see the relevance of this.

"Try that as the password."

"Oh, come on Fran, we've been at it all bloody day."

"Just one more guess."

"Alright, but this is the *last* time."

James typed "Anything Goes" into the keyboard and the screen went black for a few tantalising seconds. Eventually the file for Marianne's private journal opened.

"*You've done it!*" James exclaimed. He quickly glanced at the very first journal entry which was in 2009.

He then hugged Fran and everything that had felt utterly useless suddenly became completely worthwhile. James then released himself from the embrace and speed dialled Stafford on his mobile phone.

"Hello sir, just to say we've cracked it, the password, it's 'Anything Goes'."

James smiled broadly and Fran was able to glean that they had achieved a remarkable feat, they had pleased Stafford.

"No problem…thanks, good night."

James put his phone away before switching the laptop off. He pulled the lid down and wrote the code on a sticky note. James then stuck this on top of the laptop. Fran and James left the building together and the main door was securely locked. The outside air now had a skin tingling coolness as the sun had handed over to the moon for the night shift. They stared at each for a few peaceful moments before James asked Fran a question.

"Do you want to go for a drink?"

There was nothing in the world that Fran would want to do more.

A NIGHT OUT

James and Fran walked over to the retail centre. Fran was about to turn towards Jac & Mac's, where she assumed they were heading. Suddenly James indicated that he wanted her to stop.

"Hey Fran, there's a lovely pub about 10 minutes' walk away and they've got a late licence on weekend nights."

The words "late licence" made Fran's ears prick up like a dog whose name had just been called out. It was now clear that James wanted what enthusiastic drinkers would call *a proper drink*. This would make a refreshing change to the usual quick one followed by the "ooh, is that the time" malarkey. The night was still young and to Fran's delight it would live a lot longer than she had expected. Fran had never really explored the area past the retail centre. She didn't think there was anything there other than houses, but she gladly followed James.

It was dark and they were walking along narrow paths, so it wasn't easy to properly converse. However, Fran did not mind as she knew there would be plenty of time in the pub especially with a late licence to boot. James then led Fran down, what was to her, an unfamiliar road. A thin shaft of dim moonlight divided the lines of cars that were parked either side of the street. Eventually, they came across the pub's elevated sign.

Fran and James smiled at each other before walking inside. *The Silver Goose* had an informal cosiness that made you feel immediately at home. It consisted of one relatively small room that bent round the wooden bar in a L shape. Traditional pub furniture was mismatched with a selection of sofas, the kind that would normally belong in someone's lounge. A warm chattering ambience was at an ideal sound level, so you didn't have to raise your voice to be heard. The clientele was clearly at the older end of the age scale. There were a couple of grey shaggy beards absorbing the foam from their pints of beer. The resident black Staffy dog was sniffing around enthusiastically in anticipation of a stray crisp.

Fran was a little self-conscious in her police uniform. She therefore took off her jacket, her black and white cravat as well as undoing her top shirt button. Fran hoped this would make her profession not quite so glaringly obviously. James was scanning the room for a free table when he noticed an elderly couple finish their drinks and leave. This was the perfect spot, right next to a warm log fire whose flames were glowing magnificently. He and Fran moved in swiftly and sat down gratefully.

"What's your poison then Fran?" James asked.

Fran knew she wanted wine; it was only the colour that needed to be considered. She was torn between a light white, a heavy red or the halfway house rosé? *Oh, it's the weekend* she reasoned so she opted for the more potent drink.

"A large red wine please" Fran said assertively.

She wondered if she should offer some money. Her instinct then told her that James did not need or want payment, so she just smiled instead. As James queued patiently at the bar, she felt the fire massage her bones. The effect was like a jacuzzi bath only without the water. The weekend had arrived in style with a handsome drinking companion and wine on its way. She felt like a cat who had just been served a bowlful of double cream.

James returned a few minutes later and handed over her wine. He then supped at the lager that was fizzing away in his pint glass.

"So, what do you reckon is in Marianne's computer journal?" asked James.

Fran didn't really want to discuss the case. However, she knew that this was the normal way with a work colleague on a night out. You start off with the job-related stuff and then as the drinks flowed you moved onto other more interesting subjects.

"I've got a hunch we'll find something useful there. I can see why Stafford was so keen to get access to the file," said Fran.

"That was an inspired guess by the way."

"Thanks James, I just I wish I had twigged this morning then it could have saved us a lot of time."

"Oh, I don't think anyone, not even the royal git that is Stafford, could expect you to get it straightaway. It really is remarkable that you guessed it at all."

"So, you don't like him either then?"

"I don't think anyone likes him. He sucks all the joy out of the room like a hoover."

Despite all the problems Stafford had caused her, Fran's inclination was still to be diplomatic.

"Well, I guess that's just the way he is."

"Yes, but how far do you go with the whole 'it's just the way he is' thing Fran? I mean, I wonder if that did that during the second world war: Adolf Hitler, fascist dictator; 'that's just the way he is!'" said James with his tongue locked firmly in his cheek.

Fran laughed and took a gulp of her wine. It was a relief that James had a similar view of Stafford. She decided now was the moment to ease the conversation away from work related matters. Fran brought up something that she had overheard at a previous works night out.

"James…by the way, if you don't mind me asking, I once heard that you had your whole name changed by deed poll."

"It's true. I hated the man I was Fran, I was a bastard! I wanted to be a different person and part of that process was to change my name, give myself a new identity."

"I see."

"Be glad you know James Mallen and not my former incarnation."

Fran decided not to probe any further. Whoever or whatever he once was, she certainly liked the man presented to her now. Having broken free from work and this murder case, they began to expand their repertoire of subject matter. There was one topic that they were bound to discuss.

"Don't get married," said James.

"Well…I've got to say you're not the first person who's said that to me. To be honest, although I love romance, I've never really understood marriage, this whole idea of *the one*. I feel bad saying that as I've been brought up to believe marriage is a sacred thing. 'The two become one flesh' and all of that, but I just don't get it. I mean, there are billions of people on the planet. How can you possibly know this person is *the one* out of the whole human race? Whenever I ask my friends this they say 'you just know' but how do you *know*? I mean, what happens; does God give you a giant thumbs up sign in the sky?"

"Well, if he did, I never saw it. No Fran, in all truth your lover is only *the one* from those who are available at the time. It's just a spin of the roulette wheel. I take it you're not with anyone then?"

"Oh God, no! My whole experience of relationships has been like an airplane that's driven around the runway but somehow never got airborne."

"Whereas I got airborne, but the plane came down with such a crash that I wished I stayed in the terminal!"

There was then a pause as they reflected on their different experiences of love. The conversation then resumed and it flowed very easily. They almost forgot that they were work colleagues. James and Fran were now just a man and a woman enjoying each other's company. Several more drinks disappeared as they were losing themselves in the rhythm of the night. Fran was yet to share with any colleague her plan of resigning. Her intention was to keep it a secret, but alcohol has the uncanny knack of pushing up everything to the surface.

"James, I need to share something with you."

"Sure Fran."

"When this case is over, I'm going."

"Oh no, don't let Stafford do you out of a job."

"It's not just Stafford, I just don't think I'm cut out for this."

"But Fran, you've got great detective instincts."

"Yeah, but I just...oh I don't know James...well actually I do know and I said this to a friend the other day. It's doubt, I've got too much self-doubt so I can't follow my convictions and that's no good in this job."

James visibly sighed and put his hand affectionately on Fran's shoulder.

The midnight hour crept into the room without Fran and James noticing. James was now regaling Fran with tales of his time as a customer service advisor in a call centre.

"You see Fran, there is one golden rule for anyone who works in customer service; 'never underestimate how stupid the general public can be'."

Fran laughed, her eyes giving out a beam of joy. James continued with his diatribe.

"No, but seriously, their stupidity knows no bounds. Just when you think you've encountered the smallest IQ humanly possible someone else rings up and lowers the bar even further!"

Fran's laugh was interrupted by a loud ring from the bell on the bar.

"Last orders," the barman bellowed out like a ship's foghorn.

James looked at his watch in sheer disbelief.

"Oh bloody hell, there's no way that's the time."

But, of course, that really was the time, the night had somehow fast forwarded to this moment. After briefly pausing to absorb the reality, James then asked the appropriate question.

"One for the road?"

They drunk their final drinks and enjoyed a slightly dizzy but deeply comfortable silence. More time disappeared into the ether until they realised that all the other punters had vanished. The bar staff wore impatient faces as James and

Fran slowly stood up to leave. James explained to Fran that there was a taxi rank about 5 minutes' walk away.

They then walked outside and the stars sparkled like a million silver dots in the black sky. It felt like they were the only two souls in the universe as they walked down the road. Pure peace filled them as they gently meandered along an almost silent street. They muttered meaningless nothings to each other and then it happened. Fran was feeling the cold air on her fingertips, but this was suddenly replaced by the warmth of James's hand. An interlocking happened naturally and immediately.

The connection that had been building up all evening in the pub had been fully realised by physically joining each other. Life just stopped and in this moment everything that had happened before, or might happen after, paled into utter insignificance. The only thing that mattered now was the emotional door that had just opened within their hearts. The full force of her feelings overwhelmed Fran; it had been years since anyone had touched her like this.

Every fingertip gently pressed against every knuckle of the other one's hand as they continued to walk aimlessly. They didn't speak, they didn't need to, silent emotions did all the talking. The taxi rank came into view, but they turned away in a different direction and didn't give it a moment's thought. This was clearly not going to be their destination.

Fran felt as if she was floating in a dream. It was like she had somehow become a character from one of her many chick-lit novels. However, her ecstasy was interrupted by an anxious thought; *wait a minute, he's married*. Fran just couldn't let go of James, the emotional impulse, the craving, the need was all too much. It was now very confusing for her as she couldn't understand how something so wrong could feel so right. Her desire and her morality were at war with each other.

In the throes of romantic passion, they had wandered almost a mile without realising where they were going. Fran didn't care about being lost, but she knew that she would have to confront her niggling doubts. They kept coming back to her amongst all her bliss.

"James…this is wrong."

"Oh, I don't care, I *just don't care* Fran. I wanted you from the moment I first saw you."

This was the killer blow, no-one had ever said that to her in her whole life. Fran simply had to take this man home regardless of the consequences and however wrong it might be. She took a bit of time to work out where they were and in which direction they should walk. They ended up taking a less than direct route to her home. Neither of them cared as they were happy to drift along in a romantic haze. Finally, they reached the short driveway that led to Fran's maisonette.

Fran had to force herself to let go of James's hand so she could deal with the practical matter of unlocking the front door. She then led James into the lounge and turned the light on. James noticed the large freestanding candlestick holder that elevated a candle to about thigh height off the ground.

"Please light it Fran, I want to see your beautiful face in the candlelight."

Fran smiled and went into her kitchen to get a box of matches. She then took one out, struck the match and lit the candle. Fran switched out the main ceiling light, so the warm orange flame created a much softer lighting ambience. James and Fran then sat down on the two-seater sofa and stared at each other intensely. Silence was now present as they both waited in suspended animation for the perfect moment. There was a sweet surrender as they leant their heads forward until their lips had a tender meeting. Fran then wrapped her arms around James's neck and savoured the bliss.

After this magical kiss, they parted to draw breath. Fran then rested her on James's chest.

"Oh James, it's so wonderful to err…" Fran's sentence trailed off.

"Cwtch?" James suggested.

"Yes…cwtch," Fran replied dreamily.

Fran smiled warmly as James softly kissed her affectionately. She wanted to forget everything and disappear fully into this special night, but she couldn't. There was something that needed to be discussed so she pulled herself away from the embrace.

"What are we going to do, James?"

"What do you mean?"

"I mean your wife…your marriage."

"She doesn't need to know."

"Oh, come on, she's no doubt wondering where the hell you are right now?"

"She won't care, Fran. We're done, it's over."

"I can't be the other woman."

"No, you'll be the *only* woman, please, you must believe me."

But Fran could not believe him or at least not fully. She remembered the story of one of her friends who had her heart broken by a married man who eventually went back to his wife. The prospect of her being in a similar situation scared her.

"James, I do want you so much, but I need you to leave her and live somewhere else. It's not enough to just say you will, I need you to *actually* go and at least *start* the divorce proceedings."

"Oh, do we have to wait for all that?"

"James, I'm sorry, I'm just not comfortable with this."

James stood up and the romance in the room was instantly killed. It was not long before he ordered a taxi and left her flat. Fran then walked into her kitchen crying, opened a bottle of brandy and drank all her miseries away.

LOVE HANGOVER

Fran woke up, but only just. She lay in her bed hungover and motionless. Fran glimpsed the empty brandy bottle and glass that had somehow ended up on her bedroom floor. She could not remember how that happened. In fact, Fran was struggling to remember anything from the previous night. All she could think about was how terrible she was now feeling. She desperately needed the cool oasis that was provided by a glass of water. However, this would involve walking into the kitchen which, in her current state, would be an epic expedition. Eventually she persuaded herself to make the journey. She slowly staggered into the room to run the cold tap for a lifesaving drink.

She gulped away a few glasses greedily. Memories of her night with James then slowly came back to her. They were like a random selection of poorly edited scenes from a film. However, she recalled enough to realise that she'd had a romantic encounter with a married man. At this point, she then felt awful emotionally as well as physically. Today would be a challenging survival exercise.

Slowly, very slowly, her hangover eased but the guilt was proving much harder to shift. Fran could not deny that she loved to be in the company of James. However, she had always looked at him as off limits due to his marital status. She therefore felt she had trespassed into a forbidden area.

Fran didn't like to view herself as being full of stained-glass window sanctimony. However, her life had been conducted within a wholesome Christian moral framework or at least mostly. Last night's episode, she felt, had resulted in her clearly crossing the line. She was struggling to accept how this had happened. There was one man she really needed to speak to, so she sent him a text.

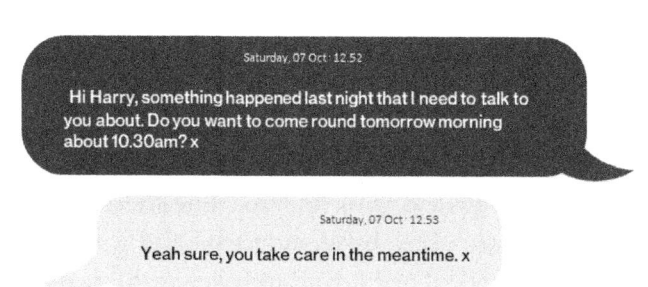

> Saturday, 07 Oct · 12.52
>
> Hi Harry, something happened last night that I need to talk to you about. Do you want to come round tomorrow morning about 10.30am? x

> Saturday, 07 Oct · 12.53
>
> Yeah sure, you take care in the meantime. x

Fran was relieved that Harry confirmed. This would give her plenty of time to properly recover, time she would definitely need. Fran was going to send a text just to say "Thanks Harry" when an idea popped into her mind.

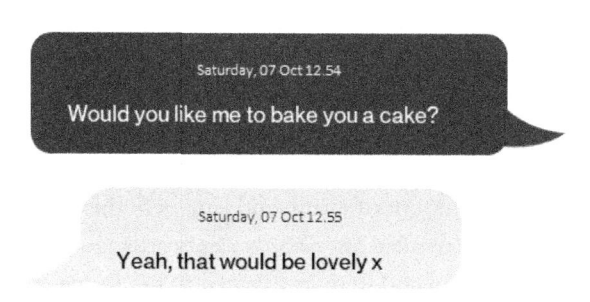

> Saturday, 07 Oct 12.54
>
> Would you like me to bake you a cake?

> Saturday, 07 Oct 12.55
>
> Yeah, that would be lovely x

In the evening, it suddenly occurred to Fran that she had hardly eaten all day. Subsequently, a takeaway chicken meal featuring two tasty sides was soon on Fran's plate. To cheer herself up, she picked out yet another soppy RomCom from her collection. Fran enjoyed watching Harry meeting Sally. However, as a British woman, she really could not imagine being as outrageous as the Meg Ryan character. There was no way Fran would ever scream out erotic sound effects in a restaurant! She then settled down for what would be a significantly better night's sleep.

The next morning Fran woke up feeling revitalised. She then proceeded with some domestic chores. Cleaning her home was tantamount to cleansing her soul. Fran then had a shower to help freshen up a bit. Afterwards, she got out her ingredients, bowl and whisk ready to create a Victoria sponge cake. Fran was a keen baker, in fact she had won prizes at village fetes. She found it hard to bake just for herself but today she would have a guest.

This would be another Sunday morning when she was not in church. It was not solely because of her arrangement to see her neighbour. Due to recent events, Fran felt that she was not worthy to go to the House of God. She could not bring herself to confess what she'd done to anyone other than Harry. She felt that he was someone who she could share this secret with and not fear scorning judgement.

After they had finished cooking, Fran took the top and base of the cake out of the oven. Once they had cooled off, a generous amount of cream and jam were then squeezed in between the two halves. Shortly afterwards, a knock on the door was heard and Fran let Harry into her home. She made a cup of tea for him before cutting off a large slice of Victoria sponge cake for him.

"You spoil me, Fran."

"Well, you know; 'love thy neighbour'."

Harry smiled at Fran's biblical reference before settling down to the treat she had served up for him. The cake was delicious with a light, fluffy texture although a little naughty on the calorie count. They then engaged in some idle chit chat. Fran and Harry both knew this was merely a warm-up for the soul-searching conversation that would soon follow.

After Fran and Harry had eaten their cake, there was a pause in conversation. Fran instinctively knew that Harry was now ready for the story of her and James. She then proceeded to tell the whole sorry tale to the best of her memory. Fran did not gloss over any parts, nor did she try to justify herself. She just took Harry through the sequence of events in chronological order. He paused for a few moments to reflect on what Fran had just told him, so that he could absorb all the information. Fran patiently waited before asking the question that she had asked herself repeatedly.

"What am I going to do, Harry? I've got to work with this man."

"And he's got to work with you. Mmm…Fran, I know this is not going to be easy, but I think you need to have a conversation with James. You've both got to work out a way forward. Otherwise, the difficult feelings will just grow and fester."

"I can't have that conversation."

"Do you want to just carry on and pretend nothing ever happened?"

"I know this is weak but yes, I do."

"It's not going to go away, Fran, it will eventually come to the fore again."

"Yeah, but I've never had a conversation like this with anyone, ever."

"It's not going to be pleasant, but I think you should both face up to what's happened."

"Harry, I just can't face this, I'm sorry, I *just can't*."

Fran put her head in her hands and was on the verge of crying. She then cut off another large slice of cake for herself. Granted this was comfort food but right now it was just what she needed as it was too early for alcohol. Besides, Fran had decided that she needed to have some time away from the booze. The shenanigans of Friday night had severely battered her liver. Harry also had another slice of cake too and they quietly munched away for a few minutes. Fran then felt rejuvenated for round two of this difficult conversation.

"Do you want to be with James, Fran?" Harry asked slightly gingerly.

"I can't have an affair…I told James that. I'm also not comfortable with him leaving his wife just to be with me."

"OK, if you don't think it can possibly work with James, then there's nothing else for it."

"'Nothing else for it?'"

"Yes, I'm afraid you'll just have to go out with Brad Pitt instead!"

Fran laughed and smiled at Harry.

"Sounds like a plan," she then replied.

"No, but seriously, I know you're feeling awful, but you haven't caused his marriage to fail, Fran."

"Yes, but I still feel like I'm interfering with the ending. One marriage should totally end of its own accord before a new relationship begins. There should not be any kind of overlap."

"Ideally yes, but we don't live an ideal world, love doesn't always fit into neat boxes."

"I know that and I'm sure some of my friends would say I'm being puritanical but I'm just not comfortable with it."

"OK, you're clear about your feelings and that's always a good thing. But it's still going to be difficult to work with James."

"Of course, I just wish I could make all this go away."

Fran then had an idea that made her stand up quite suddenly and wildly gesture before speaking once more.

"Actually…I can make it all go away. Look, I was going to resign soon anyway, so I'll hand in my notice tomorrow."

"But you don't have another job."

"Oh, I'll sort out some admin work or something. I've still got plenty of money left from the inheritance I got when my family died. This will cushion me until I find something else. No, I've got to get away Harry for my own sanity."

Shortly after deciding this, Fran got a small piece of paper and wrote out her resignation. She placed this into a white envelope and put it in her letter rack next to another white envelope containing an unopened council tax bill. Fran was now ready to end her career as a detective constable.

12a Queens Drive, Jessop's Green, Havantshire HV1 2AQ

1st October, 2023

Chief Detective Inspector Stafford
Major Crimes Unit
Jessop's Green
Havantshire
HV1 3AW

Dear Mr Stafford

I am writing to inform you that I wish to tender 4 weeks' notice to resign from my Detective Constable post at the Major Crimes Unit in Jessop's Green. I would therefore be grateful if the Human Resources Department could make the necessary arrangements to terminate my employment.

However, I would like to take my remaining 4 days' annual leave entitlement during my last work of employment. This would mean my actual last working day would be Monday 30th October, 2023.

The valuable detective experience I have gained in my current role will, I am sure, be of considerable benefit to me in my next job. I wish my colleagues every success in their future careers.

Yours sincerely

F. Jacobs

Frances Jacobs

RESIGNATION & REVELATION

Fran had an early night as tomorrow would be a big day for her. As usual, she took a moment to look at the picture of her family that was on her bedside cabinet. Fran remembered the blind spot close to the railway station where her family had the fatal car accident. Overnight, thoughts chattered away in her mind, so she was unable to slip into sleep.

Night-time overthinking had always been a problem for Fran. It was when doubts would scream at her with no distraction available. Ending her career was one of the most significant decisions she had ever made. Her personality was such that doubting herself was inevitable. She felt that her decision to resign was based on weakness and for this she was ashamed. However, she also knew that staying on at work could have dire consequences for her wellbeing.

Fran did not care how Stafford would react as he would probably not be bothered. In fact, he might even crack open a bottle of champagne; such was his animosity towards her. What she was worried about though was explaining her decision to Clara and Andy. They had both been very supportive to her and she knew they would be deeply disappointed to see her go.

She had really wanted to see this murder case through to its conclusion, so she could then have a clean break. Fran knew that someone would need to be drafted in to replace her. Alternatively, the other option would be for the team to rally round to cover her absence.

How could it have come to this? Fran asked herself. She was blind to any notion that circumstances had conspired against her and felt that she had simply failed. Fran dwelled on her perceived failure as she sipped at a cup of Horlicks in the early hours. She was also wrestling with the whirlwind of emotions that she still had about James. Their booze fuelled dalliance would make her final dealings with him uncomfortable. This could only be survived through a lot of real-life acting. Fran decided that, with all this swimming around in her brain, sleep was not on the cards tonight. She feared the groggy lethargy that occurred whenever she had stayed awake all night. Her autopilot would have to step in and ride her through the next day somehow.

To Fran's surprise, she did eventually sleep. However, extreme tiredness had deafened her to the sound of her alarm clock. Her bleary eyes slowly opened to reveal a time that shocked her. Fran then panicked and carried out a stupidly quick wash before throwing on her uniform. She knew she did not look good, but she had to leave immediately. Fran was keen to avoid the ignominy of a late arrival as Stafford was a stickler for timekeeping. She did not want another reprimand from him even though she was going to resign imminently. This was a testament to the hold that he had over her.

Fran left her flat but then remembered she had forgotten to pick up her resignation notice. She hurried back indoors and almost without looking picked up the white envelope from the letter rack. Despite her sleep deprivation, she was still able to hotfoot it into work. Fran arrived with literally a minute to spare. Stafford was thankfully in his office so did not notice that she had cut it wafer-thin fine. Fran got herself a coffee from the drinks dispenser and drank it quickly. She then took a moment to compose herself ready to go into Stafford's office to hand in her resignation letter.

She walked swiftly over to the CDI's office and took out her white envelope. It was as if she was pulling out a gun ready for a shootout. Her resignation notice was her weapon, but Stafford would not be able to fire back with anything. For once she would be in complete control. She silently gloated about this before knocking firmly on the door.

"Come in," said the voice of her superior.

Fran glanced down at her envelope and to her horror realised it was the wrong one. In her rush to leave, she had accidentally picked up the unopened council tax letter instead. She silently cursed and then froze as she frantically worked out what to do now. She really did not want to discuss her resignation without her weapon of choice. However, her knock meant she had just requested entry to Stafford's office. It would be so unprofessional to then run away like a child playing a *knocking down ginger* prank.

"Come in!" said Stafford who was clearly irritated by the delay.

Fran desperately scrambled through her mind for something to say. Eventually, she came up with an alternative. It was not great, but she had no time to concoct anything better. Fran steadied herself and walked into the office to face Stafford.

"Good morning sir, I just wondered what you have assigned for me today?"

"Is that what you've come to ask me? Fran, you know I'll come and brief everyone about this."

Stafford gave her a sharp quizzical look.

"Sorry, I just wondered...ermm. I'll go back and wait for your briefing then sir."

Fran left the office and felt like an idiot. Her nerves were already on edge, but then her heart almost leapt out of her chest when she saw James. He was looking straight at her with a sense of urgency.

"Fran, we need to talk."

He then led her away into a dark corridor adjacent to the office.

"James, please, I can't do this right now."

"Look, I just wanted to say I'm sorry. I'm a married man, unhappily married granted, but still married so I shouldn't have said and done what I did."

"Well...it takes two to tango, I'm just as much to blame."

"I know you are looking to resign soon, but I had visions of you jumping ship before you're ready, just to avoid me. I would hate for that to happen."

Fran did not know how to respond to this.

"I promise nothing like this will happen again. Our relationship will be purely professional from now on," James continued.

"OK James," Fran simply replied.

James gave a silent nod of acknowledgement before they returned to the office. Fran felt relieved and then she saw Clara who clearly wanted to speak to her.

"Hey Fran, where were you yesterday?"

"Clara, look to be honest, I need a break from church for a bit. I'm going through a tricky time."

"But Fran, it's the best place to lift you above your troubles."

Fran did not have the heart to admit that she was having doubts about organised religion. She knew it would upset Clara as this was the bond their friendship was built upon.

Instead, she gave a rather forced smile. Luckily, Stafford then called the team together for a debriefing, so she was spared from further conversation.

Stafford had assigned Fran to investigate Marianne's computer journal. She worked alone that afternoon and Fran appreciated the solitude as she could just knuckle down to some proper detective work. This could be done without all the emotional distractions that the previous weekend had given her. She typed in "Anything Goes" to access the file. She decided that she had better take a systematic approach to devour it. Fran started with the most recent entry and worked her way, one entry at a time, in reverse chronological order. The journal entries covered well over a decade so this would be a long, painstaking process. However, it was now the only thing that might provide some genuinely useful information for the murder case.

Marianne's most recent journal entry revealed how much she was dreading the funeral. However, she was clearly looking forward to gaining the inheritance. Fran noted how there seemed to be no sense of sadness at the passing of her husband. It then became clear to Fran that none of her interviewees had exaggerated Marianne's selfishness. She systematically read through some previous journal entries. These revealed how Marianne resented all the work she had to do in arranging the funeral and wake. It was also clear that she hated meeting Antony's family again. Marianne vowed this would be the final time.

Fran continued to read progressively in reverse chronological order. Eventually, she came across an entry that was from the Saturday of the August bank holiday weekend.

> **Tuesday afternoon, 22/08/2023**
>
> My plan worked like a dream. We went to the cliffs at Southcliffe-on-Sea this morning and I made sure there was no-one around. I then walked with Antony right up to the edge of the cliff and told him to look at the flying seagulls below. As he crouched down, I gave him a hard shove, so he lost his balance and fell to his death. I then gave an award-winning acting performance on the phone. The police operator believed me when I said how he had lost his footing and that I couldn't save him. There is no way that anyone could possibly prove otherwise now.
>
> I don't feel bad because I've enabled Antony to leave this earth in a blaze of glory after a successful business career. If he had lived on, he would have just deteriorated into some boring old man. I do believe that a person shouldn't live past the point of being useful. The human population is far too big without these unnecessary people wasting space.
>
> And now he's gone I will soon get what I deserve. I just can't wait to receive the inheritance; I just cannot wait.

Fran was shocked, she put her hand over her mouth in horror. This gave a completely different complexion to the case. They were investigating the murder of a murderer.

PART TWO
"THIS MURDER CASE IS KILLING ME!"

CONSEQUENCES

Fran struggled to believe what she had just read. There was nothing for it, she would have to tell Stafford immediately. Fran locked the screen and marched passed Clara and Andy who tried to engage with her. Normally she would never blank them, but she was now locked in tunnel vision mode so disregarded everything else. She walked over to Stafford's office and entered without bothering to knock on the door.

"Fran, how dare you burst in here like that!"

"Sorry sir, but this is urgent, you need to come right away," Fran said emphatically.

"What for?" countered Stafford aggressively.

"I've found something *extremely* serious; you *must* come now!"

"Why?"

"Just come with me, *please*."

Reluctantly, Stafford got up and followed Fran to her desk. She unlocked the screen of Marianne's laptop to reveal the journal entry.

"Read this..."

"Oh, come on Fran, just include it in your report."

"You *must* read this now," Fran said forcefully.

Stafford was taken aback as Fran had never spoken to him in such an aggressive manner before. He then focussed on the screen and read the journal entry. After reading it, his eyes dilated and his jaw dropped.

"Jesus Christ!"

Stafford picked up the laptop and its charger. He then gestured to Fran to follow him. They headed back to his office, he placed the laptop and charger on his desk before securely closing the door. Stafford sat down and was motionless for a few moments with his eyes closed. He then opened them to reveal a steely expression reflecting the severity of this precarious situation. Stafford addressed Fran in a cold voice to give simple but very important instructions.

"Fran, you must not talk to *anyone* about what you've just read. This information needs to be managed."

"How do you mean 'managed', sir?"

"I don't know yet, I need to work that out. In the meantime, go back to your desk and do some work. I don't care what you do, just look busy and for Christ's sake don't say a word to anyone. Is that understood?"

"Yes sir."

"OK, now go."

Fran left and walked back into the main office feeling nervous. She was not at all comfortable with having to keep such an enormous revelation from her colleagues. However, she could understand why it should be Stafford to break the news to everyone. Andy and Clara both looked concerned and tried to get Fran's attention. She avoided making eye contact with them, but this just made it obvious that something was wrong.

"Hey Fran, what's up with you, girl?" asked Clara.

Fran remained silent, but her grimace indicated the seriousness of the revelation that she was hiding.

"She's obviously found something serious in the journal...but Stafford doesn't want her to say anything," said Andy.

"Come on, Fran, we're all together in this investigation, why the secret?" said Clara.

As Fran could not answer Clara's question, she gave a dismissive gesture with her hands. She then quickly walked over to her desk and logged into her own computer. Fran gave the appearance of doing some admin tasks. In reality, she was just wasting time waiting for Stafford to make the announcement. Fran was eager to know how he would handle this situation.

She wondered if anyone had any inclination, or even knew, that Marianne was a murderer. If they did, then it might explain why Marianne ended up being murdered herself. It was obvious now why the journal was so carefully protected as it was very incriminating. Fran then ruminated about the journal in her mind. Why would Marianne write all this down? Perhaps she got some sort of sick thrill from keeping a secret document where all her dark deeds were recorded? Fran eventually concluded that these questions would probably go unanswered.

Fran was just beginning to come to terms with the enormity of the situation when Superintendent Jamieson arrived. He had a signature bushy moustache that bent round his lips and went down towards his chin. As Stafford's superior, he carried a fair amount of weight in the department. He also carried a fair amount of weight on his body too. There was something refreshingly honest about Jamieson's classic English beer belly. His protruding stomach announced itself as soon as he walked into the room.

Jamieson closed Stafford's office door for a private meeting. It was then clear to all present that there must be an urgent matter being discussed. However, no-one had a clue as to what it could be, no-one except Fran. Everyone else could not help but to glance over towards the CDI's office. They were all wishing they could be silent flies on Stafford's wall. Eventually Jamieson left and walked quickly away without uttering a word. Shortly afterwards, Stafford summoned his entire team into the meeting room. A couple of horseshoe shaped rows of chairs were set up and Stafford then addressed everyone.

"Good afternoon everyone." This was uncharacteristically polite and he appeared hesitant and nervous. Stafford looked down at the tiled flooring. His silence was held for an unnaturally long period of time. Stafford was obviously scrambling for the right words, but these were proving elusive. Eventually he decided he would have to be completely honest.

"Well, in all my years as a CDI, I've never had to announce anything quite like this."

At which point, some of the police officers feared for their jobs. They assumed this was a preamble before announcing mass redundancies.

"Detective Constable Jacobs approached me earlier this afternoon regarding an entry in Marianne's private journal. It amounted to Marianne confessing, and even boasting, about murdering her husband. Her journal entry said she deliberately pushed him off a cliff. Now, as you know, the investigation into Antony Furlow gave the verdict of accidental death. There was nothing that could really prove otherwise at the time. No eyewitnesses were present, they only had Marianne's testimony."

Stafford stopped and looked around at his colleagues. They were shocked but out of professional courtesy they remained silent so Stafford could speak freely.

"Granted, a confession is not the same as a conviction, we should never confuse the two. However, it's difficult to see why Marianne would write such a thing in her journal if it were not true. I think we must assume that our victim was herself a murderer. This is something that we all need to take into consideration with this investigation going forward."

Stafford grimaced and took a deep breath that was audible enough for everyone to his anxiety.

"Now…what I'm about to say may make some of you feel uncomfortable, but there are good reasons for it. I have been discussing this situation with my superior, Superintendent Jamieson. There would no doubt be a lot of news and press coverage if the media ever got hold of this story. Let's face it, carrying out an investigation with a bombardment of journalists is going to put us all under enormous pressure. We also must consider what would happen if we told Antony's family of our findings. Even if they kept it to themselves, it may influence what information they provide us with at future interviews. We need to tread carefully here as several of them are key suspects. As a result of all of this, we, that is Superintendent Jamieson and myself, have made a decision. We will not release this information publicly to anyone or at least not yet."

"Sir, surely Antony's family have a right to know what we've found?" said Andy, who expressed what all his colleagues were thinking.

"They do Andy but just not yet. It's in everyone's best interests that we keep this to ourselves. It's just so we can solve the case without unwanted distractions. It will also give us some space to prepare for the media onslaught that will no doubt ensue. At the appropriate time we will disclose this information but *not* before then."

Andy did not respond verbally, but the shake of his head clearly voiced his disapproval.

"I'm sorry, but this *must* be treated as classified information. If anyone says anything to anybody outside of this room, they will be disciplined, is that clear?"

No-one spoke but everyone silently absorbed this statement. The whole team knew that Stafford would make good on his threat.

"We are just managing the situation, that's all we are doing. I appreciate that normally we uphold transparency, but this just *cannot* come out…not yet."

Stafford breathed heavily once more before concluding.

"OK, that's all I have to say. I'm going to let you all go home as I don't think there's anything else we can do for now. Good night."

Stafford then walked quickly back to his office. As soon as he was out of earshot a loud cacophony of voices exploded. It was difficult to pick out individual words, but the collective dismay of the team was startling. Fran gravitated to Andy, Clara and James who had all been sat next to each other. The four of them needed the same thing, a good stiff drink.

DINNER & DISCUSSIONS

Clara phoned her husband Curtly to explain why she would be back late tonight. Andy checked his train times to ensure he could catch a later one. James was sure that his wife wouldn't care when he came home or even if he returned at all. Fran on the other hand never had to consider any of these things. Andy suggested an emergency dinner meeting and no-one needed any persuasion. Fran abandoned her pledge to lay off alcohol as today's bombshell warranted it.

The four of them entered Jac & Mac's restaurant. The well-tanned waiter was once again on shift and greeted them in his customary polite manner. James made the request for a table in a segregated booth to ensure they had some privacy. He then ordered a whiskey, Andy went for a brandy, Clara opted for a rum and Fran decided on a gin and tonic. It did not take long for the waiter to return with the drinks. Fran's 'G & T' came in a glass that looked like a miniature goldfish bowl. Unhealthy meals were then ordered as this really was not a night for salad. The restaurant was nearly empty, so they all felt safe enough to speak freely.

"I always promised myself I would never be involved in a cover-up," said Andy.

"Hey bro, Stafford did say it's only temporary whilst we solve the case," said Clara.

James took a sip from his whiskey before giving his opinion.

"You're too trusting, Clara. Yes, it's temporary for now, but I'm with Andy. I don't think they'll ever release this publicly. After all, it does highlight an investigation that failed."

"Yeah, but it wasn't *our* investigation," said Clara.

"True, but it would still bring unwanted media attention and a loss of public trust," said James. He then continued to speak whilst cradling his glass.

"That's assuming no-one outside of the investigation knows what's happened, but I really don't think they do. I'm sure the only way this story will get out is by one of us snitching."

"So, we're going to have to sit on this," said Fran.

"Or face disciplinary action," Andy added.

"No, I'm not comfortable with this, I'm *not* that person," Fran continued.

"Fran, none of us are like that normally, we're being pushed into it," James answered.

"I can understand keeping it away from the media, but I can't accept us not telling the family. Surely, they could be told privately," said Fran.

Fran then swirled the gin and tonic round and gazed into her glass. Her colleagues all correctly sensed that she'd just had an idea. She was now in a quandary as to what to say next, eventually she decided she would be bold.

"Actually…I could tell the truth without fearing the consequences, because I'll soon have nothing to lose."

"Why would you have nothing to lose?" asked Andy.

"Because I'm going to resign and leave the police for good," Fran said calmly and coldly.

"OH NO…," said Clara loudly and the waiter turned to face the table for a moment. Andy expressed his disappointment by putting his hand on his forehead and grimacing. James's facial expression gave just enough pretense to ensure Andy and Clara did not realise that he already knew Fran's plan.

"But Fran, we need you. You're the brightest one of all of us."

"Thanks Andy, but I just can't cope with the stress of this job."

"Oh…BLOODY STAFFORD!" Andy bellowed, which distracted the waiter again.

"That man has so much to answer for," Andy continued.

"Is it just Stafford, Fran? Is there anything else that's making you leave?" Clara enquired.

Out of the corner of her eye Fran now noticed that James was looking very uncomfortable. She too was feeling uneasy and this resulted in a lengthy silence whilst she calmed her emotions down.

"Well…you know…I've just got…doubt."

"Doubt…it's always doubt with you. Why do you *always* doubt yourself?" Clara asked.

Fran just sighed and sipped at her gin and tonic.

"Look I just need out," Fran eventually said.

An awkward quietness fell across the table. The faint easy-listening background music was now the only sound to be heard. Fran wore a deeply apologetic face in response to Clara and Andy's visible disappointment. Everyone was waiting for someone to say something, anything at all. It was not that they didn't have the words, but they didn't have the courage to speak up. Finally, Fran felt she should try and reassure her colleagues.

"I promise I won't leave without giving you all the heads up. Likewise, I won't say anything about Marianne being a murderer without letting you know first. At least you can then be prepared for what might follow, we'll work it out together, I'm sure."

However, the atmosphere remained tense to an almost strangling extent. The waiter then arrived and a tray full of junk food meals was distributed in accordance with the order. They ate their meals quickly and there was little conversation whilst eating. Clara left shortly afterwards as her son Brian had scored his first '50' in a school indoor cricket match earlier that day. She was a proud mother and so therefore wanted to get home to hear all about it. Andy also rushed off to catch his final train as a taxi would be too expensive.

Fran and James were now alone and they both had a bit of drink still left in their glasses. She downed the remainder of her gin and tonic quickly. Fran was about to say goodbye when James stared at her. He clearly wanted to say a thousand words, but none were actually spoken. Fran briefly wished she had met James under different circumstances before he was married. However, she didn't want to slide down the slippery slope of emotional turmoil again. Instead, she forced herself to say 'goodnight' and quickly walked away. She made sure she didn't look back as she left the restaurant.

On her way home, Fran began thinking over today's events. She suspected that there was an ulterior motive for not revealing the truth about Marianne. As was often the case with Fran, it was more feeling than fact. Nonetheless, the more she thought about it, the stronger this feeling grew. She was frustrated that she could not clearly define what this ulterior motive could be. Eventually, she filed these thoughts away into one of the drawers of her mental filing cabinet. They could always be pulled out again at a later date.

It had been quite a day and Fran wondered if it was now too late to have a chat with Harry. She decided there was no harm in at least asking so she sent him a text. Fran was delighted to see an almost immediate response inviting her up to his flat.

Fran was curious as to what she would be walking into as she had yet to go into Harry's home. She felt a touch nervous as she knocked on his front door. Harry answered and smiled warmly before leading her into a small hallway that had a grey patterned carpet. Harry then opened a door and led her into his lounge diner. A good quality light blue carpet covered the floor and was pleasantly soft underfoot. The walls had a selection of tasteful religious pictures. A josh stick was smoking away on a table giving the room a jasmine fragrance. Gregorian chant music was playing softly in the background. Fran found this most relaxing as she sat down on a comfortable well-upholstered brown sofa. Harry offered Fran a drink and she chose to just have a cup of tea. Fran wanted to be on good form for work tomorrow.

"So, what's up Fran?" said Harry.

"I had a bit of a mishap this morning and picked up a council tax letter instead of my resignation notice. The end result was that I didn't resign."

"What…after all that!"

"I know, but that's not all. James then spoke to me and I've got to say I'm glad he did. We were able to work something out so we can at least function as work colleagues."

"That's good, Fran."

"Also, please understand I can't say too much, but there has been a major revelation today in the case. After being convinced I must get out ASAP, I'm now having second thoughts. I just don't feel I can leave this investigation; it's hard to explain why. There's something about it that's convincing me that I've got to see it through it to the end."

"I see."

"It is of course a woman's prerogative to change her mind."

Fran then smiled at him a little mischievously.

"Well, *you* said it, I think I'd be in trouble if I'd made that comment," Harry replied.

"Yes, you probably would be."

Fran smiled again and took a sip from her tea.

"It just feels like everything's gone crazy. I've done stuff I would never normally do and got into situations I've never been in before. It's like I've stepped into a different life somehow."

"Try not to expect life to follow a pattern. It's your expectations that cause you distress when things don't work out as you think they should."

"Yeah, I guess so…"

Fran then decided to change the subject, partly to distract herself but also because she was concerned about her neighbour and friend.

"How are you going, Harry?"

"Ah you know, the days kind of roll into one to be honest. I get a bit lonely sometimes."

"Hey, why don't you join a group or some community activity?"

"Mmm, I guess I'm a bit stuck in a rut. I don't find it easy to connect with people for the most part, I guess I'm fearful of feeling alienated."

"Oh Harry…I just want you to be happy."

"I know, Fran, bless you."

Fran then looked around the collection of pictures and noticed Michelangelo's *Creation of Adam* on the wall. She looked at God and Adam's fingers that were just fractionally apart. This reminded her of the other thing she had wanted to discuss with Harry.

"You know I have been thinking about what you said about God. There's something else I want to ask you. I've got a lot of atheist friends and aside from all the pain and suffering in the world, there's one other argument they use for atheism."

"Now, let me guess, would this be the advancement of science by any chance?"

"Spot on, especially the notion of evolution. Do you have anything to say on that?"

"Yes, I do. It's certainly true that there are things that used to be attributed to divine intervention that science can now prove. But this is further reason why I feel that we should not view God as this almighty autocrat at the top of creation's pyramid. If you view God like that then you get into all these knotty questions. You wonder what's an act of God and what's something with a clear scientific explanation? Whereas if you view God as the *soul* of all life then there's no conflict. The divine essence is intertwined within everything that naturally happens. It's stupid to deny the existence of evolution and the facts of science, but it's all laced by a spirituality. It's like a pebble dropped into the middle of a pond with a ripple of water oscillating outwards. This divine ripple is what pushes all of life through the flow of evolution over aeons of time."

Harry had again answered a question that Fran's vicar, and other clergymen she'd met, had always sidestepped. He then continued to express his theological viewpoint further.

"It's all about having an open mind about God. You'll then see that science and spirituality don't have to be at loggerheads with each other. This genuinely is possible once you realise that everything is interconnected. Well…this is what my personal brand of armchair theology has led me to believe."

Fran took a moment to consider this before asking the other question that was in her mind.

"Actually, I've got one more question for you, Harry; what happens when we die?"

"Ooh we're going for the big ones tonight, Fran."

Harry then smiled and considered his response.

"OK, here's what I think. We all have a soul contained within our bodies and when we die this is released to the spiritual realm. No-one can possibly imagine what that is like whilst living in this physical form. It's life, Fran…but not as we know it."

Fran nodded in acknowledgment although she failed to pick up on Harry's sci-fi reference. Eventually Fran was brought down to a more mundane affair as she became conscious of the time and politely left. As she walked into her hallway, she saw the envelope containing her resignation notice. She opened this envelope, took out the piece of paper and tore it in half.

FAMILY TALES

Overnight Fran reflected on Harry's divine vision. Once again, she was torn between the traditional Christian version of God and Harry's alternative theological theory. However, she soon realised that this was something she would need to explore later. She now had to focus back onto the murder case that had taken an alarming twist. On her way into work, Fran wondered what was in store for her today.

Fran's plan was still to eventually resign and to tell Antony's family about their findings in Marianne's journal. However, she decided it would have to wait because she was committed to doing all she can to help solve this murder case. When Fran arrived in the office she took Andy, Clara and James into a corner to tell them of her new decision. All of them were relieved that she would be there until the end of the current investigation.

Fran logged into her computer and checked some emails. As she expected, Stafford then assigned her to resume studying Marianne's computer journal. Fran reckoned that, after the murder revelation, any other discoveries would be an anti-climax. However, she duly switched on Marianne's laptop, typed in the password and started reading.

It soon became apparent that Marianne was very materialistic. She had spent all her time paddling around in the shallow end of life. Fran remembered that during his interview, Kevin had mentioned Marianne's affairs. This was the other notable aspect of the journal; her numerous lovers. Fran read through numerous passages of lurid, erotic detail. Marianne's sex life made Casanova look like a monk. No wonder she kept all these stories hidden on this well protected secret computer journal. It was not the sort of thing you would post on Facebook.

Fran wondered if it was worth tracking down any of these former lovers. She eventually decided that it would not be as none of them were likely to remember much about Marianne. Each sexual encounter was just a one-night stand or, in the case of an amorous Amazon delivery man, a one-morning stand. However, after further reading, Fran then realised that Marianne had blackmailed a number of people, most notably Graham Furlow.

It transpired from Marianne's journal entries that Graham Furlow had tried repeatedly to have children with his wife Julie but to no avail. As Catholics, they didn't feel comfortable using IVF to conceive, so their dream had been shattered. This underlying frustration put a pressure on their marriage. Julie became much colder and more distant towards Graham. They were sleeping in the same bed, but sleeping was all they were doing.

Marianne had sensed Graham's frustration and she also picked up on his secret physical yearnings for her. Sometime later, Antony, Marianne, Graham and Julie all went to the wedding of a mutual cousin. Drinks flowed, Antony and Julie were engaged with war stories that a couple of elderly uncles were telling. Neither of them noticed that Graham and Marianne had slipped upstairs into her hotel room. They were not gone long but it was long enough for a lot of pent-up tension to be fully released. Graham and Marianne then returned and just carried on as if nothing had happened as no-one had noticed their absence.

Graham was overwhelmed by his lust for Marianne and so the affair continued. She was on the pill and he would normally be opposed to contraception. However, he reasoned that as adultery is equally against Catholic teachings, then he may as well just go with the flow. He told Julie that he was visiting his priest more regularly for confessions. This was most definitely not the case, even though he now had a lot more to confess.

Graham's fictitious confessionals coincided with the evenings when Antony had a business meeting. Kevin, the son of Marianne and Antony, had moved out of the family home by this time. This meant that when her husband was out, Graham could see Marianne alone. A spare hour or two was all they needed to meet up and do the deed.

Eventually, Graham's conscience and his Catholic morals returned to him. He then explained to Marianne that he could no longer continue with their affair. However, she quickly realised a financial opportunity. The revelation of their sexual encounters would destroy Graham's reputation, especially as it had been with his own brother's wife.

Marianne, on the other hand, would not have cared if the secret was revealed. For her, this would just be another man to add to her already long list of extramarital lovers. She therefore blackmailed Graham for a large monthly sum for her silence. Graham hated her for it but could not find any way out of this situation. He simply could not bear the thought of the sordid saga being revealed to his wife, family and church. However, the journal also revealed that just as Graham had been unfaithful to Julie; Julie had been unfaithful to Graham too.

***

Marianne had caught Julie Furlow in a somewhat compromising position with another man at a distinctly seedy nightclub. Both parties were obscenely drunk when Marianne saw them. However, she somehow managed to glean that this was not just a one-night fling but a full-scale affair. This was shortly after Graham had stopped 'playing away' with Marianne.

It was clear that Julie's affair was also due to their marital frustrations. As Marianne herself had adulterous affairs, Julie pleaded with her not to tell Graham as she hoped that Marianne would understand. However, as with Graham, Marianne pointed out that her husband Antony already knew about her extramarital flings. Whereas Julie had a much more respectable reputation that would be irrevocably tarnished if this were to ever come to light.

She then demanded hefty monthly payments from Julie to prevent Marianne from telling Graham. It was only Marianne's death that released Julie from paying all this money. Fran wondered if this could have spurred Julie on to actually murder Marianne? Further journal entries revealed that other members of the Furlow family were also being blackmailed.

There was an occasion when Barry Furlow stayed overnight at Antony and Marianne's home. This was because Barry had a meeting that was just a few miles from their house in Newcot. Shortly before going to bed, Barry used their PC to surf the internet and check a few emails. He used a Hotmail email address and so did Marianne.

However, he never logged out of his account but just closed down the browser. The following morning, when Marianne opened the Hotmail web page, it automatically brought up Barry's emails. By this time, he had already left to go to the meeting and Antony had gone to work. Marianne therefore took the opportunity to have a nose through. She read an email thread that revealed a secret that she knew Barry would never want to be publicly revealed.

Barry was a manager of a well-respected athletics club. Amongst his ranks was a very talented athlete who took part in the Olympics. However, this athlete had been using banned performance enhancing drugs. It was clear that Barry not only knew this but actively encouraged it. This was due to him being so desperate for the success it would bring to the athlete, the club and subsequently himself. Marianne once again sniffed a financial opportunity and blackmailed Barry into monthly 'hush money' payments. These payments also carried on until Marianne's death.

Fran then considered the possibility that Barry was the murderer as this was a strong motive. However, it was also recorded in the journal that Barry's wife Mary had been blackmailed too.

Marianne had an auntie called Deidre who lived in a care home and Mary Furlow was the well-respected manager. Deidre was one of the few relatives that Marianne actually got on with. She was therefore very sad to hear the news when Deidre had suddenly passed away overnight. Marianne also had a friend who was a care worker there. On one of their boozy nights out, Marianne learnt that the circumstances of this death were not accurately reported.

Officially, Deidre died of a brain haemorrhage in hospital. However, in reality, the elderly resident was already dead in her bedroom when the paramedics arrived. If it had been reported that a care home client died in their room, there would have been an investigation. This would have revealed that they were understaffed that night. It would also have shown that the proper procedure for handling this situation was not carried out.

The knock-on effect from this investigation would have been very serious indeed. Mary negated this by lying to the staff, residents and all relevant family members of the deceased. It just so happened though that Marianne's friend was actually on duty in Deidre's room when she died. She therefore knew for sure that this had been one big cover-up.

Marianne used this information to blackmail Mary. They both knew it would be the end of her career as a care home manager if the truth ever came out. Mary was therefore forced to pay regular substantial payments to ensure this never happened. These payments carried on until Marianne's grisly demise.

Fran added Mary's name to the ever-growing murder suspects list. She felt that the risk of losing her career and livelihood could have triggered Mary to kill Marianne. There was one final Furlow family member who also had been the victim of blackmail.

The journal showed that Antony's sister, Sue Furlow, once stayed with them for a few weeks as she had just fled from a violent relationship. During this time, they watched Sue sing in a club near Newcot. There was no band, but a backing music track had been rigged up using a laptop.

Shortly after this performance the three of them had another night out in a local pub. There was a karaoke event that evening. Antony and Marianne were baffled by Sue's refusal to sing. She insisted that she had to save her voice for her performances, but somehow this didn't ring true. When they were in bed together, Antony told Marianne that he didn't remember Sue ever being able to sing when they were growing up.

This made Marianne suspicious so, whilst Sue was asleep in their house, Marianne got Sue's laptop. Marianne listened through her headphones to the backing music tracks that were used for Sue's gig. She then realised that the recording contained not just backing music but actual vocals as well.

When Antony went out for a walk the next morning, Marianne confronted Sue about her findings. Sue was forced to admit that, in fact, she couldn't sing at all so she just lip-synched to all the tracks at her gig performances. Marianne knew that Sue could not risk it becoming public knowledge that she was only miming. The music and vocal tracks had been put together by one of Sue's friends in exchange for a lot of drugs. The gigs were Sue's livelihood, so Marianne blackmailed her into a percentage cut from every show. These payments carried on until her blackmailer had her sherry fatally poisoned. This final revelation meant that all the surviving members of the Furlow family were now on the murder suspects list.

Finally, Fran noticed that Marianne also mentioned "a nice little earner" from someone called 'Martin'. Fran could not find any more specific details about him. However, her instinct told her that this poor soul had been blackmailed too.

The one thing Fran couldn't understand was that none of these blackmail payments had shown up on Marianne's bank statements. Andy and Clara had examined them thoroughly and found nothing irregular. A quick calculator sum showed Marianne's blackmail payments would have totalled over half a million pounds. Fran wondered how Marianne had been able to hide so much money?

Stafford was updated, Fran explained precisely what she had found in the journal. It was agreed that all those blackmailed (bar the unknown 'Martin') would be interviewed. Stafford decided that they would start with Graham Furlow. Fran then called Graham to make arrangements for him to be interviewed by herself and Andy. Graham happily agreed for them to go round the next day. However, he was a little taken aback when Fran insisted that his wife should not be present.

GRAHAM

Fran took the opportunity to relax and properly unwind after work. She really needed this after what she had endured over the past few days. After catching up on the news, Fran got on her iPod to play a random selection of tracks. As the up-tempo tunes flowed into her ears, she closed her eyes and focussed on sweet imaginings. Fran had never been a junkie, but good time pop music was the drug that she injected whenever she needed a lift. She even had a bit of a dance and took full advantage of the absence of company. She might have otherwise felt a bit embarrassed.

Fran concluded her evening with a long soak in the bath. She hoped this would help calm herself enough to have a proper night's sleep. Fran then laid her head down on the pillow to try and navigate her way into the land of nod. It felt like only a few moments later when Fran opened her eyes. To her considerable relief, she saw the morning light brighten up her curtain. Refreshed and revitalized, she pulled back the duvet with more vim and vigour than usual.

Fran walked cheerfully into work and saw James looking even more gorgeous than normal in his suit. She was, however, able to quickly extinguish the fire of desire before it burned out of control. Fran's attraction to James was not going to disappear anytime soon, but she felt that she could just about contain it. Andy arrived soon afterwards and she gave him a quick informal debrief regarding yesterday's interview. Soon afterwards Stafford gave the much longer official version.

Fran and Andy then carried out a few admin tasks before driving off to Rivermead to interview Graham Furlow. The journey gave Fran plenty of time to catch up with Andy.

"How's things then?" Fran asked.

"Erm, I'm surviving…still chewing over whether I should try and drive again. Also, I'm still thinking about, you know…"

"Aw Andy," Fran said empathetically.

"It's OK, I'm sure I will get over her eventually, but don't ask me how long 'eventually' will be. Anyway, how about you Fran? Anything happening in your love life?"

Fran felt the pang of fear prick her heart and she felt torn. In many ways, she wanted to tell Andy about her recent romantic encounter with James. She felt she could trust him with this secret. If it had been with someone outside of work, then she probably would have divulged everything. However, she thought it would be unfair on James as he had not consented to this story being shared. She was also worried that it might affect James and Andy's working relationship. Fran concluded that the gossip tin opener should not open this extra-large can of worms.

"Not really Andy, I will let you know as and when it does."

Fran just about bluffed her way through that awkward moment. She then decided to employ the politician trick of diverting the subject away from the stuff she didn't want to discuss.

"Quite a revelation, Graham's affair," said Fran.

"Oh God, yes."

"It's not enough to warrant an arrest as we've got nothing to show he poisoned the sherry. However, it certainly gives him a possible motive for murder. I'm going to watch his facial expression and body language very carefully today."

"And is Graham aware that we know about his extracurricular activities?"

"No, I just said there is some more information that has come to light. I didn't want him to have time to prepare any answers. I want to see what his gut reaction is when we reveal what we know. It might just indicate whether the blackmail gave him the impetus to murder Marianne."

A few minutes later they arrived in Rivermead at Graham's beautiful house. He led them into his lavish lounge and they settled down on the red Chesterfield armchairs. No drinks were offered and Graham sat on his sofa. He gave Fran a piercing stare with a facial expression that was stone cold and serious.

"I think I know why you want to speak to me."

Damn thought Fran, as Graham would have had time to prepare answers. This meant she would not be able to surprise him with the findings from the journal.

"Well Graham, when we read through Marianne's computer journal, it described in detail the affair you had with her."

"I thought so. OK, I understand that you've got to follow this up, but you will treat this confidentially, won't you?" asked Graham nervously.

"Of course, it will only be shared with those investigating the case, nobody else will know."

"Alright. It's just as well Julie is out at a church meeting this morning."

At which point, Julie's car unexpectedly pulled up outside. It didn't take her long to put the car into the garage. Graham was now panic stricken with terror screaming out of his eyes.

"Don't say a word, don't say a word about…" Graham's sentence trailed off, but it was easy for Andy and Fran to fill in the blank. Julie then walked into the lounge and looked confused.

"Oh, hi Julie, I thought you were at a church meeting?" said Graham nervously.

"Several people were sick, so they decided to cancel it. What's going on? Why are the police here?"

"They just want to ask some more questions about Marianne."

"Oh…very well," said Julie who then sat down next to Graham. Julie was clearly a strong woman and there was an awkward silence. Fran and Andy frantically tried to work out how to tell her to leave the room.

"Well…what do you want to know?" asked Julie assertively.

Fran realised that Julie had no intention of moving so it would require a direct statement.

"Actually, we just wanted to speak to Graham, alone, please."

"Why? I knew Marianne for just as long as he did, so there's nothing he would know that I wouldn't."

Although neither party showed it, Andy and Fran were now very anxious. Even a master in the subtle art of diplomacy would struggle with this situation. Fran eventually decided that the best way forward would be to try and diffuse any offence that might be caused.

"I assure you it's nothing personal, Mrs Furlow," said Fran.

"We just feel this interview would work better on a 1-2-1 basis," Andy added, and Fran was grateful that he was backing her up. Fran realised that the statement was not quite right as technically it will be a 2 to 1 interview, but she figured it was best not to correct him.

"Come on, darling, it's a nice day. Why don't you have a nice cup of tea in the garden," said Graham.

"But I don't understand, I'm sure I could be just as helpful as you," said Julie.

"Please don't worry Mrs Furlow, it's just sometimes we like to interview people on an individual basis," said Fran who tried to sound as reassuring as possible.

There was a hesitation but eventually Julie stood up and left the room. Fran was about to speak when Graham put his hand up to stop her.

"Let's wait until she is in the garden," Graham whispered. They all remained silent for a minute. Graham then stood up, opened the lounge door slightly and peeped round the corner.

"It's alright, she's outside now. OK, let's do this quickly and quietly," said Graham.

Graham sat back down on the sofa and Andy gestured to Fran that he was now ready to take notes.

"OK, firstly, according to Marianne's journal you had a sexual affair with her. This took place between June 2012 and February 2013. Is that right?" asked Fran. She was now speaking in a sort of projected whisper to try and ease Graham's anxiety about being overheard.

"To my absolute shame, yes, that is true. I betrayed my wife; she would never do that to me".

Fran showed no emotion, but felt a little strange knowing that Julie had committed adultery too.

"We're not here to judge you, Mr Furlow, we just need to establish the facts. Marianne's journal mentions that she blackmailed you into making payments." Fran then read out an extract from Marianne's computer journal.

> **Tuesday evening, 05/03/2013**
> I arranged to meet Graham I his local pub. He had no idea what was coming and that's what made it so beautiful. I told him that unless he paid me £1000 a month I would sing like a canary about our affair. He was shocked bur eventually agreed as he had no choice. The first payment should come through in a couple of weeks' time.

"Can you confirm if this is true as well, please?" Fran then asked.

"Yes, that's also true."

"And am I right in thinking these payments continued right up to her death?"

"Yes"

"And no-one else knew about these payments?"

"I can't say for sure; Marianne might have blabbed to some of her friends, but I never said anything to anyone about it."

"Did the monthly payment amount ever change?" Fran asked with reference to the journal entry.

"No, it remained the same figure throughout."

"But that would be £12,000 a year, that's a lot of money. How were you able to pay all that without your wife being aware?"

"I set up a separate bank account that Julie doesn't know about. I found ways to transfer funds into this account. I then took out a cash payment once a month. Marianne also set up a separate bank account that Antony didn't know about. In fact, I think she said it was a Swiss account where she used a bogus name."

So that's why we never found anything on her bank statement Fran silently thought to herself.

Having established the means, Fran decided she would now focus on the effect.

"I'm sure you deeply resented having to pay out all this money," said Fran.

"Well of course I did," Graham confirmed in a dismissive tone.

He clearly felt this was a stupid question.

"I'm sure you would have wanted to find a way to stop paying her all this money."

"Yes, but there was no way out other than her revealing a scandal that would ruin my marriage and my life."

"Would it be fair to say that the only other way out for you was for Marianne to die?"

Graham clearly didn't like the question, but Fran knew this investigation required her to be a little bold and pursue the point.

"Well, there doesn't seem to be another solution, does there, Mr Furlow?" Fran continued.

"OK…I accept that as far as my personal situation is concerned, it will save me a lot of money and trouble, yes."

"Her death must have been a huge relief to you."

"Now look, I'm not a murderer!"

Graham decided to cut the chase and square up to Fran's insinuation. He stared at Fran, but he was more assertive than aggressive.

"I understand how it must look to you. I understand why this would give me a motive. I may be a flawed man, you might even say a failed Catholic, *but* I do not have the propensity to commit murder," Graham firmly asserted.

Fran did not respond immediately but took a moment to gauge his emotional response. The interview ended shortly afterwards and when she opened the lounge door Julie was stood waiting in the hall. Fran was certain Julie would ask Graham what they had been discussing. She wondered what lie he would tell her. However, this was their private matter, meanwhile Fran had a few things to discuss with Andy in the car.

Fran waited until she was on a quiet stretch of road before beginning her conversation with Andy.

"I think he's telling the truth," Fran asserted.

"Are you sure? I mean he's got a hell of a motive," Andy countered.

"He has but, trust me, I can tell a liar when I see one; the body language, facial expression, look in the eye, all of that stuff."

"You know Stafford wants evidence, not your gut feeling."

"Yes, he's made that abundantly clear."

"So, what evidence have you got for us to dismiss him from our list of suspects?"

It was a fair and pertinent question. Fran considered this as she turned onto the dual carriageway that led them back to headquarters.

"The answers he gave were plausible. He's been blackmailed for many years. If he was going to murder Marianne, don't you think he would have already done it."

"Yes, but perhaps after years of built-up pressure, he finally overlooked his conscience and Catholicism to commit the crime."

Fran could not dismiss this as a possibility and it frustrated her. She was pretty sure that Graham was innocent, not innocent as a person just innocent of this crime. However, she only had a gut feeling and not one iota of evidence. She scrambled around in her mind trying to find something that would support her case for dismissing Graham as a suspect. In the end she had to admit defeat for he had an undeniably strong motive. He also had some knowledge of chemistry which could have been used to concoct the poison.

"You know Fran, it may be that Graham and Marianne's affair was ultimately a sort of fatal attraction," Andy speculated.

"Fatal attraction?" Fran queried and was clearly intrigued.

"Only without the bunny boiling bit!"

"Eh?"

"You know the film with Michael…oh never mind."

It was clear that Fran was too distracted for Andy's movie trivia. Her mind was full of murderer musings as ideas were beginning to form.

JULIE

None of the other suspects were available for the rest of the week. However, on the following Monday, Stafford had arranged for Fran and James to interview Julie. The CDI had broached the delicate subject of making sure her husband was not present for the interview. This would be the first occasion Fran had spent some real time with James since their boozy fling. As she drove to Rivermead, James attempted to engage her in light conversation.

"So Fran, what's occurring?" he asked politely.

"Nothing really," Fran was conscious this may come over as a tad dismissive but found it hard to converse properly. Awkward feelings then travelled in the car throughout the journey. However, both parties were determined that professionalism would keep their difficult emotions at bay.

Fran pulled up near the house for the second time in the space of a week. Julie let the detectives into her home with a greeting that was polite but slightly cold. She had clearly made an effort to look her best. However, no amount of makeup could cover-up the anxiety that was now showing in her face. As with Graham, it was obvious that Julie knew or at least had a strong suspicion as to why she was going to be interviewed. It was a convenient time for Julie because Graham was now five holes into the 18 at his local golf course. There was no risk of an interruption, Julie had made sure of that. They quickly settled themselves down for the interview without any delay for refreshments. Julie never said it outright, but Fran and James correctly sensed that she wanted to get this over with quickly.

Fran took a moment to gauge how to move forward with her questioning. She concluded that preliminaries were not required, so she could go straight into the main topic of the interview.

"OK Julie, Marianne mentioned in her computer journal that during 2012, she discovered you having an adulterous affair with a younger man in an Alderham nightclub."

Fran then read out an extract from Marianne's computer journal.

Saturday morning, 28/04/2012

I couldn't believe what I saw in Nico's last night. Julie Furlow was snogging the face of a younger man. I think I can make a nice sum of money out of this...

Julie's eyes flicked down to her lush red carpet.

"Can you please confirm if this is true?"

In a way it was a totally unnecessary question. The answer was blatantly obvious by Julie's uncomfortable demeanour. However, police procedure required for it to be officially confirmed for the report.

"Yes," was Julie's simple reply.

"Her journal mentioned that she blackmailed you for a thousand pounds a month to keep her silence..."

"That's also true," Julie quickly interjected as she anticipated the question Fran was about to ask.

"It's the biggest shame of my life. There's no way Graham would have done that to me," Julie then continued.

Fran had to make damn sure she did not say what she was thinking. Instead, she just took a moment to formulate the next question.

"How were you able to pay all this money for years without Graham finding out?"

"Well…I was very fortunate that Alan, the man I had the affair with, was very rich and also didn't want this secret to come out."

"Why's that?"

"Because he was married too, and Graham knew his wife. This would have been an unbearable situation."

James gave Fran an assertive nod to acknowledge he had written this down.

"A thousand pounds a month to him was quite affordable so he would give me a regular wad of cash. Me and Marianne had this arrangement to meet in my local pub at a designated time. I would then discreetly hand over the money."

"And this continued every month for years, until Marianne died?"

"Yes, that's right," said Julie with a sigh.

She was clearly shuddering over how much money had collectively been paid to Marianne. Fran suddenly realised that, as Julie's lover, Alan was effectively being blackmailed too. She wondered whether he might also have a motive for murder.

"Julie, would I be right in thinking that Alan continued to pay you this money for Marianne right up until her death?"

"Yes…but tragically he died just before her."

Fran and James took a moment to absorb this revelation. Julie was naturally distressed by the loss of Alan but was still focussed enough to continue.

"He died in a freak fishing accident just off the coast of North Wales," Julie continued.

Fran now had to think on her two size six feet.

"OK, I appreciate this may be a sensitive matter, but I must clarify the facts, when exactly did Alan die?"

"A week before Marianne's death."

"If Alan could not make the payment to you, then how were you going to pay Marianne her blackmail money?"

"To be honest, with great difficulty."

In that moment Fran decided to pursue her murder theory as she felt Julie's admission had left her vulnerable.

"Julie, you mentioned previously that you have a degree in Chemistry."

"What's that got to do with it?"

"Well, anyone with some chemistry knowledge could have mixed together the poison?"

"Are you suggesting I killed her?" Julie exploded with vehement outrage.

"You've got to admit that her death was a very convenient solution for you?"

"Now you listen to me, young lady, I may have betrayed my husband, but I am not a murderer. And besides I did my Chemistry degree over thirty years ago. I wouldn't know how to mix poison together."

There was no point continuing the interview. Julie was too offended after the provocative murder suggestion. Fran had a feeling Julie would not react kindly to this but needed to see Julie's response. Shortly afterwards, Fran and James left her luxurious home. Julie never said goodbye or even got up from her chair when they went.

"I don't think you're on her Christmas card list, Fran," said James who was now sat beside her in the police car.

"No, she's a proud woman, clearly. It's hard to know if that was a desperate rear-guard reaction of a murderer or the outrage of an innocent person."

"No, I found her hard to read as well."

"Well…she has probably got even more motive than Graham. She admitted that she was going to struggle with making the monthly payments. I'm pretty sure she would've struggled for the rest of her life if it wasn't for that poisoned sherry."

Fran reflected for a few moments as they passed an old-fashioned stonewalled church.

"Actually no, I don't think this did drive her to murder I…" Fran's sentence trailed off.

"You what…"

"Oh…I've got no evidence."

"Don't worry about that, I'm not Stafford, what's your gut telling you?"

"Well, I don't think this murder was committed for the reason we are assuming."

"Then why was it committed?"

"Good question…oh I don't know."

"No…all we know is that it has got to be someone at the wake."

"Are you sure, James?"

"What do you mean? Who the hell else could have done it?"

"Well…the journal said there was some other guy called 'Martin' who Marianne blackmailed…"

"Fran!" James sharply interrupted.

She was rather taken aback by this slightly aggressive response. Fran had to force herself to concentrate on the road once more. James then continued with a touch of anger in his voice.

"Don't be stupid, it's got to be someone at the wake. No-one else would have had the opportunity."

This was the first time James had made Fran feel uncomfortable, normally he just charmed her. She concluded that it was a symptom of the underlying tension between them.

MARY

Overnight Fran replayed the interview conversations with Graham and Julie in her mind repeatedly. However, there was nothing worthwhile to be found in all this mental regurgitation. Fran tried to settle to sleep but another topic gatecrashed her thoughts…James. She reflected on the night they spent together or at least what she could remember of it. Fran then decided that when she leaves the police, she will cut all ties with him. She felt that she could not make the adjustment to them being just good friends. Fran had not had many romantic encounters in her life. He would not just be another one to add to her butterfly collection. Even though the experience was very short-lived, no-one had made her feel this way before. She needed to fully relinquish herself from him to have the chance of experiencing something like this again.

On the way into work the following morning, Fran felt a bitterly cold autumnal wind blow harshly into her bones. She was already feeling a tad groggy from a poor night's sleep. Fran really did not appreciate the elements conspiring against her as well. When she arrived at work, she immediately made herself a strong coffee. Through the steam of her hot drink, she saw Andy sit down at his desk. Fran then gave him an informal debrief of yesterday's interview with Julie. Andy considered this briefly before giving his assessment.

"What a charade, eh? A married couple are both adulterers but neither party is aware that their spouse is just as guilty as they are. Graham sleeps with the ultimate blackmailer Marianne and Julie hooks up with the recently deceased Alan. Subsequently they both shell out thousands for their misdemeanours, but in Julie's case it's her lover who actually foots the bill."

"Yeah, pretty much."

"It sounds like a storyline from Eastenders!"

"You watch Eastenders?" Fran enquired in a somewhat disapproving tone.

"Absolutely and so should you. It makes you realise just how talented you really are."

Stafford then marched into the room and quickly got the attention of all those present. Fran's already low mood plummeted further when she was informed that he was going to be present with her for today's interview. However, she reminded herself that she would not be in this job for much longer. Stafford would soon be nothing but an unhappy memory. This enabled her to adopt a pragmatic state of mind where she could keep her emotions in check. It had been arranged for them to speak to Mary, the wife of Barry Furlow.

There was very little conversation during their journey to Walmsbury. Stafford was busy sending messages on his mobile. Fran was relieved that he was preoccupied as she could just focus on driving. She noticed that, once again, Stafford had a bottle of water and some Polo Mints. Fran wondered whether, on her final day, she should hand him a business card with the contact details for Alcoholics Anonymous. Stafford then put down his phone and Fran sensed he now wanted to converse.

"Right, Fran, I want you to probe Mary. She's got an awful secret and Marianne blackmailed a lot of money out of her."

"She will no doubt deny everything, sir."

"Of course, but I still want you to probe her to see if her alibi is watertight."

Fran chewed this over during the final mile of their car journey.

Stafford and Fran were promptly let into Mary's modest house. She was dressed in clothes that balanced casual with smart. Her demeanour was neither prickly nor friendly but focussed and business-like. It was as if she was discussing financial affairs with her accountant. The three of them all sat down in the lounge. Mary took it upon herself to start the proceedings.

"I understand you need to ask me some questions," she firmly asserted. Fran immediately realised that no preamble was required.

"Yes, we do Mary. You probably don't know this, but Marianne had a secret journal saved on her laptop. This journal included entries revealing that she blackmailed you for a cover-up which you instigated. According to Marianne, this happened in the care home where you were the manager."

Mary's assertive façade immediately disappeared. It was as if Fran had physically pulled the mask off Mary's face. Fran was poised to swoop in like a vulture hungry for fresh meat. Mary was silent but could not control the physical tremble around her knees. Finally, Mary asked the question that was obviously preying on her mind.

"Have you told anyone about this?" Mary asked in a low tone of voice that conveyed her sense of dread.

"Only those directly involved in this investigation, no-one outside."

Mary breathed out heavily. Fran waited in expectation for her to continue but she remained silent. Fran then realised that, after this bombshell, she would have to move things along. It was clear that a certain degree of reassurance would be required.

"Mary, we are not here to investigate the cover-up. What we are interested in is the subsequent blackmail that occurred."

Mary gave a simple nod of acknowledgment.

"Marianne's journal states that a monthly payment arrangement was then set up."

Fran read out an extract from Marianne's journal.

Thursday evening, 08/09/2011

I made Mary pay for her cover-up in the care home. Like the others I demanded £1,000 a month for my silence. She had no choice but to agree, also like the others.

"Is this true?" Fran enquired.

Mary nodded her head.

"No, I need you to verbally confirm this."

"Yes, it is true," replied Mary who had to force the words out of her mouth.

"And I assume this continued until Marianne died?"

"Yes," replied Mary and she could not bring herself to look Fran in the eyes.

"How did you keep all this from your husband?"

"I paid Marianne in cash and it's money that Barry does not know about. You see, shortly after Marianne started blackmailing me, my father died. I inherited a lot of money; a lot more than Barry is aware of. Using a separate bank account, I invested this money in stocks and shares and thankfully it paid dividends. I have kept up with the blackmail payments or at least mostly."

"Mostly?"

"Yes, a few months ago I had to sell all my expensive jewellery. I replaced every item with a much cheaper replica. Barry's not got much of an eye for this sort of thing, so he never noticed."

"How much money from your stocks and shares have you got left?"

"Nothing, that's why I had to start selling my jewellery."

"But you said you had sold *all* of your jewellery, so how were you going to pay Marianne in future?"

The mood in the room instantly changed as Mary looked up and down, left, and right, anywhere except at Fran.

"Would I be right in thinking this would have been a struggle?" Fran eventually asked.

"Alright, yes it would have been a struggle, but I didn't kill her because of it." Mary's response had a significantly more aggressive tone. She then changed her tack from an intimidating aggressor to something more akin to a pleading victim.

"I couldn't commit a murder; I don't have it in me. I know in your eyes I have a motive and probably more than anyone else you have interviewed. I accept I'm a liar, but I am not a murderer."

"How do we know *that* wasn't a lie?" Fran asked provocatively.

Mary instantly realised she had dug herself into a hole. Admitting she was dishonest was a terrible faux pas. Fran could tell Mary was desperately trying to work out how to recover. She sensed this was a moment to press her point home.

"If you're a liar, how can we trust anything you've said in this interview, Mary?"

"Alright but what proof have you got? What evidence do you have? Huh, do you have anything at all?"

"We have no evidence," Fran was forced to concede.

"Right, you come back to me when you have, I think that concludes our interview."

Fran and Stafford took their cue and left her home immediately, no goodbyes were required.

"Well…that was very dramatic," Stafford opined whilst Fran was driving him back to the office.

"Indeed sir, sorry if I upset her."

"Don't be, we're not here to make friends, we're here to solve crimes."

In some ways this statement did not sit comfortably with Fran. However, she could not deny that asking probing questions would always risk the rancour of the interviewee. Experience had taught her that this was an occupational hazard.

"When we get back, I'll get the clearance for us to investigate Mary's financial transactions from this other account. I want to see if her story checks out, at least from a money point of view," Stafford continued.

The following day Stafford got the necessary clearance. He then assigned Fran to swim through the murky waters of Mary's financial history. Her secret bank account was investigated as well as the stocks and shares transactions that Mary mentioned. It was a tedious task that took hours. However, Fran eventually found that Mary had indeed inherited an enormous amount from her father. Monthly cash payments of £1000 had been taken out from this bank account up until Marianne's death.

Mary therefore appeared to have told the truth about the payments. Moreover, based purely on her gut instinct, Fran also decided that Mary was not the murderer. Therefore, this now left two remaining suspects, one of them being Mary's husband.

BARRY

Fran fell asleep shortly after arriving in her flat. When she woke up, as usual, she spent some time looking at the family photograph at her bedside. She so wished they had taken a different route that day and avoided the fatal car crash near the railway station. Fran then decided she needed to do something to distract herself. She quickly realised that once again the most available person was her neighbour, Harry. Their friendship had deepened so she now felt she could just go up at any time within reason. Harry made Fran a coffee with a horse-like kick. After swiftly drinking this, she was engaged enough to focus on him.

"What's happening in your world?" Fran asked Harry.

"Same old, nothing new."

"Nothing new…look, come on, it's not good for you to live like a hermit."

"But I'm just not used to being around people anymore. You're the one exception, Fran."

In some ways this was quite a compliment, but it still made her sad. She reflected on this as she walked up to work for another late shift. As she approached the barrier gates her thoughts turned back to the murder case.

On her arrival, Stafford told Fran she would be interviewing Barry Furlow today alongside Clara. Stafford had not informed Fran whether Mary would be present for this interview. Fran felt a bit uncomfortable about going there without this information. However, she just could not bring herself to try and confirm this with Stafford before she left. Instead, she just got in the police car with Clara and promptly drove off to Walmsbury.

During the journey, Fran was a little nervous that Clara might quiz her over her recent absences from church. She therefore took the initiative and brought up an alternative subject. Fran asked about Clara's children as she was always happy to talk about them.

"Lara took five wickets in a school indoor cricket match yesterday, I'm so proud of my girl," Clara said gleefully.

She then gave Fran an in-depth description of every wicket that Lara had taken. Fran was very bored by this detailed report, but remained politely smiling in the traditional British way. Clara then moved onto the subject of trying to arrange a trip to see her family in Antigua.

"My Mum's 60 next June, I so want to be there for her birthday party but I...," Clara's sentence tailed off abruptly.

"Oh, come on...that's plenty of advance notice for annual leave, surely that can't be declined," Fran replied. Clara did not answer but shook her head as she clearly was having doubts. Fran then decided to just focus on the forthcoming interview.

"This interview will be similar to the others but it's a purely financial situation. There was no physical relationship between Barry and Marianne," said Fran.

"Yes, but Fran, the Good Book says 'the love of money is the root of all evil'," Clara commented.

"Oh...I don't know, I just can't help thinking that in this case it's not that simple."

A few minutes later they arrived in Walmsbury and Fran knocked firmly on the front door. Barry opened it and led them through to his little lounge. He was once again dressed in his customary sports tracksuit with a blue T-shirt just visible above the zip of the jacket. Fran and Clara sat down; she sensed that Barry just wanted to get on with it.

"Before I go any further, I assume your wife is out?" said Fran.

"Yes, she is at work."

Fran breathed a silent sigh of relief as this would make the interview easier. She then quickly focussed her mind to ensure she asked the right questions.

"OK Barry. You probably don't know this, but Marianne kept a private computer journal. Some of the entries in this journal involve you." Fran then proceeded to read out an extract.

Tuesday morning, 05/05/2011

I read an email that revealed that one of Barry's athletes is using performance enhancing drugs. He obviously doesn't want this to come out publicly. I just need to work out what I will charge him to keep my silence.

There was a very uncomfortable silence and Barry turned his head away slightly from Fran. She instantly realised that Barry was completely unprepared for this interrogation. It took him quite a while to recompose himself. He was not a man who normally displayed any great emotion, but he was now a lightyear out of his comfort zone.

"Firstly, Mr Furlow, can you confirm if this is true?" Fran asked in a calm but assertive voice.

Barry remained silent and Fran waited patiently to pick the rght moment to pursue this. Clara made a note of Barry's discomfort on her pad.

"Mr Furlow, I think at this point I had better remind you that lying to the police, perjury, is a criminal offence. With that in mind may I please ask again, is this true?"

Barry looked down before finally facing Fran with an expression of surrender.

"Yes, it is true," he said in a voice almost devoid of emotion.

"Thank you."

"Are you going to press some kind of charge against me?"

"No, this is a matter for the relevant sports regulatory body, it's not a police affair. We are only interested in the murder of Marianne."

Barry seemed reassured by this and so Fran continued.

"The journal goes on to say that Marianne blackmailed you for a thousand pounds a month."

"Yes, that's right. I just couldn't bring myself to explain to Mary what I'd done or that Marianne was blackmailing me for it. She was so proud of me for my achievements as an athletics manager. It was one of the few positive aspects of our marriage. I just could not have that being ruined so I paid a very heavy price," Barry explained.

"Would I be right in thinking these monthly payments continued until Marianne's death?"

"Yes," Barry confirmed and remained icy cold.

Barry realised where this interview was heading and decided to tackle it head on.

"I didn't kill her to avoid further payments if that's what you're thinking. Yes, she exploited me as she has exploited other people but I'm not the murderer."

"Exploited other people?'" Fran enquired.

She wondered whether Barry knew about any of the other blackmail victims.

"She was always using people."

"Were you aware of her blackmailing anyone else?"

Barry paused and Fran could sense that he was weighing up in his mind whether he would divulge some information.

"Yes, I was not the only one she was blackmailing."

Fran was surprised that Barry was aware of this and she was also intrigued. As she saw it, this had to be one of potentially five other people including the ever-elusive 'Martin'.

"Who else did she blackmail?" Fran enquired.

"Well, I don't actually know their name."

Fran wondered whether Marianne blackmailed someone else, outside of the names mentioned in her journal. However, she remained silent to allow Barry to continue.

"It just came out in conversation that she was also blackmailing some Care home manager because of a cover-up."

"So, you've no idea who this person is then?"

"As it happens, my wife Mary was and still is a Care home manager. I did quiz her over this cover-up and blackmail. I just said I'd heard a rumour but obviously I didn't mention Marianne. Mary assured me that she was not involved in any cover-up and was not being blackmailed. For all her faults, and she is a flawed woman, I know Mary would never lie to me."

You don't know her like I do was what Fran wanted to say but she kept the words inside. Barry looked around aimlessly for a few moments before giving a concluding statement.

"As it wasn't my wife then I've really no idea who this manager is, sorry."

Fran decided there was not much point pursuing this but, as with the other suspects, there was another area she wanted to explore.

"How did you pay Marianne all this money?"

"Well, I have another source of income."

"Which is?"

"I do a nice little line in athletes' trainers."

"OK, but what method did you use for these payments?"

"Well, I insist on cash payments for every pair of trainers sold. I then paid Marianne with the money from these sales. I took out additional cash from my bank account, where necessary, to top up."

Fran concluded the interview shortly after this as there was not much more to discuss. Her instinct was that Barry, although certainly a shady character, was not actually the murderer. Apart from the obvious money motive that he shared with several other people, there was nothing more that could be pinned on him. Indeed, in Fran's opinion, none of the interviews had brought them any closer to the perpetrator. However, they still had one more bite at the criminal cherry.

SUE

As per the normal procedure, Fran reported back to Stafford. She also completed the relevant report regarding her conversation with Barry Furlow. Stafford had contacted Sue Furlow and an interview had been arranged for the next day. Once again, Fran began to script out the questions in her mind. She remembered how Sue immediately insisted she was not the murderer when she was last interviewed. As with all the suspects, there was an obvious financial motive that Fran knew would be strongly denied. She would have to use her detective skills to be a sleuth for the truth.

The rest of the shift passed uneventfully. Fran was pleased to see another text from Harry. He was consistent with his messages; it made her feel wanted and for this she was most grateful. After work, Fran walked slowly home, wandering and wondering. She could feel herself building up this final interview in her mind. It felt like the last roll of the dice.

Fran was not happy with how Stafford had approached this investigation. It was actually the first time she had doubted his judgement. She had doubted his people skills on many occasions. However, up until now, he had always correctly made the critical decisions that ultimately solved the crime. Something had changed and she wondered what was wrong with Stafford. However, Fran knew that she could not move the goal posts. She just had to play ball within the perimeters the CDI had set.

When she got home, Fran cooked herself a chicken casserole which she ate alone. Fran found solitary mealtimes quite difficult. She missed the way her family would all converge around the table for dinner when she was a child. Quietly munching her food alone always gave her a sense of being abandoned. It was like society had somehow dismissed her. After this lonely meal, Fran considered updating her Facebook status to distract herself, but she did not know what to say. She realised that there was nothing that was going to take her away from the dread of the forthcoming interview. Overnight, she dozed more than properly slept. In the morning, a couple of coffees and a shower were needed to perk her up for this big day.

When Fran entered the office, it was not long before Stafford assigned DI James Mallen to join her for the interview with Sue. Whilst driving over to Brock Heath, Fran focussed on keeping the conversation between them strictly professional. She was able to do this well but being in such close physical proximity with James did stir up some desires. Fran deeply wished he was not so damn attractive. As she was driving the last mile to Sue's humble flat, Fran was able to focus back on the forthcoming interview.

"James, if we're not able to pin this murder on Sue then I really don't know what we're going to do."

"Don't worry about that, Fran. Just treat it as any other interview, ask the questions, listen carefully to the answers, observe her body language and facial expressions."

"I'm sorry, I just feel under pressure to get a result from the interview."

"It's OK, just treat it like any other interview. The overall direction of the investigation is Stafford's problem, not yours."

Fran was reassured by this and then easily found a space in the car park adjacent to the block of flats. She rang on the intercom and Sue's voice crackled through the tinny speaker. The communal front door lock was then released and Fran walked upstairs swiftly with James.

Sue was ready and waiting for them by the front door of her flat. She was dressed casually in black leggings and a red top. Her face had an almost piercing seriousness and Fran knew that there would not be any bonhomie. Fran and James settled themselves quickly in her lounge. James was poised with pen and pad and Fran had her list of questions prepared in her mind. However, the first question was from Sue who jumped in before Fran had a chance to speak.

"Why are you here again?"

"Oh, was it not explained to you?"

"No, your boss just said you need to ask some more questions. What questions? I've told you everything I know."

"OK, I'll cut to the chase, Sue. Marianne had a private computer journal. We have been reading the entries which revealed that she had been blackmailing you."

Sue looked away towards her window for a moment, then to the carpet and then to the ceiling. There was a silence and Fran sensed the moment to continue and spoke softly but assertively.

"According to Marianne's journal, during July 2010, she discovered that your backing music track included the voice of another singer. And at your gigs you would lip-synch every song to give the impression that you were singing it all live."

Sue was still not making any eye contact. Fran waited for a few moments before she continued. She proceeded to read out an extract from Marianne's computer journal.

> **Monday morning, 20/12/2010**
> What a fraud Sue is, honestly, lip synching over all those songs! I forced her to give me a 50% cut of every gig to not reveal that she can't actually sing at all!

"Is this true, Sue?"

Finally, Sue turned to face Fran.

"Yes," Sue simply replied.

"Was this all paid in cash?" Fran asked but was actually sure this would be the case based on the interviews with the other suspects.

"Yes, that's right."

Fran took a moment and braced herself to lead this interview towards a very serious suggestion.

"I'm sure this would have cost you dearly and you would have been hugely resentful."

"Well yeah, obviously."

"When I came here before, you said you hated Marianne even though she had done nothing against you personally. Well, this would suggest that, in fact, she *had* done something against you personally. I think you *did* have a personal reason for hating her."

"Alright yes, I'm sorry, I just didn't want to talk about it."

"I see. Would I be right in thinking this blackmail continued up to Marianne's death?"

"Yes"

"This would have cost you a lot of money."

"Thousands of pounds."

"And Marianne's death will save you from making more expensive payments."

"Look, I told you before, I didn't kill her. Yes, I hated her but so would you if she was going to force you out of your home."

"'Force you out of your home'?"

"Yeah, you see, I have been struggling for gigs and as Marianne was taking half of what I earned I've fallen behind with my rent. My landlord is a ruthless bastard, one more missed payment and that would have been it, I'd be out on my arse!"

"So, if Marianne had not been poisoned, you would have been homeless."

"Yes, and I really don't know what I have would done then!"

The interview ended shortly afterwards. Fran walked up to the police car with James and then stopped quite suddenly.

"James, do you mind driving?"

James looked a little surprised by this but then smiled reassuringly.

"Sure thing, Fran."

James drove them away from the block of flats and Brock Heath. Fran took advantage of being in a passenger seat. She fully immersed herself in reflections on the interview that had just taken place. Eventually, she formed enough coherent thoughts to discuss her ideas with James.

"Do you think she did it?" Fran asked, although the question was aimed more at herself than her colleague.

"To be honest, I'm not sure," James replied.

"Me neither, she's a screwed up little cookie but I don't know if she really could kill Marianne."

"How did she compare with the others?"

"What do you mean 'compare'?"

"Do you think Sue is more likely to have killed Marianne than them?"

"Oh, definitely more likely. I walked away confident that none of the others committed the crime. I guess you could argue that the risk of being made homeless may have pushed her to kill Marianne. But I can only say it's only more likely, I am not sure at all."

Fran paused whilst she tried to gauge her feelings.

"Sue seems a bit out of control," Fran continued.

"Probably from years of drug taking," James replied.

"Yes, she's got that glazed expression of a stoner. Come to think of it, there was a bit in the journal that mentioned how drugs were part of the deal for the backing track recording. But no matter how much of a druggie she is, that still doesn't mean she's a murderer."

Fran returned to the office and reported back to Stafford. Unusually for him, he seemed genuinely taken aback by the findings. Shortly afterwards, he called an emergency meeting for the team and everyone quickly assembled. Stafford then made it clear that he felt Sue was probably the murderer. However, they needed to obtain sufficient evidence to warrant an arrest.

Overnight, Fran repeatedly replayed the interview with Sue in her mind. Doubts niggled into the core of Fran's psyche like a mole burrowing down into the depths of the earth. The following morning, Fran had a chat with Andy and Clara in the office before most of their colleagues arrived.

"I don't think Sue is the murderer," Fran firmly asserted.

"Well, you were the one who interviewed her, so you've probably got the best insight."

"Thanks Andy."

"Yeah, but Fran, we've got no-one else, girl," said Clara.

"Yes, I know, damn it. This murder case is killing me!" said Fran.

"Well I hope not or that would be another investigation," Andy joked.

Fran and Clara smiled and Fran took a sip from what was her third coffee of the day.

"I think that as she is so unstable, Stafford suspects she lost the plot and committed the murder," said Andy.

"Yes, but it takes a certain kind of person to actually kill a human being. Most of us have basic moral and behavioural boundaries that prevent us from doing such a thing. Now if you're unstable you're more prone to drink, drugs or maybe acting inappropriately. But committing a murder is on a different level," said Fran.

"OK, but if Sue didn't kill Marianne, then who did?" asked Clara.

Fran's frustrated frown framed her face. She gulped some more coffee in a desperate attempt to find some inspiration. A thought then crash landed into her mind.

"Maybe someone else at the wake, outside our list of suspects, committed the crime? I mean any one of them could have poisoned the sherry," said Fran.

"But none of them had a motive," said Andy.

"Maybe they did have a motive, but we just haven't found it."

"Come on Fran, we can only work from the evidence we've got," said Clara.

"That's it, that's the problem, we don't have the evidence we need," countered Fran.

"Where do you suggest we look then?" said Andy.

"Oh…damn it, I don't know," Fran despaired.

Fran realised the lack of evidence was too much of a stumbling block. She could not approach Stafford to suggest he is making a mistake. And even if she did, he was far too proud and truculent to listen to a lower ranked officer like her. Eventually, Fran concluded that she had better just let it go and follow the orders of her superior as normal.

LEAVING & CLOSING

After work, Fran, Andy, Clara and James went for a drink in Jac & Mac's. They found a relatively quiet corner and sat down together. Pints of beer and glasses of wine soon arrived at their table. The group stared at each other in silence as they had all reached the same conclusion. It was just a case of who was going to stick their neck out and actually say it first. James took a large gulp of his lager and decided he would be the one to confront the truth.

"This investigation is going nowhere. We may suspect it's Sue, but we just have not got any evidence. I don't think there's any way we can find it. Stafford is going to have to let this case go."

"He won't do that easily. He's a proud man and it's been years since he had an unsolved murder," said Clara.

"Yeah, but there comes a point where enough is enough," Andy reasoned.

"I don't think he's been on his 'A game' with this one. I still think we should have considered the possibility that the sherry was poisoned the night before. But damn it, he's just not open to that idea," said Fran.

"Yeah, but Fran, there was no break-in and it's a really remote location. There's absolutely nothing to suggest anyone went there before the wake. I think we can rule that one out," said James.

Fran disagreed but she knew she didn't have anything she could use to counter this argument, so she remained silent.

"It's also a shame for Robbie that his final case has ended like this, you know he's leaving next Friday," said Andy.

"Really? I knew he was retiring soon but I didn't realise it was next week," said Fran.

"Yeah, apparently the house sale has been completed and so he's moving to Southcliffe-on-Sea over the weekend."

The group all went to their various homes after just the one drink. Fran luxuriated in the warmth of her bath and wondered if, and when, Stafford would pull the plug on the investigation. She decided that she would hand in her resignation the next working day after the case was closed. She was now firm in her decision to move on.

Fran went to visit her friend Jane on the following Saturday. This helped to remind her that she had a life outside of work. She promised herself to make time for other things to try and regain some semblance of work/life balance. On Sunday, Fran considered going to church as it had been a while since her last attendance. She knew she would not feel right there but at the same time felt bad for not going. Eventually, she chose not to go so instead she popped upstairs for a chat with Harry. She knew she could discuss this dilemma with him.

"I suppose because I have been going there for so many years, I can't help feeling guilty that I've stopped going to church."

"No, I can understand that Fran. Personally, I like to think of the whole world as a church; a church without walls with a congregation of 8 billion people," said Harry.

Fran had never considered this before, but perhaps this was a way to help her move on from organised religion. She could view the entire planet as the House of God and not just certain holy buildings. It gave her plenty of food for thought as her weekend gently eased away.

The following morning at work, Clara pulled out a card from her rucksack.

"I've got this for Robbie."

Fran and Andy signed the card with a simple message wishing him well for the future.

> To Robbie,
>
> All the very best for your retirement
> Andy
>
> **Happy Retirement!**
>
> Enjoy your retirement in Southcliffe-on-Sea
> Fran x
>
> From the Major Crimes Unit Team

"Stafford is going to get a present for him too if you want to contribute," Clara continued.

Both Fran and Andy gave a ten-pound note for the collection. They were curious as to what Stafford would get him. As Robbie had been so aloof, she doubted anyone would know what to buy him. However, giving a voucher would be a bit lame for a man who had served for so many years. Reports were completed, admin tasks were done, but the whole team could sense this investigation was now winding down.

The following Friday, which was Robbie's final day, Superintendent Jamieson arrived and went into Stafford's office. It was clear that the investigation was pretty much over. About half an hour later, Jamieson left Stafford's office and swiftly walked away. Stafford then called a meeting and the whole team duly assembled. Everyone knew what was coming, the divorce of the Major Crimes Unit from this case. Thankfully, this divorce would not involve an acrimonious court case or expensive alimony. Fran was intrigued as to what Stafford would actually say to finalise everything. She did not have to wait long as the Chief Detective Inspector stood straight backed to face his team.

"Hello everyone. I have spoken to my superior, Superintendent Jamieson, and we have agreed that, regrettably, we must end this investigation. We feel that we, or should I say *you*, have done everything reasonably possible. However, the lack of physical evidence has proved to be too much of a stumbling block for us to progress any further. I thank you for your time and effort, but this murder case is now closed."

Fran could not believe how matter of fact he was about closing the case. It was like he did not care about the outcome. Surely this unsolved case would reflect badly on him. It had originally seemed a relatively straightforward investigation with only a small number of possible perpetrators.

"There is one other thing, as you know, Detective Constable Robbie Jones is leaving us today. Robbie has given an excellent service for over 30 years and we have got a little something for him."

Stafford then turned round and from a bag he pulled out a card and a present that had been gift-wrapped in shiny purple paper.

"Come here, Robbie…"

After a pause, Robbie gingerly stepped forward to take the card and present from his superior. A spontaneous round of applause broke out in the room. The applause ended abruptly in anticipation of some kind of speech from Robbie. However, he just smiled, nodded his head in acknowledgment and then sat back down without saying a word.

"And with that, I'll let you all finish early today. There really isn't anything else to stay for now. Have a nice weekend," said Stafford.

Robbie gave a quick wave before he swiftly walked out of the office for the final time. It felt far too abrupt, but the team knew that he just wanted to slip discretely away into his retirement.

Fran then went home and looked forward to a peaceful weekend. She wrote out her resignation notice and placed it in an envelope. Fran felt an enormous sense of relief as she put the envelope in her letter rack ready for Monday morning. She then sent a group text to Clara, Andy and James. This briefly explained that she would soon be handing in her resignation notice. Reassuring and supportive messages were sent back by all three of them.

When Sunday morning arrived, she remembered Harry's notion of a "church without walls" to excuse herself (in her mind) for staying at home. The following morning, she made sure she picked up the right envelope, the one that contained her resignation letter. As Fran walked up to the barrier gates, she was ready for the conversation she would have with Stafford over resigning. However, she really was not ready for the large number of photographers and journalists that had unexpectedly assembled outside her workplace.

AND IN OTHER NEWS...

The photographers and journalists swarmed over Fran as if she were some famous politician caught up in a scandal. There were blinding white flashing lights from a plethora of cameras. A cacophony of questions were shouted out and bewildered Fran. Everyone was speaking at the same time making it difficult to pick out what was actually being asked.

"What's happened?" Fran eventually bellowed out.

A young male journalist with a small portable recording device then spoke. The others were now just about quiet enough for him to be heard.

"We understand that the Major Crimes Unit are investigating the murder of Marianne Furlow who killed her husband. So, what's happening now in the case of the murder of a murderer?"

Fran froze out of fear, how could they possibly know this? Someone from her team must have given them the tip off but who and why? Those questions would have to wait, she first had to deal with this crazy here and now situation. Fran was not trained to deal with the media, it was at least a mile above her pay grade. She was worried that anything she did say could come back to haunt her.

"I'm sorry, I am not in a position to comment on that. Now if you'll excuse me, I have to go," Fran said assertively.

The journalists were very persistent and she had to fight her way past them. Eventually she was able to place her badge on the device that opened the electronic gate. Whilst it was opening, Fran turned round and stretched out the palms of her hand. This was to signal that they were not allowed to follow her into the grounds of the building. Thankfully, they got the message and although questions were still being hurled at her, she was able to safely walk away. Fran entered the building and sighed relief from the bottom of her boots as the door closed behind her. She took a few deep breaths to absorb what had just happened. Fran then marched up the stairs and on entering the office she saw Stafford who was clearly dismayed.

"What the bloody hell's going on out there?"

"They know sir?"

"What do you mean, *'they know'*?"

"They know about Marianne killing her husband."

"Oh, you're kidding me!"

"I wish I was sir."

"Oh Jesus!"

Stafford disappeared into his office and slammed the door behind him. Fran knew that he would be on the phone to Superintendent Jamieson. She also realised that now was absolutely not the moment to hand in her resignation. One by one, members of her team came in looking shellshocked. Everyone had received a media bashing when they arrived outside. They were now all wondering who was the traitor that had snitched? No-one dared address the matter directly as they were all too intimidated. However, the elephant was definitely in the room and trumpeting loudly with a raised trunk. Eventually, Andy decided to face up to the situation and spoke to the team.

"It must have been one of us, no-one else knew. Someone in this room must have leaked the story to the media."

Fran then had a brainwave. She had to dig deep to find the courage to speak. Fran feared some of her colleagues might object to this idea.

"Actually, there is one other person. The man who left on Friday."

"Oh no way would Robbie do that!" said James.

"Look, I'm sorry but it does seem a bit of a coincidence that the media knew nothing before he left, whereas now they're fully aware. Let's face it, Robbie had nothing to lose, no possible consequences to his career. He would have got a nice little payment for this information, I'm sure."

Fran sensed the team accepted that her idea had credence despite being an uncomfortable proposition. Their working careers had given them all a good insight into just how awful human beings can be. Stafford remained in his office for over an hour and anxiety spread around the room like an aggressive cancer. There were reports that still needed to be completed for Marianne's case. These would have to wait as everyone was too distracted by the media intrusion to concentrate. Eventually Andy, once again, stood up to the plate to suggest an idea.

"Why don't we call Robbie? Don't make any accusations as he will no doubt deny it. Just ask if he knows anything and then see how he reacts?"

"Yeah, I've got his number saved in my mobile. You see, he gave it to me it a while ago when I had to give him a lift to work. It was just in case anything happened last minute," said Clara.

"Put the phone on speaker so we can all hear him," said Andy.

The whole of the Major Crimes Unit crowded around Clara's modest mobile phone in an attempt to listen in on her conversation. She speed-dialled Robbie's number but it never rang, instead Clara just got a pre-recorded female voice message.

"I'm sorry but the number you have called has not been recognised. Please hang up and try again."

"What? But this is a saved number, how can it be?"

"He's changed his number; he's changed his number so none of us can contact him," said Fran.

"The bastard!" Andy shouted.

"He's not on social media, he never gave his new address to anyone. We could look it up but even if we did, we wouldn't have a legal right to conduct an interview. He's not committed a criminal offence, there's nothing we can do," said Fran.

At which point Stafford walked in with trauma screaming out of his face. It did not take long for his team to realise that he had an announcement to make.

"OK, well I think you all know what's happened. I will be holding a press briefing today at 4pm as the media have questions that need to be answered."

Stafford had a swallow of drink from his water bottle. Fran wondered how much 'Dutch courage' this bottle contained.

"Now if you'll excuse me, I need to go and prepare my statement for them."

As Stafford walked away it suddenly occurred to Fran that she may not get another chance today to hand in her resignation. Stafford would no doubt be busy dealing with the media. This placed Fran into a quandary as she knew Stafford wouldn't want to be disturbed. However, she didn't want to hand her resignation in any later than today. Fran was worried that this would invalidate the employment end date mentioned.

"Damn it," said Fran before marching off towards Stafford's office. Andy and Clara wondered what had upset her, but she was now focussed on the conversation she was about to have. Fran gave a rhythmical knock on his door and waited on tenterhooks for a response.

"Come in," Stafford said reluctantly.

Fran got into the mode of an actress. She would walk onto the stage, deliver the lines and act out the role of a detective constable resigning. She certainly would not get a round of applause at the end of her performance. However, it would enable her to get the damn thing over and done with.

Scene 1: Stafford's Office

Fran enters from the equivalent of stage left and walks downstage to face the other protagonist in this production.

Fran:	(Boldly) Sir, I know this is not a good time, but I've got to do this today. I don't think there will be another opportunity.
Stafford:	(A little taken aback) What is it Fran?
Fran:	I'm sorry sir, but I have to give you this.

Fran pulls out a white rectangular envelope and stretches out her hand in close proximity to Stafford. He snatches the envelope without uttering a word and quickly opens it. An excruciating silence falls between them as he reads it. He then puts the letter on his desk and turns to face Fran.

Stafford: Right…I get it, so you've snitched to the media, made a nice little earner and now you're running away with the money.

Fran: (Outraged) Sir, I swear I didn't!

Stafford: (Sneering tone) Really?

Fran: (Assertive) Yes, really. I would not do that to either you or the team.

Stafford: Then who did?

Fran: Well…we think it was actually Robbie. He's left his job, changed his number, left no forwarding address or anything, he's just upped sticks and gone.

Stafford: I know the real truth, Fran…but obviously I can't prove it. Just keep your nose clean for your remaining days. Now get out.

Fran promptly exits the stage through Stafford's door.

The curtain had now fallen on Fran's performance. Whilst their relationship had never been easy, Fran still expected Stafford to have shown more decorum. She was appalled, even by Stafford's standards this was vicious as well as false. Fran wanted to walk out of the building that very moment and never return. It was only a sense of loyalty to her friends in the team that convinced her to stay.

Fran was thoroughly demotivated and subsequently did very little work on the case reports. A few hours disappeared into the ether before she saw Stafford leave the building. He was obviously on his way to the media conference at a location he had not disclosed. In Stafford's absence, James acted up and used his authority to send everyone home early. This was so they could all catch the edited highlights of Stafford's press conference on the local news that evening.

As she was walking home, Fran thought about Robbie and was now stone cold certain he had leaked the story. She concluded that it was like he had left the building but then thrown in a grenade. An explosion of media activity would now ensue, but Fran decided she would just take one day at a time to serve out her notice until her last working day.

Fran had a bath before slipping into some comfortable lounge wear. Some would say it was far too early to put on her night clothes, but having bathed she could not see the point of getting dressed again. Fran quickly whipped up a tuna pasta meal with a sprinkling of sweetcorn. It was now just before 6.30pm and she switched on the TV awaiting the start of the local news. Whilst she utterly loathed the man, she could still see that Stafford was in a precarious situation. He would have to explain why this murder case, that had now drawn so much media attention, had to be closed.

The news programme started, the initial headlines were given and were punctuated by some over dramatic sound effects. Smartly dressed presenters with neatly coiffed hair gave a friendly but serious introduction. This quickly cut to an image of Stafford sat at a long desk surrounded by microphones. Directly in front of him was what appeared to be a glass of water. Fran wondered whether it might actually be vodka. The voiceover then introduced this story or rather their slant on it. A carefully constructed snippet from Stafford's interview quickly followed.

"Yes, it is true that we discovered a document that alleged Mrs Furlow killed her husband. However, this is completely unsubstantiated; our investigation found no evidence to support this claim."

Fran could not believe what she just heard although Stafford had not actually lied. Outside of Marianne's journal entry, there really was nothing to prove or even suggest that she had pushed her husband off the cliff. It just made no sense that she would write a fictionalised and deeply incriminating account.

A few seconds later there was another soundbite from Stafford.

"I can assure you that my team have carried out a painstaking investigation into the poisoning of Mrs Furlow. There is no evidence that anyone at the wake had poisoned her drink. We must therefore conclude that she was not murdered but had tragically committed suicide."

Fran was now convinced she was watching a film and that this could not actually be happening. Who on earth commits suicide by poisoning themselves apart from spies and desperate characters in Shakespeare plays? The news moved onto the cost-of-living crisis and then Fran heard her mobile phone ring. It was Andy who was equally as outraged as she was by Stafford's interview. He spent a good half an hour pounding Fran's ears with expletives. After this conversation had finally ended, Fran poured out a gigantic glass of wine and thanked God she was leaving her job.

FOOD FOR THOUGHT

The following morning, Fran got up quite slowly and only just arrived for work in time. It was not long before Stafford called everyone in for a meeting. He then explained that as there was no real evidence of anyone else poisoning the sherry, suicide was the only logical conclusion. Nothing was said, it was his decision and no-one felt they could change his mind. Shortly afterwards, Andy, Fran and Clara came together in the office to discuss the situation.

"What do you think?" asked Clara.

"Well, if this really was suicide then Marianne chose a very painful method," Andy replied.

"No, I can't believe Marianne would do that to her herself. Someone has literally got away with murder and I don't think they knew Marianne was a murderer herself," said Fran.

There was a collective agreement about this between the three of them. Fran was sure the rest of the office would also agree but this still wouldn't change anything. The team was then assigned to another case, but Fran could not properly engage with it. She just did the bare minimum required as she wished the time away.

A couple of days later she went for a drink with Andy. She promised him that she would go to his birthday party. This was a few Saturdays after her final working day. Andy also informed her that he heard on the grapevine that Stafford had somehow cleared all his debts. This depressed Fran and convinced her that there is no justice in the world. Fran's last few weeks drifted by drearily. She felt like a cork bobbing around in the ocean waiting for the tide to carry her to shore. It was frustrating because she was eager to move onto the next chapter of her life. At one point she was even tempted to just go AWOL and never return. Once again, her loyalty to her friends prevented her from doing this.

On the Saturday before Fran's final working day (which was a Monday), she had a kind of 'almost there' celebratory dinner with Harry at Jac & Mac's. This was the first time they had a pre-arranged rendezvous away from their homes. They both took the trouble of sprucing themselves up a bit for this event. A table had been booked for an early evening slot when it was still quiet. It did not take long before their plates were covered by an enormous burger and a gluttonous helping of fries. Fran chinked her wineglass against Harry's pint of lager and they smiled at each other warmly.

"So, it's all over on Monday," said Harry.

"Yes, I'm sad in some ways but I've got to get out of there, Harry."

"I know you do."

"And it'll give me a chance to review a few things, work out what I'm going to do next."

Fran took a sip of her wine and then remembered what she wanted to discuss with Harry.

"When I said, 'work out what I'm going to do next', I didn't just mean my job but in other ways too."

Harry smiled at Fran, with his eyes as much as his mouth, and she was reassured by this. It gave her the emotional safety she needed to express, what was for her, a difficult truth.

"You see, I feel a little lost, spiritually."

"I can tell you're looking for something."

"Yes Harry, I am, it's just…oh this might sound stupid, but I'm not actually sure what I'm looking for."

"It can be confusing sometimes. Don't worry, just take your time and eventually you'll undo the knots in your mind."

"I think my problem is that I really struggle to follow my convictions. I'm always having these internal dialogues where I frantically try to explain myself to those with opposing views."

"You don't have to justify yourself."

"But there's something inside that makes me feel that I must make it right to them, somehow. Oh, this is where I hate myself, Harry. I just can't find the inner strength to let it go and just be me. I keep asking myself what if I am wrong and the atheists are right?"

"OK Fran, let's look at that possibility, shall we? Let's suppose that there is no God of any kind, all spirituality is a delusion and when you die, that's it!"

Harry had a sip of his lager and took a moment to compose his thoughts, he then continued.

"Well…if the atheists are right, and at the end of our lives we all just switch off like lightbulbs, then you'll never know you were wrong."

Fran considered this for a moment before she reached her conclusion.

"So basically, I've got nothing to lose."

"Exactly. If your beliefs help you to get through your life and they're not impinging on the lives of others, then let it roll."

"Ah that's what I love about you, Harry, I can talk about this stuff. Spirituality has always been a major part of who I am. If it is a delusion, then it's a damn good one as it helps me to get the best out of myself."

"Absolutely and you can go your own way regardless of what anyone else thinks. You are at liberty to do that, they don't own your mind."

"I know but I…" Fran's sentence trailed off. She took a sip of wine and paused for a moment whilst she figured out what she actually wanted.

"I wish I could just go with the flow and not be so afraid all the time."

"Fear is the mind killer, so use your detective skills to prevent this murder."

Fran smiled and then looked around to savour the ambience of the restaurant before continuing.

"The thing is it's not just my secular friends that I disagree with. I actually have some different views to my Christian friends too."

"Yes, I can imagine they wouldn't appreciate the sort of spiritual ideas I've been giving you."

"No, they wouldn't Harry but there's more to it than that. They tend to put enormous emphasis on having the right belief and this really upsets me because…"

"…most of your friends have different beliefs to you," Harry interrupted.

Fran had never told Harry this, but he instinctively guessed.

"Yes, Harry, most of them do. I just hate the whole 'us and them' dichotomy of believers and non-believers. There must be a better answer than this."

"Well Fran, once again I'm going to give you an idea that a lot of religious people would find challenging. Although beliefs may be precious to a person, God doesn't give a damn what you believe."

Fran remained listening but said nothing. She just took a sip of her wine as Harry continued.

"If God has an exclusive contract with one religion, then most people would be excluded. You see, the world is split amongst a number of religions. None of them has the majority of the global population. No, we are not divided by belief, we are not divided by anything; in the eyes of God we are all one."

Fran reflected on this for a few moments and then was compelled to ask another question.

"Actually, what do *you* believe, Harry?"

"I don't fit easily into a category but let me put it this way. George Harrison once said that 'all religions are branches of the same tree'. Well, rather than just one branch, I believe in the tree; the tree of life, if you will."

Harry took a sip of lager before continuing.

"But that's just me, you have to find your own way with this, Fran."

"Yes, but to do that I need to have conviction and I've just got too much doubt. It's not just religion but pretty much everything in my life. I mean if I had more conviction, I'd really overturn the tables regarding the case of Marianne. It's a farce, no way would she have poisoned herself. I just can't understand how Stafford came to that conclusion."

Up until this point, Fran had been careful not to discuss the case with anyone outside of the Major Crimes Unit. However, she decided that as it had been in the news, she was more at liberty now. Fran had also reached a point where she didn't really care anymore.

"The suicide verdict is going to annoy me for a long time," Fran continued.

"Do you think the investigation overlooked some key evidence?"

"Oh, I don't know, there's just something really not right about…*key evidence*!" Fran suddenly screamed.

As she said this, she suddenly stood up. In doing so, she knocked her glass off the table spilling the wine onto the floor. Fran did not even notice as she was so transfixed by the revelation that had just come into her mind.

"Oh God, oh my God, why didn't we think of that?"

"Fran, what's the matter?"

"I've worked it out. I've worked out how the murder was committed!"

"What?"

"Yes, the sherry was poisoned the night before the wake."

"But how?"

Fran looked left and right to make sure no-one else was listening and then explained her theory to Harry.

"Bloody hell, are you sure?"

"I just know, Harry, trust me, it all adds up."

"But can you prove it?"

"Well, it might be possible if I can…oh what am I on about? The case is closed, and anyway I'm not allowed to do my own investigation."

"You may not be allowed, but that doesn't mean you can't do it, Fran?"

"Sorry?"

"You could break the rules and just do your own investigation without them knowing."

Fran went silent, she knew Harry's suggestion was definitely possible. However, this level of rule breaking was an intimidating prospect. A waiter come over and picked up the glass. To his surprise, Fran then ordered a straight treble vodka. When the drink arrived, Fran gulped about half of it down in one go and then breathed out heavily. The alcohol helped to relieve her from her piercing anxiety.

"I'm scared Harry. I've never done anything like this before in my life."

"There are times in life where you should break the rules. After all, Jesus broke the rules when he healed a leper on the Sabbath."

Fran sipped a bit more of her drink but still looked very nervous.

"Fran, there's a murderer out there and how do we know that person won't murder someone else, someone much more innocent?" Harry continued.

"Oh God, Harry."

"Well, this is the reality and you've got to face it. Besides, if they fire you then you would not have lost anything, you were going anyway."

"But I might be totally wrong about this."

"You just said you *'know'* and it *'all adds up'*."

Fran took another sip from her glass and looked Harry square in the eyes.

"If I do this, will you help me, Harry?"

"How can I? I'm not a policeman?"

"I mean emotional support."

"Oh, in that way, I'll back you up a hundred per cent."

Fran drained the remainder of her vodka and in that moment made her decision. She simply had to follow her hunch and investigate… whatever the consequences may be.

SCHEMING

Fran and Harry left the restaurant shortly afterwards. Once again, a cold choppy wind blew in menacingly from the hills and chilled them both to their bones. Fran did not care about the harsh weather. She was far too preoccupied by the unorthodox investigation she was about to embark on. She was frantically figuring out how she would get the necessary evidence together. Fran needed to prove her hunch or at least have sufficient grounds to warrant an arrest.

When they reached home, Fran invited Harry into her flat and he duly accepted. Fran poured herself a glass of water. She was not drunk but this would help her to make an early start the next morning. Harry declined her offer of a drink and she then sat next to him on the sofa.

"It's not just breaking the rules that's the problem. I've never arranged my own investigation; I've only ever worked under the direction of Stafford."

"So, you don't know how to go about this?"

"No."

"You need to speak to one of your colleagues."

"Agreed but who?"

"Obviously I don't know them, but it's got to be someone you can really trust?"

Fran immediately narrowed it down to three choices; James, Clara or Andy.

James was a bit too high up the food chain as a detective inspector. Fran would feel more comfortable in confiding to someone who was the same rank as her. There was also the emotional situation between them that would be tricky as well.

Clara was of the same rank and a good reliable friend. However, Fran decided that she would probably be too uncomfortable with the rule-breaking aspect of the plan.

Fran concluded therefore that Andy would be her best bet. He was also trustworthy but was more likely to ride along with something that was completely against the book. As it was Saturday night, she could not be sure that Andy would be available or sober. This was a chance she would have to take.

Fran speed-dialled Andy on her mobile, there were several rings but no answer. She feared it would cut to an answerphone message, but he picked up just in time.

"Hey Fran."

"Andy, do you have a few minutes?"

"Yeah sure, I was just having a Hitchcock film night. It's OK, I can watch this woman get stabbed in the shower another time. What's up?"

Fran went silent as she was not sure where or how to begin.

"Hello?" said Andy who wondered if he had lost signal.

"Sorry Andy, ermm…"

"Are you OK Fran?"

"Well…I'm a bit overwhelmed to be honest. Andy, I think I've worked out how the murder of Marianne was committed?"

"But Fran, the case is closed."

"Yeah, I know, but come on there was no way it was suicide. There's a murderer out there."

"Agreed but we can't do anything about this?"

"You can't, you could lose your job but I'm about to leave anyway."

Andy went silent for a moment.

"I'm not going to ask you to get involved, Andy, I just need some advice," Fran continued.

"OK Fran, but first of all, how do you think the murder was committed?"

Fran explained her theory to Andy.

"Yes…yes, brilliant, that makes perfect sense," said Andy sincerely.

"So, what do I do Andy?"

"Sorry to give you a boring old chestnut but you need to find evidence."

"Mmm…actually yes, there is one way. It's a long shot and it wouldn't be absolute proof. However, it could show if someone was at least heading towards Marianne's house on the night before she died."

"That would be a start, what's the plan?"

"I'm going to visit Stuart Larkin. He might just have a film that I need."

Fran felt it was too late to make another call, so she went to bed. This extraordinary situation would make sleep virtually impossible. However, Fran relaxed her body as best as she could to restore some energy.

Early the next morning, Fran remembered that she did not have Stuart Larkin's phone number. Stafford had made the arrangements for the previous interview with him. She could turn up unannounced, but she suspected his carer would want some notice. Stuart might otherwise get anxious by an unexpected intrusion. Fran decided that she should get the number and ring first, but that would mean going into the office. She realised that as soon as she swiped through into her workplace it would automatically be recorded. However, if anyone asked, she could just pretend that she had left something behind and had only gone there to collect it. Fran knew where to find Stuart Larkin's phone number and it would not take long to get it.

She quickly walked to work but then a thought occurred to her. She knew it would seem a bit strange if she turned up outside Stuart's property in her own car. Fran eventually settled on a plan where she would park her vehicle a small distance away from the bungalow where it would not be seen.

Fran went to the office and retrieved the required number. She called Stuart's landline and thankfully got straight through to the carer on duty. After Fran explained why she was calling, a somewhat distracted sounding man said he could not give his permission for her to use the film. He felt that Fran should come over to explain to Stuart in person why she needed it. The carer explained that Stuart does not like speaking on the phone. An arrangement was then made for her to visit him at 12 noon, just before his Sunday lunch. This would buy Fran a couple of hours to work a few things out.

Fran wanted to get all the evidence required today so she could challenge Stafford's decision about the case. This conversation would have to be done the very next day as she would then be leaving her job. Fran reasoned that if she did find what she was looking for, it would be compelling enough to force him to reconsider his verdict. She was prepared for the reprimand she would undoubtedly receive for breaking police procedures. Fran quickly walked home after what had only been a very brief visit to the office. She then made herself a cup of coffee before calling Andy as she really needed his advice. Fran confirmed to Andy that she had arranged to meet Stuart. She then moved onto discussing her dilemma.

"Alright, I've got to find out whether Stuart was filming for owls the night before Antony's wake. And if he was, I would then have to explain to him why I need to see his film even though the case is closed."

"Mmm, yeah that is a tough one, but I agree. Somehow, you've got to get old Bill Oddie to hand over the bird footage!"

"We'll have to come up with something quickly, Andy, as I'm seeing him at noon."

An awkward conversation followed, there seemed no easy explanation for Fran asking for the film. It would be quite incredulous to say the case was reopened just a couple of weeks after it had been very publicly closed. Eventually, Fran had an idea, but she was a little unsure about it.

"Maybe I could pretend that our investigations raised the suspicion of illegal activity taking place in the adjacent fields on that night. We therefore need the film to see what happened," Fran suggested.

"OK…well, to be honest it's a bit weak but, damn it, I can't come up with anything better."

Fran checked her watch and sighed.

"Andy, I'm due to meet him in about an hour and a half. Look, if you do come up with a better idea, call me, otherwise I'll just have to go with that story."

The phone call then ended and she got changed into her work uniform. This was partly because she wanted to appear official to Stuart when she went to his home. It would also help her to get into the detective constable zone. Fran hoped that neither Stuart nor his carer would realise that if this really was an official visit, there would be another police officer present. The prospect of doing all this alone was uncomfortable, but she would have to just push herself. Fran then went upstairs as she wanted to discuss her situation with Harry.

Harry realised that aside from the obligatory coffee, Fran could also do with a sweet treat. He therefore gave her a few of his delicious Belgian chocolates. Fran then explained her plan to him and he listened carefully.

"I know it's a lame excuse, but damn it, if he does have a film then I've got to have it as that's the only way I can get some evidence," said Fran.

"Yeah, but how do you know that film is even going to show the road?"

"I don't, it's a chance I'll have to take."

There was not much further conversation, but Fran remained in Harry's flat as she simply did not want to be alone. Time tantalisingly ticked towards the moment she would have to leave and drive straight into an enormous uncertainty. Fran wished to God that someone else, Andy, Clara, James or anyone could just go there and get the film for her. However, she knew it had to be her. She had the liberty of only having one working day left so effectively had nothing to lose. Fran may end up with a poor reference from Stafford, but she reckoned this was probably going to happen anyway. She glanced at her watch and realised she had to go. Fran then nipped back into her flat to pick up a memory stick before driving off.

TACTFUL PERSUASION

On the way to Stuart Larkin's bungalow, Fran drove past the blind spot near Jessop's Green station where her family were killed. She briefly reflected on their fatal car accident. After all this time, she doubted that she would ever find out the identity of the reckless driver who caused it. Fran then focussed her mind back onto the visit she was about to make.

She arrived promptly at Stuart Larkin's bungalow. Fran doubted whether she could convincingly carry off the pretence of an investigation into fictitious activity in a nearby field. However, she now had no choice but to take the risk. Fran knocked on the front door and waited impatiently. A young, gaunt and somewhat vacant looking man dressed in jeans and a black T-shirt answered.

"Oh hello," he said almost apathetically.

"I'm Detective Constable Fran Jacobs, I've come to speak to Stuart."

"Aren't there supposed to be two officers for this sort of thing?"

Fran was already highly anxious, but this question propelled her into a 'fight or flight' mentality.

"Yes, that would normally be the case but unfortunately my colleague has just been called away on an emergency," Fran swiftly lied.

The young man seemed convinced by Fran's fictional statement and showed her into the lounge. Stuart Larkin was sitting down and inevitably reading a book about owls. Fran noticed that his beard was bushier and even more unkempt than at their previous meeting.

"Hello Stuart."

Stuart did not respond immediately, but eventually he acknowledged the police presence and put his book down.

"This time, I don't want to interview you. I've actually come to ask a favour."

He appeared a little puzzled by this idea.

"Now, you may have heard on the news that the investigation into the death of your neighbour has the verdict of suicide."

Stuart gave a simple nod of acknowledgment. Fran took a moment to brace herself for the outrageous lie she was about to tell. She could not believe what she was about to say, she just prayed that Stuart would.

"You see, the thing is Stuart, although that case is closed, something else has recently come to light. Our investigations have revealed some new evidence. It would appear that illegal activity took place in the field across from your home on the night before Marianne's death. So, to clarify, this was the night of Thursday 21st September."

Stuart's facial expression instantly became a veritable oil painting of confusion.

"What…errm…illegal…what….what illegal activity?"

Fran had no answer for this, she could not think of anything resembling a credible lie so instead she opted for a professional bluff.

"Unfortunately, I'm not at liberty to divulge that information, but I promise you it's a serious matter or I wouldn't be here."

"But what's this…got to…errrm…ermm…got to do with me?"

"Well, when I was here last time, I heard someone say that you sometimes film owls overnight. The reason I'm here today is to ask you if you were filming on that particular night?"

There was a pause, Fran felt as though her heart was going to burst clean out of her chest as she waited for Stuart to answer.

"Maybe…but…look…you…you've got to understand…no-one goes…in that field…except me and…"

At this moment, Stuart pointed to his right. Fran realised this represented his former neighbours Marianne and Antony.

"…And they're both…"

Stuart then made a crude cutthroat gesture to signify that they had both died.

"I know it seems strange, Stuart, but trust me I do have a very good reason to see your film," Fran countered. She felt relieved to finally say something that was actually true.

"Why can't you…you…you tell me…what this is all about?"

Fran realised he was not going to give in easily and so dug in for a battle.

"Stuart, there are very strict laws on what the police can divulge to members of the public. Trust me, it really is for your protection that I must withhold that information."

"But you're not making any sense."

Fran noted how Stuart had lost his stutter with the last statement.

"To be honest, even if I did tell you I don't think you'd believe me. Between us two I'm onto something that's very unusual."

Stuart frowned again and was silent. It soon became obvious he was going to need prompting.

"Well Stuart?" Fran gestured with her hand to gently signal that she wanted him to answer her request. She could sense that he was deciding whether he would allow her access to the film. Her investigation hinged on this moment, but she said nothing. Instead, her eyes desperately pleaded to him like a starving child asking for food.

"Oh…go on then…it's on…" said Stuart who did not finish his sentence.

"His computer in his bedroom," said Stuart's carer who had been listening silently to the whole conversation.

"Thank you, I really appreciate it."

Stuart then led Fran to his bedroom and switched on his computer. She waited anxiously as he opened the subject folder that contained his many night owl films. He had only said "maybe" when asked if he had filmed on the night in question. This created a niggling uncertainty in Fran's mind. The films were all saved with the date in the title. Everyone one of them was placed in chronological order. Fran searched meticulously but there was no title containing the right date. Eventually, Fran was forced to give up and she put her head in her hands in utter despair.

This was it, the end of the line, her enquiry was over. She still had her theory about how the murder was committed. However, without proof that someone was actually there on the night it was useless. After thanking Stuart, Fran traipsed dejectedly through the hallway and opened the front door ready to leave. She was about to walk away from Stuart's bungalow and her whole investigation when a thought suddenly came to her. Fran then turned round and went back into Stuart's bedroom where he was still sitting at his computer.

"Sorry Stuart, just one final thing. Am I right in thinking that you would have downloaded these files from your camera to your computer?"

Stuart nodded his head to confirm.

"Just so we cover all bases, can you go to the downloads folder of your computer for me, please?"

Stuart co-operated and accessed this folder immediately. Fran looked carefully through the various downloads that he had there. She scrolled down the dates of the downloads. Eventually she came across a film that was downloaded at around noon of the day Marianne had died. Stuart had clearly forgotten to transfer the film over to his night owl folder as it remained untitled.

"Do you mind opening this file please, Stuart?"

Stuart opened the file and the film appeared on the screen. Thankfully, it had been shot in suitable 'night vision'. It showed a view of the old barn where he had clearly hoped an owl would fly over to and land. The trajectory of the shot meant that the road was clearly visible at the bottom of the screen. In the top right-hand corner was the date and time, 10.35pm on Thursday 21st September. This confirmed it was indeed taken from the night before Marianne's death. It was perfect, exactly what Fran needed. To her considerable surprise and delight, Fran's investigation could now continue.

AN ENDURANCE TEST

Fran swiftly saved the film file from Stuart's computer onto her memory stick. She thanked him for his co-operation and she sincerely meant it. Fran then left through the front door and when she got outside sunshine streamed down from the heavens. She walked quickly down the road to her car. The small electronic device that contained the critical night film was safely secured in her pocket.

The drive home was full of picture postcard scenery. This was accompanied by relaxing tunes seeping out of the speakers to caress Fran's ears. On her previous trips she had not really taken in the beautiful surroundings as she was too preoccupied with the case. However, as she was now in a much more relaxed state of mind, she could savour the splendour. She picked a route between the hills on an empty twisting road. Fran felt she was moving in a positive direction, spiritually as well as physically.

When she got home, Fran took out her laptop, placed it on the table and switched it on. Fran reflected that she now had a chance to solve the crime. It was still only possible rather than probable, but realistically she could not have hoped for more. Fran took out the memory stick and slotted it into the USB port. A yellow square loaded up in the middle of her screen, Fran double clicked into it. She then scrolled down to the untitled film that she knew contained the night footage. Fran settled herself down to absolutely concentrate on the screen. She double clicked on the file and waited for it to load up...but it was not to be. Instead, an error message popped up on her screen.

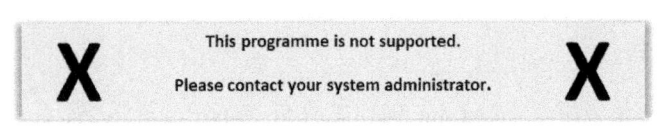

> **X** This programme is not supported.
> Please contact your system administrator. **X**

Fran curled her hand into a fist and banged it firmly on the table. She tried rebooting but to no avail as she kept getting the same result. Fran grew increasingly frustrated and felt like reprogramming her laptop with a hammer.

The peaceful serenity of her car journey had pretty much disappeared into the ether. She was dealing with the nuts and bolts of tedious technical issues and it was proving impossible. Eventually, she called Andy who talked her through downloading several programmes based on Google searches. It took an excruciating hour to find something that would support the film file. Finally, when she was on the verge of giving up, she downloaded one albeit at an annoyingly expensive cost.

Fran opened the film file using the newly downloaded programme, *please God* she silently prayed. There was a tantalising few moments where she just saw an empty screen, but it eventually loaded up successfully. She could now see a view of the road with the date and time in the top right-hand corner. Relief then instantly massaged her whole body. It was like a masseur was rubbing her down with sensual fingertips. Fran was then ready to concentrate on the film.

Fran skipped an hour on the timeline to see if the camera angle changed. She was pleased to see it was still focussed on the same shot. She checked several other points during the film's duration but the view did not alter one iota, it was therefore a static shot. Fran noted that the end time showed 5 hours 27 minutes and 13 seconds. She was conscious that this marathon slog would require her total and undivided attention. If a car did go past, it would do so in literally a second. Meticulous diligence would be essential.

Fran decided to watch the film in short 30-minute sections. She reckoned this would make it easier to maintain a high level of concentration. Having settled on her approach, Fran pressed play and began watching. This was no popcorn movie, the monotony of the still shot soon became irritating. Fran stuck with it and was determined to remain focussed. It was excruciatingly hard work and the minutes slipped by slowly, agonisingly slowly. By the end of her first viewing session, Fran felt like she had metamorphosed into a zombie.

There was nothing for it, so, once again, she drank an extra strong coffee. It was the only way Fran could get the energy to stick to the task. The second viewing session was even more tedious than the first and the one after that was somehow worse. There was no sign of a car and this lonely pursuit was proving too much for her. Fran then decided that, as it was now late afternoon, she would order a takeaway. She knew a couple of places that delivered food all day on a Sunday.

Fran flicked through various take away menu options on her mobile phone for her early dinner. It needed to be delivered quickly, contain an obscene amount of calories and be totally unhealthy. Thankfully, her local kebab joint ensured all three requirements were satisfied. Fran munched on the greasy grub gratefully. It then occurred to her that she had eaten more junk food in the last month than she had in the previous year. She reasoned that this extraordinary case justified a temporary alteration to her diet. However, she promised herself that when it was over, she would then eat salad for a few weeks.

After finishing her meal, Fran returned to the film and finally saw something to break the monotony. A beautiful tawny owl flew in and landed on the barn. This was just what Stuart Larkin was looking for but unfortunately it was of absolutely no use to Fran. She continued watching but stuck to her routine of taking a break every 30 minutes. After watching five soul-destroying hours of the film, Fran was convinced that her hunch was wrong. She was certain that no-one had driven up to Marianne's house on that night. Dark despair washed over her and negative thoughts presented themselves as the objective truth.

After a brief break, Fran then settled down for what would be the final viewing session. When there was 10 minutes left, Fran was tempted to immediately stop watching. She wanted to save herself from the humiliation of watching until the bitter end. It seemed positively stupid to continue but something, pure insanity perhaps, persuaded her to keep going.

When there were only 10 seconds to go, Fran found herself giving a countdown. It was as if there was a spaceship about to blast off. The final few seconds ticked by and *hang on* thought Fran as the film finally ended. She reckoned it was just a case of wishful thinking, but she could have sworn she saw something move. Just to satisfy her curiosity she played the last 10 seconds again. She then realised it was not her imagination, something *definitely did* go past about two seconds before the end. Fran played and replayed this moment until eventually she was satisfied that the moving object was indeed a car.

After her deep depression, Fran was instantly catapulted up to euphoric elation. The vehicle had to be travelling to Marianne's house as this was at the end of the cul-de-sac. However, as the film was shot in 'night vision', it was hard to determine the make or model.

Fran then moved onto the next logical stage in the process which was to identify the registration number. She proceeded to play this very short extract repeatedly, almost frame by frame. She wanted to get to the moment where she could see the licence plate but this was an arduous challenge. The best angle was the split second where the car had almost gone past. This was when you could just see the rear end of the vehicle sticking out. It took numerous attempts, but Fran eventually paused the perfect image on her screen. She then zoomed in to try and read the letters and numbers, but they were not quite legible.

Fran then phoned Andy on her mobile and he answered almost immediately. She was mightily relieved by his quick response as she really did not want to wait for a call back.

"Hey Andy, there *was* a car driving up to the house on that night – I've just seen it on the film!"

"Great work Fran."

"Thanks, but there's one problem, the registration number is not clear."

"Ah!"

"It's OK, I'm sure our IT team could probably get a better image. Who can I call about this?"

"If I were you, I'd go for James."

"Yeah but…" Fran stopped herself in mid-sentence. She did not want to explain to Andy the reason why this would be awkward.

"Is there a problem, Fran?"

"Oh, I just feel bad dragging him into all of this."

"Under these exceptional circumstances, I'm sure he'll understand."

"I guess so. Alright I will make the call."

"Let me know how it goes."

"I will do, bye."

Fran then released the line and dreaded the next call she had to make.

IDENTIFYING THE MURDERER

Fran had hoped to have minimal contact with the Detective Inspector before saying goodbye to him forever. Fran took a few minutes to work out exactly what she would disclose. She then fought against her emotional discomfort to carry out the simple act of speed dialling him.

"Hello, Fran." said James who was clearly surprised.

"Hello, James."

"What's occurring?"

There was a long silence, Fran was struggling to speak as she was so intimidated. She had completely forgotten the script she had mentally written.

"I'm not sure how to tell you this…"

"Why, what's happened?"

Fran noticed the background noise had suddenly gone. James had clearly walked into another much quieter room.

"Alright, something's obviously upset you, take your time," said James, who was at least trying to give reassuring empathy.

"James, I never accepted that Marianne committed suicide by poisoning herself, so I did my own investigation."

"You did what!?"

"I did my own investigation."

"Come on, when a case is closed, it's closed, that's it, you move on."

"But I couldn't accept the outcome. I figured that, as I'm leaving on Monday, I'd just have a go at investigating the case myself."

James audibly sighed down the phone, he was clearly annoyed. He had instantly ditched the empathetic approach.

"But it's come up trumps. I've found a film that shows a car approaching Marianne's house the night before the murder."

"Oh Fran, you don't know what you're getting yourself into."

"I just had to do this!"

"Damn it…have you told anyone about your investigation?"

"No, you're the first person I've spoken to," Fran lied instinctively.

"Well, that's something, alright now just sit tight, I'll come over and see you."

"You don't have to do that."

"Look, this is not something we can do over the phone. I'll be there in about twenty minutes. In the meantime, don't talk to anyone about this."

The phone call ended and Fran immediately called Andy.

"Hi Andy, I spoke to James, he's on his way to see me."

"To see you?"

"Yeah, I know, I thought we'd just work it out over the phone."

A thought then struck Fran.

"Andy, I'm probably just going off on one, but there's something I want you to do for me."

They talked for a few more minutes and then Fran decided she had to go. She then waited with an overwhelming sense of dread for James to arrive. The uncomfortable feelings she had about him returned with a vengeance. Fran knew that somehow she had to ride it all out for the sake of solving the crime and catching the murderer. She made herself another coffee, she wanted something stronger but felt she had to stay sober to do the work required. Fran did not know whether to stand or sit. Eventually she elected to pace around hoping the movement would somehow shake off her anxiety. And then there was a knock on the door.

Fran froze for a few seconds, but then let go of her fear just enough to let James in. He was dressed in black trousers, black T-shirt and a black jacket. Fran gave a falsely polite smile as James walked with her into the lounge. She sat down on the sofa, but he remained standing. The mood was a world away from the last time he was in her flat.

"Fran, why the hell have you done this? What made you think you could suddenly solve the crime?"

"Because we overlooked the key evidence."

"What *'key evidence'*?"

"*Literally* a key. You see, we decided the poisoning had to be done at the wake because there was no sign of a break-in. However, if you have a key, you can obviously just let yourself in."

"Yeah, but her son Kevin is the only one who has a spare key."

"And his house was broken into the night before the wake. Don't you see what's happened, James? Whoever did this, broke into Kevin's house which was not secure and got the spare key. They then drove over to Marianne's home to poison her sherry. Afterwards they returned the key back to Kevin's house before leaving again. Hence Kevin woke up the next morning to find that there had been a break-in but inexplicably nothing was stolen."

James took a few moments to consider Fran's idea before replying.

"But Fran this is pure conjecture, you've got no proof."

"Not proof but I have a film here, James. It proves that someone was driving towards Marianne's house in the middle of the night in question. There's nothing else up there, so if we can verify who the driver was then they will have a hell of a job explaining themselves."

James listened carefully and was clearly considering his next words.

"Fran, please, this is all on the back of an unauthorised investigation. Now, for God's sake, delete the film. I will pretend that we never had this conversation."

"I'm not doing that, James."

"You've *got to*."

"Why have I *'got to'*? What can Stafford do? Tomorrow is my final day so if he fires me, I will just finish a day early, it's no big deal."

James pleaded with his eyes, but Fran remained resolute and shook her head firmly.

"There's a murderer out there James, and I just know it was the person driving that car."

James slumped into Fran's armchair with his head bowed down. A few unpleasant silent minutes slipped past where neither party could look at each other. Eventually James decided that a new approach was required.

"OK, let's have a look at the film."

Fran opened her laptop and cued up the image for him to see. The detective inspector stared hard at the screen and then he returned his gaze back to Fran.

"No, it's too unclear an image," James said dismissively.

"What! Come on James, you know what our IT guys can do. They've had much worse images than that."

James grimaced and Fran then continued assertively.

"We're going to catch the murderer James, bring them to justice."

Fran then went off into a trance as she considered who the murderer could be?

Was it Graham; Marianne's ex-lover who paid dearly for his adultery with her?

Was it Julie; Graham's wife who Marianne caught having an affair with another man that Graham knew?

Was it Mary; Barry's wife, the care home manager who lied about the death of one of her clients?

Was it Barry; the athletics manager who had a drug cheat athlete in his club?

Was it Sue; the sister of Barry and Graham who pretended to sing at gigs but was actually just lip-synching over a backing track?

All of them had been blackmailed by Marianne. All of them therefore had a motive. All of them knew that Kevin was the only person with a spare key.

Fran could not decide which one committed the murder. However, she was now confident that the identity of the car owner and, ipso facto the murderer, would soon be revealed. James looked deeply distressed and wandered around the room aimlessly.

"I need a drink," he finally declared.

In that moment Fran decided to give up her plan of staying stone cold sober. She poured them both a generous measure of brandy. It quickly warmed their throats and gave some relief in this crazy situation. Fran briefly looked outside her window at the early evening sunset. She then turned to face James once more.

"Oh my God, I really don't want to get involved in this crap," said James.

"Look, if you feel so uncomfortable, I'll just pass it to the tech guys and pretend we never spoke."

"Fran, I can't let you do that."

"Why?"

"Well…apart from anything else, there's no need."

"What do you mean 'there's no need'?

"I know whose driving that car."

Fran struggled to comprehend what she had just heard.

"Excuse me?"

"I *know* who's driving that car," James repeated.

"How can you possibly know that? The film is in night vision, you can only just make out the shape of the damn thing."

"Just trust me, I *do* know."

"I don't get it."

"I can't explain, all I can tell you is that you need to delete that film right now."

"No!"

"Please Fran, this is for your protection."

"What do you mean, 'my protection'?"

"You're going to have to trust me. As I know who the driver is, I will get Stafford to lead the direction towards…that person. But you really must delete the film."

"Don't be stupid, James, you will need the film for evidence."

"Oh just delete the bloody thing Fran!"

"No! What is wrong with you?"

"Fran, you don't understand…"

"Have you got some kind of connection with the murderer?" Fran asked suspiciously.

"Don't go there."

"Are you under some kind of pressure? James, we can help you."

"There's only one way you can help me and that's by deleting the film."

"I just *can't* do that," Fran said emphatically.

James again pleaded with his eyes, but Fran remained stony-faced. He then gave a facial expression of surrender. Fran sensed she could now press forward to get the information she wanted.

"Now…if you honestly do know then tell me. Just tell me, James, tell me what I want to know; who is driving the car?"

James then braced himself for what he was about to say and do.

"Me!"

And then, in a flash, he pulled out a gun from his jacket pocket and pointed it at Fran.

ON A LIFE EDGE

Fran stared in silence at the weapon that was now being directed towards her chest. She was not actually afraid of the extreme threat that she now faced. It was so overwhelming that her sense of reality cut out. This released her from what would have been a terror like she had never known. It was like she was in a dream except her eyes were wide open.

"When I said, 'you don't know what you're letting yourself in for', I meant it!", James continued.

"James, why are you holding me at gunpoint?" Fran said coldly.

"Isn't it bloody obvious, Fran?"

Fran said nothing so James then continued.

"I'll give you full detective marks for your correct deduction. I carried out the murder exactly as you described it. I got the poison from a criminal contact I made. He owes me a favour as I overlooked his crimes. I knew Marianne and her habit of having a sherry aperitif every evening. I also found out the date of her husband's wake. Hence, I put the poison in the sherry bottle the night before knowing that Marianne would drink it that evening. This would make it appear that one of the guests at the wake must have poisoned the sherry."

"But we could have arrested an innocent person."

"No, you were never going to find any evidence on any of the guests because there was no evidence to find. And there was no way you'd get evidence linking me to her murder. I made sure of this by wearing full protective clothing when I poisoned the sherry. Consequently, there would be no fingerprints or anything else incriminating left behind."

"Why did you do this, James? What has Marianne ever done to you?" Fran asked.

"She's done nothing to James Mallen, but remember...I used to be somebody else."

It took a few moments, but Fran eventually worked out what James was referring to.

"Your deed poll name change. Wait a second...*Martin*...you're the 'Martin' that Marianne was blackmailing. Of course, that's why you said that we should not pursue him...or should I say *you*."

After a moment's pause, something else occurred to Fran so she continued.

"It also explains why you dismissed my idea of the crime being committed the night before the wake."

"You're putting the pieces together. Yes, I was keen for everyone to focus the investigation purely on the day of the wake. Just to explain, I had my name changed to give me a new lease of life after I...did what I did."

"What did you do?"

James seemed a little reluctant to answer at first, but decided that as he had been found out to be a murderer then he may as well confess.

"Years ago, I caused a fatal car accident because I was drunk."

"And presumably Marianne was blackmailing you for this. How did she find out?"

"Because she was in the car with me! You see, I had an affair with her too. This happened a year before she began keeping her journal. That's why, immediately after you guessed the password, I checked the date of the first entry to make sure."

"Oh my God, James!"

"I never told her my new name, but she still knew what I had done, as well as where and when I did it. For years I felt that I only had two choices, to continue paying the money or risk a prison sentence. It's only recently that I started to consider the third option…"

"Killing Marianne."

"Yes."

"But how come you've waited all these years then?"

"Taking a human life is not something I would do lightly. It took me a long time before I truly accepted that the world would be better off without Marianne. You see, recent events finally persuaded me that I was justified to kill her. Also, as my marriage is failing, I knew I would need more money for the alimony after the divorce. Now, that's enough questions, delete that film and then empty your deleted folder. I want to make sure it's completely removed from your laptop."

Fran carried out this task without question as she did not want to risk a fatal consequence.

"Have you emailed this file onto someone?"

"No."

"Mmm…I'm not going take your word for it, let me see your emails, both work and personal."

Fran again obeyed the instruction immediately. The inbox and sent folders for both her work and personal emails were checked. Eventually James was satisfied with this and Fran folded down her laptop on his instruction. Five excruciating minutes then passed in total silence. James was clearly contemplating something, eventually he spoke to give the verdict.

"It's no good Fran, you've left me with no choice."

It was as this moment that the terror, which Fran had pushed to the back of her mind, began to overwhelm her.

"James…*please* don't…"

"Why did you have to investigate this? All you had to do is what any other normal person would have done in your situation. Serve out your notice, do a half-arsed job and then leave."

James stared at Fran in utter despair before continuing.

"But no, you had to stick your nose into something that had nothing to do with you."

There was another terrifying silence, and in her panic, Fran was tempted to try and jump out of the window. However, she quickly realised this would only result in her being shot.

"You see, I can't rely on you to keep this to yourself," James continued.

"But James, after all we've been through…doesn't that count for anything?"

"Not enough for me to spend years in prison."

"I won't tell anyone about this."

"Oh, *you will* Fran, you couldn't live with allowing a murderer like me to get away with it, even though I only murdered another murderer. You would snitch, your sense of duty will make you grass me up."

"I won't, I won't, I won't…"

"You will, you *know* you will. There's only way I can stop you."

James cocked his gun. Fran knew there was only one other option, one final thing she could say, it was literally do or die.

"You're being recorded," Fran said loudly and clearly.

James looked totally nonplussed by this comment. He slightly lowered his gun whilst he tried to take on board what Fran had just said.

"*You're being recorded*, James," Fran repeated to emphasise the point.

"Don't try and trick me."

Fran pulled out her mobile phone from her pocket. She then held the phone out so James could see the ticking timer that showed the call had now lasted over 20 minutes. At the top of the display was the name 'Andy'. It was also set to speakerphone mode meaning every word of the conversation had been heard.

"I knew something wasn't right when we spoke on the phone. So that's why I got Andy to listen in and record our conversation. 'Why are you holding me at gunpoint?' was a stupid question, of course. I only asked that to make it clear to Andy what you're doing."

"Andy…as in our detective constable?"

"Yes. Andy, are you still there?" Fran called out.

"Yes, I'm still here, Fran," Andy said loud and clear.

"Are you still recording this conversation?"

"Yes, it's all been recorded on my laptop."

"Oh, and how can he do that?" James asked.

"I have a sound recording programme and I also have a computer microphone. This call is being played out through my speaker phone. Subsequently, every word is being recorded."

"And have the police been contacted?" Fran asked.

"Absolutely. I sent a group text to the whole unit and Clara texted back to say she's called them. They will be there at any moment."

"No, you're just bluffing!" James interjected.

At which point a voice from outside was heard and it was amplified through a powerful megaphone.

"James Mallen, this is the police, we have the place surrounded, come out with your hands up!"

James looked startled and Fran noticed he was distracted. She realised this was her one and only chance. Fran dropped her mobile phone and lunged forward to put both her hands on his gun to point it away from her.

"Come in now!" she screamed at the very top of her voice.

James then physically overpowered Fran and threw her against the sofa. He aimed his gun at her and she closed her eyes expecting immediate death.

"Drop it!" bellowed one of the marksmen who had just burst through into the lounge. He was now holding James at gunpoint using a semi-automatic weapon. James then realised that he would not be able to turn and shoot this man. If he tried, James would be immediately shot, so he dropped his gun defeatedly. A few moments later he was arrested, handcuffed and bundled into one of the police cars waiting outside. Fran peered from her window to watch him being driven away.

"Hello, hello, Fran are you still there?" said Andy through Fran's mobile that was still on speakerphone. Fran walked over and picked up her phone.

"Yeah, I'm here, Andy."

"Oh, thank God."

Fran had a brief conversation with him. She found it hard to say anything intelligible as she was on such an emotional edge. Several crime scene officers remained in Fran's home. Fifteen minutes later Stafford pulled up outside Fran's property and quickly walked in.

"What the hell happened Fran?" Stafford asked firmly.

"Well sir, I'm afraid our detective inspector is a murderer."

Stafford was shocked and almost motionless as he absorbed this statement.

"How did you find this out?"

"I did my own investigation."

"You did what!?"

"Sir, it was just something I had to do."

"I see…OK, well, talk to me, how did you find out that James committed the crime?"

Fran then explained how she got the film and what it revealed. She also explained how James came over to her home, held her at gunpoint and eventually admitted that he was Marianne's murderer.

"My God!" Stafford said after hearing this extraordinary tale.

Harry then came down and knocked on Fran's door as he was naturally very worried about her and wondered what had happened. Stafford then assured him that the situation was now under control. After Harry went back to his flat, Stafford sat down in Fran's armchair and stared vacantly at the wall. Eventually, he decided on what the next course of action should be.

"Fran, do you think you can face James in an interview room?"

She was torn, she wanted to see this case through to its logical conclusion. On the other hand, Fran really did not want to see James's face ever again.

"I know this would be very hard for you, but you're the best interviewer I've got."

Fran noted the rare compliment from Stafford and in that instant, she made her decision.

"Alright sir, I'll do it."

Fran was still dressed in her police uniform. She had been so absorbed by her secret investigation that she never thought to take it off. This was fortunate as she was required to wear it for the forthcoming interview. When Stafford and Fran arrived at their Head Office building, James was being held in a police cell.

James had used his one permitted phone call to ring his lawyer. It was clear that he would not say a word in an interview unless this person was present. Stafford was informed that it would take at least an hour for the legal professional to arrive. Fran used this time to properly calm herself down from the life-threatening situation that had taken place in her flat. She considered what questions she would ask and tried to predict what James might say.

Thirty minutes later, Andy also arrived as a police car had been dispatched to pick him up. He brought his laptop with him as it contained the vital evidence of the recorded interview. Stafford played a brief extract of the interview and was pleased with the sound quality. He then listened to the full recording and made notes, Fran did likewise. Stafford and Fran were now good to go for the interview, but they were still waiting for James's lawyer to arrive. Fran got frustrated, she just wanted to get this damned thing over and done with. Stafford turned to Andy who was sitting at a computer nervously sipping a glass of water.

"I'll get that dispatch car to take you home Andy. There's no point in you being here now."

Andy gave an acknowledging nod to Stafford and then turned to Fran with concern written clearly on his face.

"Are you going to be OK, Fran?"

"Don't worry, I'll be fine." Fran replied although she was not sure if she was telling the truth.

Andy then went home leaving Fran with her superior. As they were both ready for the interview neither knew what to say to the other. Fran was relieved that this would be the last time she had to do anything with Stafford except her exit interview. Tomorrow, her final working day, would no doubt consist of relatively straight forward admin tasks. She was confident that she could waltz through that easily enough.

It was just after 9.30pm when the lawyer finally arrived. He introduced himself as 'Mr Simpkins' and apologised for being so long. He was a middle-aged man dressed smartly in a blue tailored suit, a white shirt and a conservative looking brown tie. His years had reduced his hair to just a little curly grey flurry around the lower half of his head. He had striking gold framed glasses that gave a sense of intelligence to his icy blue eyes. Mr Simpkins also wore a serious expression which was appropriate for this situation. One of the police officers doing the night shift took him down to meet his client.

Neither Fran nor Stafford knew how long it would be before they could start the interview with James. This resulted in another awkward silence as both parties were now impatient with the delay. Finally, the police officer who led Mr Simpkins to his client then reappeared with a simple message.

"They're ready for you now."

Fran told herself (in her mind) to just carry out the interview like any other. Tonight, she had learnt that the man she had a fling with is a murderer. However, it was essential that she completely blocked this to be calm, focussed and professional. She picked up Andy's laptop and her notes before following Stafford. They went down the stairs and along a narrow hallway to the interview room where James and his solicitor were waiting.

INTERROGATION

Fran and Stafford walked in assertively and James was sat at a desk with his lawyer right next to him. The room was small with pitch black walls. These were contrasted by the harsh white light that beamed down from the ceiling. A camera was placed high up in a corner and was angled down to get a view of all those present. There was also an audio recording device that was primed ready to capture the words that were spoken.

Stafford and Fran wasted no time in sitting down and the CDI pressed record. He announced the date and time as well as the names of everyone in the room. Whilst he gave his introduction, Fran stared at James who had a neutral almost lifeless facial expression. She could not believe he was indifferent to the severity of this situation. Fran reckoned that he was just drawing on his previous police experience of not showing emotion during interviews. She was equally pokerfaced and just waiting for her cue to begin.

"Detective Constable Jacobs…" Stafford simply said.

"James Mallen, you have been arrested on suspicion of the murder of Marianne Furlow. For the benefit of the tape recording, I am about to play an extract from a recording of a phone conversation that I had with the subject earlier this evening."

Fran then pressed play on the laptop that had been queued up ready. They all listened to the extract together in total silence. It started at the moment where James admitted the vehicle on the film was his car. The extract ended after Fran was asked to delete the film off her laptop. Fran pressed 'stop' and then looked James straight in the eyes.

"Do you deny that this was your voice on the recording?"

James turned to his lawyer before responding.

"I will confirm that it is me on the recording, yes."

"Thank you. Now, on the recording you are clearly heard saying that you murdered Marianne Furlow. Can you please confirm if this is true?"

"No comment," James said dismissively.

"If it is not true then could you explain why you would say such a thing to a detective constable?"

"No comment."

"During the extract you are heard saying that you caused a fatal car accident because you were drunk. Could you elaborate further, please?"

"No comment."

"You also said that Marianne Furlow had blackmailed you, could you give more specific details?"

"No comment."

"OK, let's return to the crime that you are arrested for. You held a detective constable, namely myself, at gunpoint and it required police intervention to diffuse the situation. If your murder confession on the recording is not true, then why would you do that?"

"No comment."

Fran felt the frustration rise within her and this propelled her to ask a somewhat unprofessional question.

"Have you got anything to say other than 'no comment'?"

"No comment." James then gave a sinister smile before continuing.

"Actually no, no I do have another comment to make. I'd like to point out that this interview is compromised because I have had a romantic liaison with the woman interviewing me."

Fran was shocked and deeply wished she had guessed James would have played this card. If she had, then she would have never agreed to carry out this interview. Stafford then sharply turned to face Fran. He was doing his best to stay professional but was clearly unnerved by what he had just heard.

"Is this true?" Stafford calmly asked.

Fran racked her brain for the best damage limiting response possible.

"Romantic liaison is a bit of an exaggeration, sir. We had a few drinks and a bit of affection was shown," Fran replied.

"Oh, very good Fran, just try and play it down. For the record, I was kissing Detective Constable Jacobs in her flat after midnight."

Fran and Stafford were speechless, neither knew how to respond to this. Eventually Fran's superior turned to her once more.

"Did this really happen, Fran?"

Fran again scrambled around in her mind trying to think of a suitable response.

"Well…not for very long!"

"Oh, for God's sake!" Stafford said in despair.

"Yeah, but you're not in a position to judge," said James.

"Excuse me?" replied Stafford sternly.

"You're not in a position to judge Fran."

"What do you mean?"

"I mean you can hardly start judging Fran when you deliberately misled this investigation to ensure I was not caught."

"I beg your pardon!"

"You took a bribe, didn't you?"

"I don't know what you are talking about."

"Oh, but you do know John. You know that I paid you £15,000 to focus the investigation solely on the day of the wake. This way no-one would ever find out it really happened the night before."

"I totally refute that."

"I thought you might, but I have evidence."

James then pulled out his mobile phone from his pocket. The lawyer had made a special request that James could have his phone during the interview as it would be used for evidence.

"No, you don't," said Stafford.

"Let my client play his evidence," Mr Simpkins said assertively.

"For the benefit of the tape recording, I am about to play an extract of a conversation that I secretly recorded on my mobile phone," said James.

He loaded up his recorded file, put his mobile into speaker phone mode and pressed play.

"Look John, I know you are being chased for a debt you owe. I also know some very unpleasant people are chasing you for it. But here's the good news, I can get you £15,000 tomorrow."

"Really, what, as a loan?"

"No, a payment, you won't have to pay me a penny back...but I want something for my money."

"What do you want?"

"Well, it's probably best if I don't go into too much detail. Let's just say I have a vested interest in the murder of Marianne Furlow. For personal reasons, I don't want the murderer to be caught. I can tell you the poison was placed in the sherry bottle the night before the wake. I want you to focus the investigation on everything that happened on the day Marianne died. This should ensure the truth is never revealed. You can be your usual fastidious self with searching the house. You won't find anything, the murderer knows all about investigation procedures and used his knowledge to ensure there would be no incriminating evidence left. Oh, and one other thing, I want you to eventually reach the conclusion of suicide due to there being no proof that anyone else poisoned the sherry."

"Oh God, James, I can't…"

"Look John, if you are having a moral dilemma then let me tell you something. I have a friend who investigated the forensic evidence of this case. He knew Marianne must have pushed her husband off the cliff by the way Antony's body landed. However, without any witnesses, there was not enough evidence to arrest Marianne. You and I have both been in this business long enough to know that there are certain people who really don't deserve to live. I can promise you that Marianne definitely fits into that category."

"Well, I'm not surprised she killed her husband. I know what money can do to people."

"So come on, you don't want to get beaten up by the heavy mob for the sake of catching someone who was a murderer anyway."

"Alright…I'll do it, but make sure you pay me all the cash tomorrow."

The recording then ended and James faced Stafford who was visibly shaking.

"Do you deny it was your voice on the recording?" asked James.

"Alright…I will confirm I am the man you were speaking to," Stafford said defeatedly.

"You see John, I couldn't be sure that you would be true to your word, so the recording was a bit of insurance. However, as I've now been arrested, I'm going to take you down with me. Fran, in light of what you've just heard, you now need to carry out your duty."

It took a few moments for Fran to realise what James meant. She could not believe what she was about to do but knew she was obliged to do it. Fran stopped the recording of the interview and arrested Stafford.

The chief detective inspector was then taken to a cell and James was also returned to his. Superintendent Jamieson was called as this extraordinary situation warranted his immediate presence. Twenty minutes later he arrived and he took Fran into Stafford's office. On Jamieson's insistence, Fran explained everything that had happened. This included her embarrassing dalliance with James. Inevitably the revelations were not well received. Fran had to push herself to tell the whole story without sugar coating any details. Jamieson was not an 'ends justifies means' sort of person so he was angered by what Fran had done.

"Look Fran, you know there are strict procedures and practices in place. You can't just go off and do your own rogue investigation," Jamieson insisted.

"With respect sir, this was an exceptional case that would never have been solved via normal investigative procedures."

"Yes, but what you've done amounts to gross misconduct."

"I solved the crime and we've caught the murderer. We've also got a corrupt chief detective inspector to boot! Does that not count for anything, sir?"

Jamieson did not respond immediately but was silently seething.

"Yes, you solved the crime, but we can't have our officers behaving like this. What kind of precedent would that set?"

"As I said, this was an exception, a one off, sir."

Jamieson did not like what he heard one iota. However, his wealth of experience made him realise the need for pragmatism.

"Alright…I'll take Stafford's place in the interview room as he's err…not available."

"Very good sir."

"Just focus on extracting the information we need."

"Of course, sir"

Fran was still a little shaken from the unbelievable event of arresting her superior. However, she was determined to remain on an even keel. She walked back into the interview room with a sense of purpose. Jamieson took the seat where Stafford had previously sat. James and Mr Simpkins had now both returned to their original seats too. Fran swiftly started the recording and recommenced the interview. Having spoken the preliminaries, she was about to ask a question when Mr Simpkins gestured at her to stop.

"My client has something he wishes to say," Mr Simpkins firmly asserted. It was clear that during the interval James's lawyer had given him further advice on how he should approach the current situation.

"On the advice of my lawyer, I now wish to make a confession regarding the previously mentioned drink driving incident. I drank well over the limit and my judgement was severely impaired by the alcohol. I was driving on the wrong side of the road approaching a blind corner.

Subsequently, I pretty much forced an oncoming car to swerve straight into a large tree. I should have stopped and checked to see if everyone in the car was OK. However, in my drunken and deeply selfish state, I didn't stop and just carried on driving. This car crash resulted in three fatalities."

Fran paused to consider her next question.

"Where did this incident happen?"

"It happened at the blind spot near the railway station just up the road from here" James continued.

"I see. What made you…" Fran abruptly stopped her question.

"Yes..?" James queried.

Fran suddenly started to visibly shake.

"Fran?" Jamieson asked in concern.

"Oh God…oh dear God…no...no, please God, no!" Fran was only just coherent as she was clearly traumatised.

"Fran, what's wrong?" asked Jamieson.

Fran ignored her superior and instead focussed on James.

"And did this happen on Christmas eve in 2006?" Fran asked.

"Yes, how did you know that?" James replied.

An image of Fran's dead family came into her mind.

"You bastard!" Fran screamed.

Fran was incandescent with rage and overturned the table. Superintendent Jamieson had to physically force her out of the room into the adjacent hallway. She briefly explained to him that her family were the ones killed in the accident. Fran then explained in no uncertain terms that she was leaving and never returning. Without so much as a goodbye she stormed out of the building.

And that concluded Fran's career as a detective constable.

REFLECTIONS

Shortly after arriving home, Fran collapsed into her bed exhausted and fell asleep almost immediately. However, during the night, she had several nightmare flashbacks. These were of James holding her at gunpoint and the traumatic interview that followed. The next day she did not get up until lunchtime as she was so drained both physically and emotionally. She went upstairs to see Harry and give him the full story of the previous night's events and this concluded with her overturning the interview room table.

"I've never done anything like that before, I just lost it. I am supposed to be at work now for my final shift but well…I don't think Jamieson would want me to come in after my little performance."

"Come on, Fran, those are really extreme circumstances."

"Yeah, but actually overturning a table."

Harry had a wry smile before he replied.

"Jesus did the same thing."

Fran then smiled too.

"Well yes…except I did it in an interview room instead of a temple."

Shortly afterwards, Fran told him that she needed some time to herself for a while and left. Later that day Clara came to see Fran to give her a leaving card and present. Fran then gave Clara her uniform and her ID badge to take back to the Head Office. This was very much an affirmation that Fran's police career truly was over. In the evening, Andy called her to confirm that both Stafford and James had been charged. Andy also explained that Superintendent Jamieson had contacted Antony Furlow's family to inform them of all the developments. Jamieson felt that it was better that he did this himself rather than the details being leaked out through the media.

The following morning, Fran was expecting to be contacted regarding an exit interview. However, Jamieson was far too busy dealing with the turmoil that had ensued following recent events. No-one in the team could believe what their detective inspector and chief detective inspector had done. As a result, Fran's exit interview slipped through the net. This was highly irregular but then so was the way the Major Crimes Unit had been run. Fran was very grateful as it meant she could make good on her word; she actually never would return.

The next week drifted by peacefully as Fran just relaxed. She had nothing to do but really enjoyed doing nothing. After the extreme nature of recent events, she needed some serious time out. On the following Thursday afternoon, she felt ready for something mildly constructive and went for a walk. Fran arrived at her local lakeside café not long before it was due to close. Whilst cradling a cup of hot chocolate she watched a sunset. The orange sunrays reflecting on the water were truly life affirming.

Fran then realised that although the revelation about James was shocking, within it was something that made her very grateful. For years she had been upset that the driver who caused the death of her family had got away with it. Whereas now, James had been caught and Fran was confident he would be brought to justice. Having settled that in her mind, she then considered what she would do for her future work. She also spent some time addressing some spiritual matters. Everything started to click into place, she had a plan and a vision which uplifted her enormously.

When she returned home, she wasted no time and loaded up Google to start researching. Fran then remembered that Andy's birthday party was scheduled for the following Saturday night, so she sent him a text.

> Thursday, 30 Nov · 17.17
>
> Hi Andy,
>
> Are you still having your birthday party at the Fox & Vixen on Saturday night? x

> Thursday, 30 Nov · 17.18
>
> Yeah Fran. It's from 7.30pm onwards, are you still coming? x

> Thursday, 30 Nov · 17.19
>
> Definitely, I could do with a night out, see you there. x

Fran genuinely did feel this party would be good for her. It had been a long time since she had really let her hair down apart from that crazy night out with James. On Friday, she had a relaxing day and could feel that was she returning to her normal self.

The next day, after buying Andy a birthday card, Fran popped upstairs to see Harry.

"How are you going Fran?" he asked.

"I'm alright, thanks Harry. It's been good to have some time off to put everything into perspective. I've figured out what's important and who is important. You are one of the most important people in my life, Harry. You're always there, you're not too busy, you make time for me. It makes a difference; it *really* makes a difference," said Fran with heartfelt sincerity.

"No worries, Fran. You're the only friend I have so I'll move Heaven and Earth for you."

"Thanks, but I do think you need to meet some other people too."

"It's funny you should say that because I have just joined a book reading group. You're right Fran, as weird and as alternative as I am, I do need to join in with the local community."

"That's great, good for you."

Fran stayed with Harry for another couple of hours and she discussed her future plans with him. She really wanted him to join her tonight but, as he was in his 70s, he was a bit too old to go out partying.

Eventually, Fran left to focus on the delicate operation that was getting ready for a night out. It took a while but eventually she accepted what she saw in the mirror. She then flicked through her wardrobe for dresses and found a glitzy, gold number. It was a touch short, but she decided that as this was a birthday party, she was at liberty to show a bit of leg. She was pleased to find some shoes of a very similar colour and a matching handbag.

Having settled on her outfit she then ordered a taxi. Fran was definitely not going to drive tonight and it was an awkward venue to get to by public transport. The fare would be expensive, but she was armed with a debit card. She could always just do a tap payment whilst looking the other way. The taxi then took her safely to a remote country pub called The Fox & Vixen.

It was a friendly enough place run by a family who valued every drink that was bought. There was a large function room with a dancefloor and this had been hired out for the occasion. Andy said a buffet would be laid on, but Fran was a little unsure as that word covered a multitude of sins. There were 'buffets' where you can easily eat your fill. However, there were also 'buffets' which amounted to little more than peanuts and pork scratchings. Fran was relieved to see a decent selection of both savoury and sweet food, so she would not go hungry. She promised herself that after tonight she actually would eat salad for the next few weeks.

She then saw Andy dressed in black trousers and a screamingly loud shirt. She handed over his birthday card and gave him a peck on the cheek.

"Thanks Fran, but I've got bad news I'm afraid. Brad Pitt just called and he can't make it tonight."

"Oh Andy, I got all dressed up and everything."

"Yeah, these Hollywood celebrities are so unreliable. Actually, for your information, your favourite man is in one of my favourite films."

"Which one?"

"I can't tell you."

"Why can't you tell me?"

"Because the first two rules state I 'can't talk to anybody about it!'"

Fran had a little sip of wine and briefly pondered.

"Fight Club."

"Hallelujah! You finally got one of my film references."

Clara then joined them wearing a much more conservative long purple dress. No-one else from work was present at the party. Fran preferred this as she could focus on her two genuine friends from her former workplace. After a glass of wine and a couple of platefuls of food, she sat down for a catchup chat with Andy and Clara.

"Hey, I do miss you, girl," said Clara.

"Me too," said Andy.

"Thanks, but I just had to get out of there."

"I know but it just seems such a waste. You genuinely do have great detective skills."

"Thanks Andy, but I've actually got a plan. I don't know which position to apply for yet, but I know where I want to work."

Fran took another sip of wine. Clara and Andy both stared at her as they were eager to learn more.

"Never repeat this…" Fran said very seriously. She then mouthed 'MI5' silently, but it was clear enough for Andy and Clara to understand.

"Excellent!" said Andy who was genuinely delighted by the news.

"Yes, but Fran, to do that you've really going to have to…", Clara's sentence ended abruptly.

"It's OK, I know what you're thinking and yes, I am going to have to overcome my self-doubt."

"You do that, girl, fight the good fight," said Clara.

"I know I do have good detective skills."

This statement was quite a step forward for Fran, actually speaking positively about herself. She took a moment before continuing.

"I'm sure these skills are transferrable and can be put to good use there. It's just a case of working out what job would be best for me and what I would need to do to get this job. That won't happen overnight, of course, but I will make it happen somehow."

Clara and Andy smiled warmly and were clearly pleased by her new found confidence.

"How about you Clara, do you have any news?" Fran asked.

"Yes, Brian and Lara have been doing really well in their school indoor cricket matches. They both have a trial for Havantshire's under 11s team. I spoke to Jamieson about my annual leave request. He has granted me the two weeks off that I wanted. HR have pushed it through so next June I'm off to Antigua for my Mum's birthday. Brian and Lara are really excited as Mum said she will show him the house where Viv Richards used to live."

"Viv who?" said Andy.

"Oh, believe me bro, he was a very special cricketer."

Andy then bought Fran another glass of rosé wine and asked if he could have a private word. Fran agreed and they popped outside where the moon and stars lit up the sky like a Van Gogh painting.

"Sorry Fran, but I'm going to have to ask you this. When you spoke to James that night, you said something about 'all that we've been through', can I ask you what happened?"

Fran then told him the full story of her and James despite it still being a point of shame for her.

"Obviously I had no idea what he had done but…I don't know, I guess I just have a weakness for attractive men," Fran concluded.

"I see, I'll make sure I'm very careful around you then."

Fran laughed before taking another sip of wine and Andy had a gulp of his lager too.

"Oh Andy, I'm not sure I'm cut out for this whole 'love' thing. Well, I'm not saying it will never happen, I just don't think I can rely on it. Some people just don't find their soulmates."

"Yeah, but Fran, don't forget it's not always good, sometimes it destroys people. I mean I had a lot of problems with Suzie long before we broke up. Don't think everyone who is in a relationship is happy, that's definitely not true."

"Mmm, I suppose I've got to stop being negative and just make the best of this single life of mine."

"Absolutely, being single is not a crime."

Fran smiled before clinking her wineglass against his pint of lager.

"Oh, and Fran, on the subject of making the best of things. I've decided to move on from my car accident, I'm going to start driving lessons next Wednesday."

"Excellent, Andy!

Fran then gave Andy a hug and immediately after their embrace another thought popped into her mind.

"You know, one other thing I can't help thinking about. If James had started his car journey five seconds later, he would have got away with it. Stuart's film would have ended before we saw James drive up the road. Come to think of it, we would have never realised Stafford was corrupt either."

"Yeah, it's crazy…but so was the whole investigation. Our detective inspector and chief detective inspector both turned out to be criminals. Robbie cashed in big style for the murder information he leaked to the press. You know, with all these bent coppers, we're going to have to get that grumpy Irishman from 'Line of Duty' on the case!"

Fran laughed again, the evening was justifying the expense of her taxi fare.

"I was wrong about one thing though Fran. Do you remember I told you that I didn't think you'd ever arrest any of your colleagues? Well, you actually did, can I ask what that felt like?"

"Weird…I wouldn't recommend it!"

Andy was then called over by some rowdy lads in equally loud shirts. The DJ turned the music up to try and encourage some dancing on the currently empty dancefloor. A fair amount of time had been given for the consumption of alcohol. This is, of course, essential to get British people to dance. It doesn't make them better dancers, but it does help them to overlook their inability. A couple got up and bravely danced alone to the funky disco tunes. This was seen as permission for other people to get down and shake their booty too. Fran went back inside and Clara then came over to see her.

"Hey, Fran, are you having fun?" said Clara who was now projecting her voice so it could be heard over the music.

"Yeah, great!" Fran replied. This was actually the truth instead of a polite British lie. Clara then looked at her watch and was clearly concerned.

"I don't want to stay out too late. I've got to make sure I'm up for church in the morning."

Clara looked Fran deeply in the eyes. Fran braced herself as she knew what question was about to be asked.

"Hey Fran, when are you coming back to church?"

Fran then decided it was time to tell the truth.

"I'm sorry Clara, but I'm not coming back to church or at least not as a regular member."

Clara grimaced and Fran felt she had better explain.

"Church services don't do it for me anymore. You see, deep down, I've been looking for something for years, but I've only recently realised what it is. I want to find and connect with a more progressive spirituality. A spirituality that acknowledges all the pain and suffering and doesn't just brush it all under the carpet. A spirituality that can work alongside the advancement of science. A spiritualty that does not have a dichotomy of believers and non-believers but views us all as one. A spirituality that is in tune with our complex modern world."

Fran took a sip of wine before continuing.

"Now I don't know how all that actually works, but this is what, in my own little way, I want to explore. I'm sorry Clara, I just don't think the church is geared up for this."

Clara was now slightly looking away, so Fran tried to engage her.

"Hey, look, I know you're disappointed that I'm no longer the traditional churchgoing Christian, but can I give you the other side of the coin. I've got a whole load of secular friends who are equally disappointed that I'm not some atheist who believes solely in science. I can't be what I'm not, I am what I am and I have to live my life as that person."

Fran gave her friend a warm smile to try and reassure her.

"I know you don't agree with me but that's OK, we can still be friends. Clara, people have been disagreeing over this subject for thousands of years but please let's not argue…let's just dance."

And with that the two ladies moved onto the dancefloor. They were soon joined by Andy and the three of them danced together. The DJ then played The Pointer Sisters 'Jump for my Love'. After a bit of a persuasion, Andy shimmied like Hugh Grant famously did across an arched hallway in 'Love Actually'. If he had done this move on Strictly Come Dancing, Craig Revel Horwood would have torn him to pieces. However, it was Andy's birthday party, so his efforts were much appreciated by Fran and Clara. They both whooped like a couple of over-excited teenage girls.

Happy pop songs continued to play. Fran really connected with the music and she then felt a positive energy in her soul. For the first time in her living memory, Fran honestly believed that she was not just good enough but, in her own way, beautiful. She was now released, like a butterfly breaking out of the chrysalis and flying freely away. Fran was totally in the moment and love filled her heart like the air in a balloon. She danced and danced and danced, and it was as if the whole world was dancing along with her.

Fran found herself and found all of life too.

Acknowledgements

I would like to thank my 'bestie' and fellow novelist Ruth Masters. Aside from her assistance with the images in the first few pages of the book, she also gave me plenty of encouragement, advice and was there when I needed her.

I would also like to give an enormous vote of gratitude to the undisputed Queen of grammar that is my mother Sheila Card. She spent many hours of painstaking editing with a hawk eye diligence. I am sure this novel would have been of a much poorer quality without all of her hard work.

In addition, a sincere thank you to my natural father Roger Tilley for his support.

Special thanks also go to Tim Hirst, Geoffrey Card, Jamie Stephenson and Thames Valley Police.

And finally, thanks very much to you my kind reader.

Also by Nick Card

Loving, Laughing & Living

A collection of poetry and prose that encompasses an enormous variety of subject matter. Nick Card uses his often quirky, but always accessible style, to share a distinctly sideways view of the world. The book is split into two halves to enable the full range of material (both humorous and serious) to shine through. The humour has a large focus on the hilarity of everyday situations including social satire and media ridicule. Card also has the ability to describe carnal activity using creative innuendo that's often incongruously polite. These comedic poems are sharp and punchy often concluding with either a strong pay-off or an unexpected twist. The serious material has a strong focus on the truth, clawing through social facades. Despite the uplifting theme, difficulties, darkness and demons are also tackled with an honest sincerity. Romantic yearnings and encounters are sensitively recalled and spiritual matters are explored in an inspiring and prettily worded manner. *Loving, Laughing & Living* is essential reading for anyone who wants to explore all the elements of life's rich tapestry.

That Special Place
Is ours to share.
Your heart is the compass
That leads you there.

www.amazon.co.uk